City Gone Askew

A Brooklyn 8 Ballo Mystery

Novels by Matt Cost
aka Matthew Langdon Cost

The Goff Langdon Mainely Mysteries
Mainely Power

Mainely Fear

Mainely Money

Mainely Angst

Mainely Wicked

The Clay Wolfe / Port Essex Mysteries
Wolfe Trap

Mind Trap

Mouse Trap

Cosmic Trap

Pirate Trap

Historical Fiction
I Am Cuba: Fidel Castro and the Cuban Revolution

Love in a Time of Hate

At Every Hazard

The Brooklyn 8 Ballo Mysteries
Velma Gone Awry

City Gone Askew

City Gone Askew

A Brooklyn 8 Ballo Mystery

MATT COST

Encircle Publications
Farmington, Maine, U.S.A.

Editor, Encircle Publications: Cynthia Brackett-Vincent
Book and cover design by Deirdre Wait
Cover photographs © Getty Images

Published by:

Encircle Publications
PO Box 187
Farmington, ME 04938

info@encirclepub.com
http://encirclepub.com

*To those who fight for
equality, peace, and love.*

Chapter 1

8 Ballo didn't usually find himself in a speakeasy at eight in the morning. And this was a real blind pig, the type of place where you had to check to make sure your shoelaces hadn't been stolen when you got up to leave. He had a whiskey in a dirty glass on the counter in front of him, but that was more so he wouldn't be thrown out, and not because he had any desire for it. He did like the occasional tipple, just not this early, and not in a cesspool like this.

He'd brought along the *Brooklyn Eagle* to peruse as he waited. It looked like Judge Landis had ruled to ban New York Giant's player Jimmy O'Connell and Coach Cozy Dolan from the game of baseball. This was a sore spot for 8, as the two had tried to bribe an opposing player to throw a game, a game which might've allowed the Dodgers to win the pennant. Instead of his team going to the World Series to play the Washington Senators, the hated New York Giants would be going.

It looked like the bribe had fallen through, the Giants winning the pennant fair and square, but a faint reek of corruption surrounded the victory. Had they successfully bought other games and stolen the pennant from 8's team, a team that he'd loved since he was a young boy?

His reading and rumination were interrupted as the door was flung open, and the hospital night shift poured in. The man he was waiting for was the third person through the door. Joseph Grady was of average height, but that was all that was normal about him.

It looked like his shoulders had been hollowed out and his cheeks deflated into his skull. The man sat down at the bar and ordered gin. His eyes were sullen, and there was a sneer on his lips that looked to be permanent.

8 slid over two seats. Grady looked sideways at him with blue eyes stained dark by life. "What do you want?" he asked.

"Are you Joseph Grady?" 8 asked.

"Who the hell are you?"

8 put his right hand onto Grady's skeletal shoulder and gave a squeeze. "My name is 8 Ballo." Grady winced under the grip and tried to pull away and failed. 8 had always been strong. Big. Ever since the day he was born, according to his mother, anyway.

"What do you want?"

"You Joseph Grady?"

"Sure."

8 released his clasp of the man's shoulder and patted him gently on the back. "I want to help you out," he said.

"Yeah?" Grady said. "Why ya wanna do that?"

"I got a lady friend who's a telephone operator. She sits right next to a woman named Jill Grady. Your wife, I believe."

The man nodded.

"My lady friend tells me that this Jill Grady has been showing up to work about once a month with fresh bruises on her face. She won't say how she got them, or makes some excuse about being clumsy, but me and you both know that isn't the truth, don't we?" 8 cupped Grady's neck with his hand, giving a little squeeze.

"What's it to you if my wife has a hard time standing up sometimes?" Grady asked. He slapped at 8's arm holding his head, but it had as much effect as trying to topple a redwood tree with a penknife.

"How about you, Joseph?" 8 asked. "You have a hard time staying upright sometimes?" He smashed the man's face down into the bar.

The bartender looked over and decided that there was business out back for him to take care of. Only two others even appeared to have noticed, neither showing any signs of caring. 8 plucked Grady's head back up from the bar, his nose bleeding, splinters in his cheek.

"I care," 8 said.

"What the fuck?" Grady spluttered.

8 mashed his face into the bar again. "I will be checking in on the welfare of Jill Grady. You best hope she stays accident-free, because, if I hear of or see so much as a scratch on her, I'll be paying you another visit."

8 stood up, went over and grabbed his newspaper, picked up the untouched whiskey, and set the grimy glass down next to Joseph Grady. "Here. Have a drink on me."

It was just over three miles back to his PI office in Bushwick, and 8 set out through Fort Greene Park with a long stride. He was two inches over six feet and forty pounds over two hundred. It was hard to find suits off the rack that fit his large frame, and thus, they were often tight, especially around the shoulders. He was clean-shaven, had a slightly round face, and dark eyebrows.

Given the chance and time, he'd always walk, certainly before taking one of the elevated cars that clunked and clattered their way above and through the streets of Brooklyn. Some of his best thinking occurred when he was walking the streets. 8 saw no real reason to buy a motorcar as it seemed too much of a hassle and just another tool getting between him and his thoughts.

That fellow, Henry Ford, was spitting out automobiles from his factories real cheap these days. Heck, for $300, 8 could get himself a brand-spanking-new, 1924 motorcar, but that was still a pile of dough. And it wasn't all that safe. Crossing the streets, especially at intersections, meant putting your life on the line, unless there was one of the towers on the corner with a copper holding up different colored lights for stop and go, not that half the people knew which each color meant what. Throw in horse and buggies, farm carts, and pedestrians—well, driving was a whole lot more dangerous than being a PI.

8 didn't much care for men who hit women. Perhaps that had to do with his three sisters and four, now three, brothers. Or his mother, who'd showered him with the love that he never got from his father growing up.

His mother had been so certain that he was going to be a girl to even the scales, four girls, four boys, that she had no name prepared when it was a boy who emerged into the day. Margit was to be her given name, but there was no male equivalent in Hungarian. His father, Mr. Ballo, was off to sea, and thus, his mother, Mrs. Ballo, merely wrote down the number of the child he was. She meant to revisit that with a real name, but had never gotten around to it, so his name was 8.

With a grin creasing his face, and thinking of the reasons for his unique moniker, 8 emerged from the park and onto DeKalb Avenue. Now, on the 3rd of October, it'd finally cooled off enough to be bearable in the city.

It was past nine when he got to his office on Bushwick Avenue. His private investigator business was on the second floor, above a tavern, which, because of Prohibition, no longer served alcohol, unless of course you went through the coat closet and down to the basement where a juice joint was located. His apartment was on the third and top floor.

"Morning, Millie," 8 said to his receptionist as he walked through the open door, hanging his bowler on the hat rack to the right. He'd hired Millicent Winter last year after the Hartmann mob war had blown up, taking her job as maid along with it. She had chilly blue eyes, short black hair, and a sunny disposition that belied her eyes.

"Morning, boss," she replied. "You're late."

"Had to stop out to Fort Greene this morning," 8 said. "Needed to give a fellow a close up look at a bar over that way."

Millie wrinkled her nose. "Bit early for the juice joints, isn't it, even for you?"

"If you're looking for rats, the best place to search is down in the sewer."

"*Quatsch*?" Millie said in German, looking perplexed, and then repeated it in English. "Whatever. There's a woman waiting for you in your office."

8 looked at the open door leading into the office. Until hiring Millie last year, he'd kept his desk out here, and the interior room had been mainly for storage. He was just getting used to being buried in the back away from the front lines.

"Yeah," he said. "Client?"

"That would be my assumption," Millie said. "Unless she's your long lost and wealthy aunt. Who happens to be a couple of years younger than you."

"Wealthy?"

Millie gave him the stop-being-a-pain-in-the-ass look and bent back to whatever paper or form she was busy filling out. Since hiring her, his PI business had been much more organized and efficient, even if interfering with his nap times and solitude. 8 figured that life was all about trade-offs, or something like that.

8 stepped into his office. It was a spacious enough room that was largely barren of decoration. A single light was attached to the ceiling casting a faint glow over the room, aided by the window looking down upon Bushwick Avenue. There were three chairs, one behind his oak desk and two across. A bookshelf against the wall was filled with some of his favorite authors. That dame from England, Agatha Christie, the fellow he'd met the previous year, F. Scott Fitzgerald, D.H. Lawrence, and many more.

The woman standing by the window held a cigarette holder in one gloved hand, the accessory about a foot in length, a Lucky Strike glowing at the tip. 8 guessed that she was about thirty, a very attractive thirty in a mysterious, sultry, sort of way. She wore a cloche hat with a brim that allowed her straight black hair to escape down one side of her face. Her lips were a dark red and her eyes brown. She wore a blue velvet coat with a white fur collar, and around her neck hung a gold necklace with purple amethyst gems and pearls adorning it.

"Good morning," 8 said.

The woman turned, her eyes studying him from head to foot. "Nothing small about you, now, is there?" she said.

"My name's 8 Ballo," he said, moving behind his desk. He gestured at one of the chairs across from it. "Won't you sit down, Miss..."

"Theda Lazar Vogel." The woman waved the cigarette holder in small circles as she spoke. "And, of course, I know who you are. Dorothy Parker sent me to you."

Ah, that made sense, 8 thought. "Please, Miss Vogel, sit."

Theda took three flowing steps from the window and settled into the proffered chair. "Mrs. Vogel, at least until last week I was, but you must call me Theda."

"Until last week?" 8 asked.

"My husband was killed in a hit-and-run incident, not accidental as the police suggest, but rather, an intentional act of murder. I suppose I'm still a Mrs., though, I'm not sure." Theda pronounced each word carefully, her mouth polishing each one before sending it out into the world.

Hmm, 8 thought, this was not the case of a cheating spouse that he'd expected when he walked into his office. It'd been some months since anything of interest had come across his desk. "Your husband was killed in a motorcar... incident?" he asked.

"Yes. A week ago this past Wednesday. Karl was on his morning walk just down the street from our home."

"Where do you live, Theda?"

"Brooklyn Heights."

"Your husband was walking along the sidewalk and was struck by a motorcar? And killed?' 8 wondered how a motorcar would be going fast enough on a crowded Brooklyn Heights' thoroughfare to strike and kill a man. Seriously injure, yes, but kill?

"According to the coppers, Karl was crossing the street, and two automobiles came whizzing down the roadway. The first one smacked him, sent him tumbling to the ground, and the other one ran right over him." A tear ran down her dimpled right cheek, the droplet pooling within this tiny indentation. "He died on his way to the hospital."

8 imagined it was the same hospital he'd been across from just this morning, the place where Joseph Grady was a night janitor. "And these motorcars didn't stop?"

"One of them stopped, and the driver went to Karl—but then hopped right back in his car." Theda sobbed, and 8 handed her his handkerchief. "Sped off down the street like it was a raceway or something."

"And there were witnesses?"

"Yes."

"And you think that your husband was targeted? That these motorcars purposely hit and killed him?"

"Yes."

Theda stood up, delicately put out her cigarette in the onyx ashtray on 8's desk and walked to the window. As she walked, she put another Lucky Strike in her cigarette holder.

8 approached her and held out a light. Her lips trembled as she inhaled. "Why do you think that it was something other than a couple of imbeciles driving faster than they should, racing down the road, who struck your husband by accident, and thought it best to just keep going?"

"Karl had been acting strange for a few weeks before the incident," Theda said. "Maybe a month or longer, I'm not sure. But there was something dark hanging over him."

"Did he say anything, maybe he was worried, or he was afraid that his life was in danger?" 8 asked.

Theda blew out a ring of smoke. 8 smelled tobacco mixed with a vanilla and berries scent. Her brown eyes, he saw, were flecked with flashes of amber. "One night when he was well into his cups, he told me that they were after something that he cherished."

"They?"

Theda shook her head. "I didn't ask at the time. I was more interested in what it was that he cherished, thinking, you know, it might have something to do with me. But, it didn't, really, now, did it?"

"And what would that be?" 8 asked.

"I suppose it can't hurt to tell you now," Theda said. "Now that Karl is dead, and it has gone missing."

"You think that these men who hit Karl took the missing item?"

"Yes. That is exactly what I think."

8 drummed his fingers on the desk. "Something valuable enough to kill for. And you know what it is."

"When Karl was stationed in Germany after the armistice, he came across a very rare artifact." Theda glanced over at the window, as if the outside had the ability to help her form the story. "He was part of a detail sweeping for bandits in the countryside. His regiment engaged in a skirmish with one such group. All of them were killed, and Karl was tasked with the burial detail. Inside a sack one of them had carried was an Aquila."

"An Aquila?" 8 asked.

"He didn't realize it at the time, the importance of what it was. It was a gold and silver eagle, originally attached to the top of a standard to be carried into battle, but now just the statue remained, about thus big." Theda held her hands to show that it was a bit under a foot tall by a foot wide. "There was a book with it that told the history of this Aquila. It was used as the Roman Legion Standard for many years, carried into battle, and was more than a symbol, but almost a religious emblem, the soul of the Roman soldier. Only a handful of these were ever lost in battle. The book tells of a barbarian Germanic tribe, the Batavi, who revolted against the Romans in 69 A.D.

"The Batavi were led by a man who'd had experience fighting with the Romans, having been conscripted into their army at a young age, and thus knew their strategies, which allowed him to use that against them. Anyway, they ambushed and destroyed two legions and captured the Aquila. The Romans returned in greater force and crushed the rebellion, but a group of men tasked with keeping the Aquila safe escaped.

"This group of men started off as outlaws hiding in caves but over time changed into a secret society that called itself the Batavi. As the years progressed, they migrated south, ending up in Cologne, where they flourished. They had grown in power throughout the centuries, with members holding key positions in important industries and sectors of society. Then, with the defeat of Germany at the end of the Great War, they were forced again to go into hiding, which was not much of a problem for them being the clandestine organization that they were. Karl surmised that the occupation of Germany had put the Aquila and the book in danger of being found and that they were in the process of moving it when his detail came upon them. When ordered to halt, they fought back in desperation, not wanting the Aquila discovered."

8 processed this load of information as Theda swung her desperate and determined eyes back to lock onto his. "And this, uh, Aquila," he said, "is quite valuable?"

"It is the only one left in the entire world," Theda said. "As a matter of fact, there are very few people who know of its existence. The group of Batavi. My husband, now dead. Me. And now you."

"A gold and silver Standard carried by Roman Legionnaires into battle almost 2,000 years ago," 8 said. "The last of its kind."

"It is priceless," Theda said.

"So, you think it was the Batavi who killed him?"

"The day before he was killed, Karl said it was the Americans he feared, not the Germans."

"That means somebody else knows of its existence," 8 said. "Did he say who these Americans were?"

Theda shook her head no. A sob escaped her lips. A tear rolled down her cheek.

Chapter 2

8 couldn't really be considered a regular, but he did pop into the Algonquin Round Table lunch about once a month, ever since the year before when he'd met and become fast friends with Dorothy Parker. After his meeting with Theda Lazar Vogel this morning, a woman who'd been recommended to 8 by Parker, he thought it a good time to pay the caustic wit a visit.

The doorman nodded to 8 as he entered the twelve-story building on 44th Street. When he walked into the Rose Room, the Round Table was already in full swing, Dorothy Parker being the center of attention. This was normal.

"Heterosexuality is not normal, it's just common," Dorothy was saying as 8 slid into a seat next to her. She paused in what she was saying and looked over at him. "My darling 8, so good of you to join us."

"Oh, great," Robert Benchley said. "The bean shooter from Brooklyn."

8 grinned at the man. They often engaged in a bit of back-and-forth insults, but he guessed that he might actually be growing on Benchley. "Better a bean shooter then a two-bit actor and has-been writer."

Those at the table laughed, none so loudly as a curly-haired fellow about the same age as 8. The man mimed throwing a rope to Benchley and then reeling him in hand over hand to the enjoyment of the group of writers around the table.

"My darling 8," Dorothy said, "I don't think you've met Harpo Marx. Harpo, this is 8 Ballo. He's a gumshoe from down to Bushwick."

Harpo held his hand across the table, about six feet from 8, and pretended to shake his hand at a distance.

"Harpo is an actor who doesn't speak much," Dorothy said. "Perfect for silent pictures but a bit more of a problem for a future career in the moving pictures, I'd think."

"That's not quite true," the man next to Harpo said. "He's got a line in his new moving picture coming out next year. What is it, you say, my dear chap?"

Harpo stood up and looked at the man. "You sure you can't move?" And then he pretended to punch him.

The patrons at the table whistled and clapped as Harpo took a bow and sat back down.

"Can we speak for a moment in private?" 8 said to Dorothy.

"Are you suggesting we get a room upstairs?" Dorothy asked, raising her eyebrows.

"Maybe just step out to the lobby?"

"My, how risqué." Dorothy stood up and led the way out of the Rose Room, finding two chairs in a corner of the lobby where she sat. "And what, pray tell, do we need to discuss in privacy, my darling 8."

8 sat down next to her and leaned forward. "I got a new client this morning. She said that you recommended me."

Dorothy shook her head sadly. "Poor dear Theda. Quite a shame what happened to her husband."

"Terrible," 8 said.

"And she thinks that it was more than an accident?" Dorothy asked. "That perhaps poor Karl was... murdered?"

"She believes that he may've been killed for something he had in his possession." 8 saw no reason to delve into the theft of a priceless and mysterious eagle symbol called an Aquila.

"What a shame." Dorothy shook her head. "What is the city coming to? It seems that it has gone all askew of late."

"Perhaps you can fill in some of the blanks," 8 said. "Tell me what she didn't tell me about who she is."

"Well, how would I know what she didn't tell you?"

"Theda told me that her husband worked for the Brooklyn Hospital and that they live in Brooklyn Heights. Not much more than that. What kind of people are they?"

"Theda never saw a cocktail party she didn't like," Dorothy said. "She loves to have people up to their apartment and can be quite the flirt. She is quite a jazz fan and not above traipsing up to Harlem and the Cotton Club. None of the low brow places, not for Theda. The fancier and snobbier, the better."

"Would you say she was a flapper?"

Dorothy snickered. "Not in the slightest. She considered herself upper society, which, frankly, was a stretch. There is nothing flippant or reckless about Theda. She is intelligent, conservative, and manipulative."

8 chuckled. "So, you recommended this conniving social climber to me?"

"I thought the two of you would get on marvelously." Dorothy scoffed. "You have a way with difficult women."

"I suppose that you would be the expert on that," 8 said. "In what way is Theda conservative?"

Dorothy appeared to ponder this for a few moments.

"The modern flapper sees little distinction between man and woman, doesn't give a rat's ass about people's sexual predilection or skin color, and has a general disdain for conventional behavior. Theda embodies the exact opposite of these beliefs."

It was 8's turn to ponder. "How about the husband that got run down?" he asked. "What was he like?"

"Karl was a bit of a fanatic on pure, white European bloodlines being superior to everybody else. I got myself cornered by him one evening when I'd drank a bit too much gin and was regaining my composure on the sofa, by that, I mean the ability to stand up had left me, and he sat down next to me. According to him, the United States was being overrun by people of inferior genetic blood, and these people were breeding with the good European stock, which in turn was creating diluted and bastardized offspring. Or something like that, I was a bit into my cups, as I said. He was also going on about there being proof that criminals, handicapped, and perverts begot more of the same when they mated."

"More of the same?"

"I took it to mean their babies would be criminals, blind, deaf, and perverted."

"Sounds like a real charmer," 8 said.

"He was quite the sweet talker, actually, most of the time. That was the one and only time I got a hint at what was underneath the hood, if you know what I mean. You'd never guess that, under the surface, this normally delightful chap was an intolerant bigot—or at least was capable of ranting away like one." Dorothy stood up. "I seem to have left my gin behind and must go and find it before sobriety gathers me into its desperate clutches. Will you be going back in?"

8 looked at his pocket watch. "No, I got to be getting on."

"Maybe we could get a drink tomorrow?"

"I'm meeting the lads at Pearle's house to listen to the World Series game on the radio."

Dorothy snickered. "Without the Yankees playing, what's the point?"

"Or my Dodgers?"

"I believe the name being used this year for that wastrel of a team is the Robins," Dorothy said. "Meek little birds that they are."

"They had a better record than the Yankees this year," 8 said to her disappearing back.

Chapter 3

On Saturday afternoon, 8 walked over to his buddy's house. Pearle Hill lived in the burgeoning neighborhood estate agents were starting to call Bed-Stuy. His house was large, if not enormous, but was expensively furnished for comfort rather than elegance. Pearle had done well for himself, having laid the foundation for a business empire before going off to the Great War, and then bursting forth upon his return.

He was almost as thick as 8 through the body, but half-a-foot shorter and not as muscular. A thin mustache wrapped around his mouth and merged into a goatee adorning his chin. Round spectacles and a wide grin gave the impression of a carefree and genial man. Sometimes others took this to mean he was soft—that was a huge mistake.

8 had first met Pearle when they were not yet teenagers. 8 had joined a stickball game, avoiding his own neighborhood for his father frowned upon him playing games, and the two had hit it off. They'd become fast friends, growing up together, had their first drink together, shared secrets of crushes on girls and, later, on lovers, and had each other's back in many a fight.

A confirmed bachelor who claimed he'd never marry, Pearle was a snazzy dresser who was often dating multiple women at a time while retaining his independence. He had a billiards room with a bar, darts, and a Westinghouse tube radio with batteries which was currently tuned to Game One of the World Series from the Capital between the New York Giants and the Washington Senators.

The voice of Graham McNamee flowed from the radio, his rich baritone balancing the crackling reception. *"We are about to get underway here at Griffin Stadium in the Capital of our fair country. President Calvin Coolidge has made his way out to the pitcher's mound to throw the first pitch."*

"Okay, boys, time to place your bets," Pearle said. "I'm taking the Giants to beat up on the Senators. Who wants some action?" He and McGee were playing billiards while 8 and Marty sat off to the side.

"Bang on, lad, I'll take some of that," McGee said. "Those cheating Giants are gonna get what they got coming to them."

In the last weekend of the pennant race, the Dodgers could've pulled it out by winning their last two and the Giants losing their last three. And then one of the Phillies had come forth with the bribery attempt 8 had been reading about earlier, ensuring the Giants a pennant. He'd declined the offer, the Giants won anyway, but there was a murkiness about the entire matter, perhaps left-over resentments from the 1919 World Series scandal. Especially if you were a Dodgers fan.

"Where's the money, big mouth?" Pearle asked.

"I got it right here in my pocket," McGee said. "Five bucks."

"Let's see it," Pearle said. "Better yet, give it to me now, might as well get it over with. You know that when they talk about the luck of the Irish, they're not talking about you, don't you?"

"I'll give it to you now, alright," McGee said. The Irish beat cop made a fist and waved it under Pearle's chin.

8 chuckled, watching the two friends trade insults. He sat in a comfortable armchair next to the fourth man, Martin Hoffman, a journalist for the *Brooklyn Eagle*. "Picked up a new case this morning," he said to Marty.

"Yeah? Cheating husband or wife this time?" Hoffman was a Jew from the Rhine River area of northern France and western

Germany. Not too far from where the Batavi had rebelled against the Romans, wiped out two legions, taken their Eagle Standard, and lived in secret for almost 2,000 years. He was short, small, slender, and possessed a cracking wit and sharp tongue that went with honeyed words.

"Hit and run death," 8 said. "The widow doesn't think it was accidental."

"You mean the fellow was murdered?" Marty took a sip of his gin, and 8 did likewise with his whiskey. "What for?"

"I suppose that's part of why I've been hired," 8 said. "To find out who and why."

"Any reason to think he was purposely killed?"

8 shrugged. "Don't know. Haven't even really gotten started looking into it."

"What'd the fellow do for work?"

"He was a doctor. But it sounds like his murder didn't have to do anything with that."

"Yeah? What then?"

"Have you ever heard of the Batavi Rebellion against the Romans in 69 and 70 A.D.?"

Marty shook his head. "Something tickles my brain about it but can't say for sure."

"Theda thinks that her husband was killed while being robbed."

"Theda, huh?" Marty raised an eyebrow with a sly smile below. "Got right to the first name basis with the grieving widow, did you?"

"I'm not sure that Theda Vogel is my type," 8 said. "I like myself a short blonde woman."

"How's Asta doing?"

"She's great," 8 said. "I plan on seeing her tomorrow."

"Say hello for me. What'd the thieves get?"

8 cast a glance at the billiards table. Marty and Pearle knew the meaning of discrete. McGee couldn't keep a secret, his face giving away his hand at cards, a pathetic liar, and his mouth having no

filter. He leaned closer to Marty. "Theda tells me that Karl Vogel returned from Germany after the war with the only known Aquila, or Eagle Standard, in existence, taken from the Roman Legions some 2,000 years ago." He gave Marty the quick version of the Batavi Rebellion and subsequent secret society.

"And that ball is out of here," the deep voice of Graham McNamee crackled over the radio. *"High Pockets Kelly has just hit a home run here in the top of the second inning with nobody on and no outs to give the Giants of New York a 1-0 lead."*

"Not too far from where my people came from," Marty said. "I remember now hearing a story of that rebellion. They were in the Rhine River delta."

"You think you could dig around a bit and see what you can find out about the Batavi and the Roman Eagle Standard?" 8 asked.

"I assume I get first crack at the story when it goes public," Marty said.

"Of course."

"Next victim," Pearle said, plucking McGee's dollar bill, the bet on the billiards game, from the edge of the table, and putting it in his pocket. "You want to pay up for the ballgame now as well, you poor unlucky Irishman?"

"Go ahead," 8 said to Marty. "I'm going to wait until the shark is drunk to take my turn at him."

Marty groaned but stood up. "Might as well get the beating over with," he said.

"That was brutal," McGee said sitting down next to 8. "He's a real *cute hoor,* isn't he, that Pearle Hill. Sits home and practices his billiards play every day just so he can take our money."

8 chuckled. Lit a cigar. "Cost you a dollar so far. Correct me if I'm wrong, but that's your third Irish whiskey of Pearle's you've drank so far with several more to come. Plus food. Consider it your entrance fee."

"Got to make sure I get my money's worth," McGee said. "Got

a fiver on the baseball game, which the Senators are currently throwing down the drain."

"You got any buddies in the Brooklyn Heights precinct?" 8 asked.

McGee went to speak, paused, and looked at 8 over the rim of his glass before taking a slow and measured sip. "Sure. Why you ask?"

"Lady hired me this morning to look into the death of her husband in a motorcar incident."

"A crash?"

"Nope. He was walking across a street and a motorcar came racing along and struck him, knocking him senseless, and then a second car ran him over and mashed him into the road."

"And Walter 'The Big Train' Johnson has struck out the first two batters he's faced in this fourth inning," Graham McNamee said over the radio. "Up to the plate steps Bill Terry. He's had a tough year, hitting only .239. The Big Train goes into his windup, and here comes the pitch, and Terry crushes one to left field. Deep. And it's over the fence. The Giants take a 2-0 lead."

"Bollocks," McGee said. "I can't afford to lose any more money or Aine is going to be some pissed at me."

"You should know better than to bet against Pearle. I don't know if I've seen him lose more than a few times in the twenty-five years I've known him."

McGee shook his head. "I just figure lady luck has to change direction and come my way at some point."

"Can you ask your buddies up to Brooklyn Heights what they know?" 8 asked. "Guys name was Karl Vogel. Maybe find somebody willing to have a chat with me?"

"Sure thing," McGee said.

"Time for ole 8 ball to step up and play some 9-ball," Pearle said as Marty walked disgustedly away from the table.

8 rose to his feet and went over to the bar and poured another two fingers of whiskey into his glass. "How about we play for a sawbuck?" he asked.

"Ten dollars on one game?" Pearle said. "You must be lining up for the poor house."

"But you got to play blindfolded," 8 said.

"Fat chance of that. Even if I could probably still beat you."

8 chuckled. "One dollar is fine with me, then. Price of admission."

After 8 took his beating at billiards, he and Pearle sat sipping whiskey and smoking their cigars while McGee went about whipping Marty at darts. 8 told him about the stolen Aquila and the rebellion of the Batavi Rebellion and the clandestine organization as he knew it. Pearle was a history buff, and 8 knew that his friend would dig further into this as it was right up his alley.

In the bottom of the 9th inning, the Senators from DC tied the score to force extra innings. McGee was quite excited about this turn of events, and the four of them hung on to every word of the radio broadcast as Johnson and Nehf battled into the 12th inning where the Giants scored twice in the top of the inning. The Senators came back in the bottom of the frame, scoring once, and had Bucky Harris on third base, when Goose Goslin grounded out to end the game.

Pearle Hill waved off McGee when he offered up the five dollars, suggesting that he use it to buy his children something special. It was just another night in Brooklyn.

Chapter 4

At just past ten the next morning, 8 Ballo walked into the Butler Street Police Station. McGee had come and pounded on his door earlier, having set up a meeting with Captain Archipoili, chief of detectives of the precinct. There was a lazy morning energy in the police department as the officers began a new day that had not yet grown chaotic. That would more than likely occur later that night.

Captain Archipoili was a thick-set Italian with intelligent eyes and a ready laugh. He had his own office in the back of the precinct, his desk neat and organized, a coffee pot in the corner, from which he offered 8 a cup of joe. It was strong enough to erode the brick walls of the building.

"McGee said you were a no-account, good for nothing Hungarian who'd sell his friends down the river if a pretty lady gave you a tiny smile," Archipoili said once they were settled across from each other.

"That Paddy is the one who went and sold himself to a woman," 8 said. "And believe you me, Aine is his master in every way, and when she says jump, that lad, he jumps."

Archipoili laughed loudly from the belly, the sound vibrating up through his body and crashing forth like a wave dashing against the rocks. "He said you been hired to look into the death of Karl Vogel."

"His widow doesn't think his death was an accident. She believes he was targeted."

Archipoili read from the single paper on his desk. "Vogel was out on his morning walk. It was early and there was little to no automobile traffic. He went to cross over Livingston Street. Witnesses said he seemed preoccupied and didn't look up until he heard the racing engines of two motorcars. At which point, he stopped, looked, and froze. The first vehicle sent him tumbling and the second ran him over. One witness, a Mr. Axel Theisen, believed that the two automobiles may have been racing each other." Archipoili shrugged. "Pretty open and shut."

"Did either motorcar stop?"

Archipoili looked at the report. "It says that the second motorcar pulled over and a man got out and went to check on Vogel. Then he got back in and raced off."

"Is the police department doing anything about it?"

"Man gets hit crossing the street and dies." Archipoili shrugged. "It's a shame, but even the fact that Karl Vogel was a local doctor isn't going to encourage the brass to expend manpower on this."

"Would you mind if I spoke with some of the eyewitnesses," 8 said. "If nothing else, to appease the grieving widow?"

8 decided to start with Axel Theisen. The man lived just two blocks down the street from where Vogel had been killed. He opened the door of his apartment with an annoyed look as if he'd been disturbed doing something very important. He was of medium height, compact, and had a pencil mustache that was carefully clipped and trimmed.

"Mr. Theisen," 8 said. "Can I ask you a few questions about the incident you witnessed on Livingston Street?"

"The incident? You mean the two hooligans racing along Livingston who killed that man?" Theisen bristled with indignation.

"Yes. Karl Vogel. His widow believes that this might've been done on purpose. Did you see anything that might make you believe the drivers meant for this to happen?"

"I have to get down to my shop," Theisen said.

"I've already told the police everything I saw."

"Do you mind if I walk with you?"

"As you will. Wait here for a moment." Theisen turned, leaving the door open, and disappeared into the interior. He returned a moment later carrying a satchel.

"What is your business?" 8 asked as he led the way down the stairs.

"I'm a furrier. Mostly women's hats."

"Would you mind repeating to me what you saw that morning? No detail is too small."

Theisen scoffed. "Whatever. I was on my way into the shop as I had several projects to complete before it opened for the day. I was just in front of the grocer on the corner of Livingstone when I heard racing engines. I looked up in time to see a man, standing frozen in the street, and then he lunged to the side, and an automobile caught him a glancing blow, sending him tumbling toward the sidewalk on the other side."

"Toward the sidewalk?" 8 asked. "Was the second car that far to the side of the street on the wrong side? Were there parked automobiles?"

Theisen paused his hurried strides, pursing his lips. "I believe the second motorcar swerved toward him. Yes, I'm certain of it. Not only did it veer in the direction of that poor fellow, after it trampled over him, it scraped alongside another automobile."

"And did they stop?"

"The second car, the one that ran him down, it did. A man got out and walked back to the fellow who got hit. He bent down over him to check if was alive, and then must've thought better of it, and stood up and hurried back to his car."

"What did the man look like?"

"I told the police all this," Theisen said. "I didn't get a good look at the chap. It all happened so quick. He had on a derby and a trench coat—Aquascutum, if I'm not mistaken—with the collar turned up. Might've been dark hair peeking out from under his cap, but I couldn't say for certain. Never caught sight of his face."

"Tall? Short? Heavy? Thin?"

"Ah, yes, I believe he was quite tall and thin. A real daddy long legs."

"Taller than me?"

Theisen glanced sideways at 8. "Yes. By a few inches I'd say. But not nearly so big as you."

"Is it possible that this man took something from Vogel?"

"What? What do you mean?"

8 didn't want to put words into the man's mouth, so he spoke carefully. "You said that the man got out of the yellow motorcar, approached Vogel lying in the street, and bent down over him. Is it possible that he took something from his body?"

Theisen seemed to contemplate that. "I suppose so. I thought that he was checking if he was okay, and that my approach scared him off, but it is possible that he was robbing the poor fellow. Was his wallet missing?"

"No, I don't believe it was."

"Well, then, I guess he didn't rob him, now, did he?"

"Do you know what model the motorcars were, Mr. Theisen?"

"No. I'm not much of an automobile person. I believe the first one was black and the second one was yellow. Just standard looking if you know what I mean."

"Any chance the second motorcar was just trying to avoid hitting Mr. Vogel, and inadvertently struck him when he was knocked sideways?"

"I supposed anything is possible," Theisen said, stopping. "This is my shop. I'm sorry I can't be of any more help."

"How about the parked motorcar that was struck? 8 asked.

"It was red, I believe. Yes, most definitely. Red."

8 spoke with two more witnesses, several others not being home this morning, before walking over to where the *Brooklyn Eagle* office was located just under the Brooklyn Bridge. As 8 walked, he

processed the information he'd gained. The second witness had said that the front motorcar, the black one, was a Sheridan Touring automobile, built in Muncie, Indiana. The man seemed to know what he was talking about. The second one, the car that had run over Vogel, was a Kissel Gold Bug Speedster, 8 learned, and also per this motorcar aficionado, there was no way in bloody Hell that if the two were racing that the Gold Bug would've been trailing. Not with sixty-one horsepower pushing six-cylinders.

The third witness was a woman who'd been coming back from the grocer where she'd run down to get some eggs, seemingly having neglected to get some the day before, and her husband was just a bear if she didn't make him eggs for breakfast. He could be quite irate on any number of topics, the woman said, but at least when he was eating, he shut up for a bit, and then, he'd be off for work, and she didn't have to deal with his applesauce. 8 didn't think the slang quite fit her and wondered that she might be slipping out into the flapper arena when the husband wasn't around. After forty-five minutes, she finally ventured forth with some information about the man who got out to check on Vogel. She'd caught a look at his face and said that it was long and grave like that of an undertaker.

Not bad work for the morning, 8 thought, as he neared the offices of the *Brooklyn Eagle*. A black Sheridan Touring automobile struck Kurt Vogel, knocking him sideways, and a Kissel Gold Bug swerved to mash him into the ground, in turn, hitting a red motorcar parked on the side of the street. More than likely, then, he was looking for a Gold Bug Speedster streaked with red paint. He had a partial description of one of the drivers, and it was possible that the lanky man in the trench coat had taken something from Vogel before speeding off.

Marty Hoffman had agreed to meet him for lunch. 8 knew that he'd be paying, and that this was the cost of gathering whatever information his friend may have dug up regarding the Batavi Rebellion. The newsroom was a busy and noisy place with people yelling, typewriters clattering, even if the presses weren't currently running. Luckily, Marty saw him coming and came loping over to him, the tiny man's legs able to somehow cover immense distances with each stride.

"About time you showed up," Marty said. "I'm starving. Let's go." He led the way back down the stairs and out the door.

"Where we going?" 8 found it hard to keep up with the shorter man, whose haste was not borne of hunger or busyness, but rather because Marty always walked fast.

"Round the corner," Marty said. "Kaan's Deli. Fantastic fatty meat on mouth-watering and buttery bread."

"Did you find out more on the Batavi Rebellion?"

Marty just rolled his eyes. "The Revolt of the Batavi," he said, "was one of those true David and Goliath stories that is almost hard to believe. The Batavi were skilled warriors, but under the rule of the Roman Empire, who had far superior weapons and manpower. As the Batavi had little ability to pay tribute, they supplied soldiers to the Legions."

"Ha," 8 said. "You're telling me that the Romans trained the men who revolted against them."

"A tale as old as time," Marty said with a grin. He turned and pushed his way through a glass door claiming kosher deli meats on a sign. He bypassed a few milling people, went to the counter, and placed an order, before turning back to 8. "Let's sit outside. They'll bring it to us." 8 shrugged and followed.

Marty plopped into a chair at a table on the sidewalk and continued speaking before 8 was able to sit down. "Their leader was a man by the name of Gaius Julius Civilis, obviously not his birth name, who cut his teeth in the Roman Legions during the invasion and conquest of Britain in 43 AD. But by 69 AD, he was home in Batavi, and unhappy with Roman rule."

Two sandwiches, the two wedges of thick rye hardly able to contain the sliced meat they held, came out along with two lemonades. Marty immediately took a huge bite of his and kept talking while he chewed. "Civilis took the opportunity of disarray in Rome during the time of the Four Emperors to rise up against the Legions stationed in his home region. Knowledge of Roman fighting strategies and confusion in their ranks allowed him to rout and destroy these two commands, capturing at least one Aquila, maybe two."

"So, the story told to me by Theda could be true? Karl Vogel might've gotten his hands on an Aquila, an artifact that is most likely the only one to survive history?"

"As Theda told you, if it is true, the Aquila is priceless."

8 realized that Marty had almost finished his enormous sandwich and hurriedly took a bite of his own. "Any luck finding out anything about a secret society of the Batavi?"

"Not yet, but the story has merit," Marty said. "There does seem to be a lot written about this German fellow, a real rabble-rouser named Adolph Hitler."

"He have something to do with the Batavi?"

"Doubt it. He was born about 2,000 years too late." Marty stood up. "I take it you got the bill?"

Chapter 5

The four men sat away from prying eyes in the center of Fort Greene Park. They all wore overcoats and caps. Two of the men, one thin and the other quite rotund, had heavy German accents.

The American doing the talking wore a cowboy hat. "We have the statue," he said.

The heavyset man did the speaking for the Germans. "The Aquila," he said softly. "The symbol of independence and *mut...* what is the English word? Courage. The symbol of independence and courage of my people."

"Well, fellow, y'all didn't hold out so well in this war, now did you?" Cowboy Hat said.

"We Batavi have not, nor will we ever, accept the *diktat* treaty of Versailles."

"It is not us who dictated the terms of the peace."

"There will be another war, *mein Freund*, and when that time comes, you Americans will want to be on the right side. We *Chermans* will rise from the ashes and conquer the world. Blood and soil. *Der Heimat!*"

"You are weak. Crippled. Occupied." Cowboy Hat took out a cigar and lit it, puffing several times. "But the Teutonic peoples are hardy. I trust that you will rise from the ashes like the Phoenix. Perhaps that should be your new standard. Not some Latin name for eagle."

"The *Phönix* would be very appropriate for our return to dominance."

"That possibility exists if you ally yourself with the United States of America. Not the sissies, but the real Americans. An American-German alliance would surpass the Roman and British Empires for greatness."

"Our Führer is ready to join together with a cause that has similar aims."

"As are we, ready to ally ourselves with your Führer and the Batavi."

"What is it you want?" Rotund German asked.

"We want to work together," Cowboy Hat said. "Share research science, real resources to build a superior race of human beings. Ally yourself with us, and we will return your Aquila. Then, together, we will build a Phoenix to rise from the polluted mud in which we live and cleanse the blood of all humanity to forge one master race."

"We greatly admire the work you are doing," Rotund German said. "And while we have encountered a small setback in our own country, the *Cher-man* people will soon have a new leader, who, like the *Phönix*, will rise from the ashes and create a new world order. One based upon the work which you have carried out and so generously share."

"Here is a list of men we'd like to meet with," Cowboy Hat said, handing over a piece of paper. "When we meet them, we will return to the Aquila to you. I am that certain that we will be able to come to an accord once we are all together in the same room. After all, it is for the salvation of the human race."

* * *

That afternoon, 8 stopped by to borrow Pearle's Nash 690 Touring Car so that he could take Asta out on the town. It was a bit gaudy for 8's taste, the exterior in purple and white with orange rims on the white-wall tires. It was, however, right in character with Pearle's flashy presentation. He dressed, worked, and played loudly at all times.

Asta Holms lived on Ellery Street in the northwest corner of

Bushwick in a third-floor apartment. 8 parked on the street and carried a bouquet of wildflowers up the stairs. Asta opened the door as soon as he knocked. She was short for a Dutch woman, barely five feet, with the blonde hair and stunning blue eyes typical of her nationality. There was a tousled look to her that was normal, and her eyes, if stunning, were sleepy and content, like the cat who'd got the cream.

"They're beautiful," she said, taking the flowers and turning on her heel with 8 following.

Asta found a glass vase, filled it with water, and put the flowers on the table. Asta lived here with a roommate, a woman who spent most weekends with her parents in Connecticut, so 8 had only seen her a few times.

"Once in a golden hour," he recited, "I cast to earth a seed. Up there came a flower. The people said, a weed…"

"Whose words be you stealing now?" Asta asked.

8 chuckled. "That would be Lord Tennyson."

"So, are you suggesting that you've brought me weeds?"

"The poem goes on to tell of how the flower grew tall and beautiful and then was stolen by thieves. I believe it is a metaphor for his own poetry, and how people criticized it, and then stole it and claimed it for their own."

"How about we forget all that nonsense and enjoy their beauty," Asta said. "What plans does my 8 have for me this evening?"

"Hmm. I have many a notion of what we may do together tonight," 8 said with a chuckle.

"How about we first stick to those plans that involve us wearing clothes," Asta said, smiling coyly at him.

"I have Pearle's automobile outside. I thought first we'd go see a moving picture."

Asta clapped her hands excitedly. "Wonderful. Colleen Moore is starring in *Flirting with Love* down to the Colonial Theater."

"As is *The Arab*," 8 said.

"What's that about?" Asta asked.

"A Bedouin tribal leader saves an orphanage from an evil Turkish army."

Asta wrinkled her nose. "I suppose if you're paying, we can go to the swords and horses thingy instead of the silly picture about love."

8 very much liked it when Asta wrinkled her pert little nose at him as it made his legs weak. They decided to flip a coin.

Afterwards they drove to a jazz club for dinner, both agreeing that the moving picture had been wonderful and entertaining.

It was a warm October evening, the top was down on the automobile, and the stars were vivid in the sky above.

"I paid Joseph Grady a visit Friday morning," 8 said. "We came to a mutual agreement that he'd stop beating his wife."

Asta wrinkled her nose. "Jill told me yesterday that he came home with a swollen nose and two black eyes. Said he got rolled in the street by a gang."

8 chuckled. "Let me know if you hear anything. I'm pretty sure that Mr. Grady got the message, but just in case."

"Will do," Asta said. "And thank you."

"Can you do me a favor?"

"Of course."

"Can you keep your ears peeled down to the telephone company about anything to do with a man being run down by a motorcar in Brooklyn Heights?"

"You got a new case?"

"Yep. Hired by the widow of the fellow who was killed. Karl Vogel. Sounds like he was targeted. Maybe for a rare artifact he had in his possession."

"What would that be?"

"A gold and silver eagle about one foot tall." 8 pulled the Nash to the side of the road just down the street from the *Dog House*, the club they were going to.

"Is it worth a lot of dough?"

8 chuckled. "If it exists, it is the only surviving standard of the Roman Legions."

"Standard?"

"Something each Roman division displayed going into battle to show they were the official representatives of the Emperor of Rome."

"So, the answer would be yes." Asta wrinkled her nose. "Enough to be killed for it."

8 got out and walked around, opening her door, and offering his hand. "Karl Vogel may've stolen it from a clandestine organization in Germany that has existed for the last 2,000 years for the sole purpose of keeping this heirloom safe."

"How'd that work out for him?" Asta asked cynically. "And if that's true, your statue thing and the people who took it are probably long gone back to Germany by now."

"Very possible, but I've a hunch that it's still around."

"Those famous 8 Ballo instincts." Asta kidded as they walked up to the door.

"I believe you give yourself to them and trust them to your own satisfaction," he said with a grin.

Asta hit his arm. "I just pretend to for your ego."

"Thank you for that."

"Anybody I know playing music tonight?"

"Sure do," 8 said. "The Hawk is playing here with Bessie Smith and some new fellow by the name of Louis Armstrong."

"Wow," Asta said. "We going to be able to get in?"

"Invite only," 8 said. "Guess it pays to be friends with Coleman Hawkins."

"Smack going to be there?"

8 grunted, something that may've been a no. Fletcher 'Smack' Henderson had met Asta the previous year and had been instantly smitten.

Asta snickered. "I suppose if he was playing, then *I* would've gotten a private invite."

8 and Asta dined, danced, drank—and found their way back to his apartment sometime after midnight. If the night had been delightful, the early morning hours were delicious.

*   *   *

Bettie Young didn't want to go down to the free clinic and stand in line with a whole bunch of sick people, but the pain in her stomach wasn't going away. She lived with her aunt and the woman's boyfriend of the month, as well as three cousins. She had a boy, seven, and a girl, five, who also lived there. Neither one of their fathers was around. It was only a couple blocks down to the clinic near the Brooklyn Hospital, but at the sight of the line leading out the door, Bettie decided to keep walking.

Her aunt had been telling her for months now that if she didn't start contributing money to the household, she and her two children would be out on the street. She'd never known her father, but after Bettie was born and he left the scene, her mother had turned to prostitution to keep food on the table and a roof over their heads. When Bettie was ten, she got a job in the pencil factory to help out, and then at twelve, found work as a maid for a wealthy family in Brooklyn Heights.

When Bettie was thirteen, her mother died of syphilis. She moved in with her aunt and the current boyfriend of the month as well as her three cousins. Her aunt had kicked her out seven times over the past ten years, only allowing her back when she had money in hand. Those had been the times she'd been forced to do favors for men. Down in Fort Greene Park or in cheap rooms that charged by the hour.

But this was not the life that Bettie wanted. She had dreams. When she was fifteen, Betty had been working in a brothel that had a wonderful piano player, a young Black man nicknamed Peaches, and sometimes she'd sing. And she'd been good. The Madam had spoken with her about spending less time on her back and more time serenading the other girls as they lay with their men.

And then Bettie had gotten pregnant with her son, and those dreams were dashed. She'd been urged to end the pregnancy, by Peaches, her madame, her aunt—just about everybody she knew. But she couldn't, not with God watching. After he was born, Bettie found work in the glue factory for a quarter an hour. It was a toss-up which was worse, the brothel or the factory. But she still had dreams of being a singer. She joined the church choir for a time. Then her daughter was born, and she'd lost her job.

A racket erupted up above, and Bettie realized she'd made it down to Fulton Street and the elevated cars were clattering overhead. A pain suddenly gripped her insides, and she bent over gasping. After a few minutes, it subsided. There was talk of an impending strike up on the docks, but those jobs usually were filled by men, certainly not by a Black woman with some sort of stomach issue.

Tomorrow, Bettie decided, she'd get to the clinic. Tonight, she'd take a walk through Fort Greene Park and see if she couldn't make a couple of dollars to appease her aunt and keep the woman from kicking her and her children out onto the street.

Still, Bettie had dreams. She could see herself onstage, the music washing over her, the crowds in front, her mouth opening and caressing the world with her heart's song.

Chapter 6

Monday morning found 8 again walking to Fort Greene, this time not to the speakeasy, but across DeKalb Avenue from it to the Brooklyn Hospital. The hospital was an impressive and eerie sight. Perched on a small hill, it consisted of a cluster of three- and four-story buildings with gable roofs. The buildings rose into the sky, visible through a smattering of hardwood trees. This was where Karl Vogel had worked as a doctor.

A wrought iron fence stretched around the grounds. 8 went through the gate and up the driveway. It was an overcast day, the clouds cloaking the tops of the buildings in a murky embrace. With the help of two different hospital personnel, 8 eventually found himself seated in an administrative office across from a slender, balding man in a suit. A placard on his desk proclaimed that he was Vice President Ronald Dankworth.

"What can I do for you?" Dankworth said in a peevish tone.

"My name is 8 Ballo, and I'm a private investigator." The chair was undersized and rickety for his large frame, and he worried it might collapse to the floor at any moment. "I'm looking into the murder of one of your doctors."

"I don't know of any doctors here at the Brooklyn Hospital who have recently been murdered." Dankworth put down the clipboard he'd been pretending to look at. "Are you sure that you've come to the right place?"

"Karl Vogel."

Dankworth cleared his throat. "Dr. Vogel was a victim of an unfortunate accident."

"He was intentionally run down by two motorcars and killed. That is murder."

"I have spoken with the police on this matter, Mr. Ballo, and they assured me that it was nothing more than a terrible mishap."

8 leaned forward, resting part of his bulk on the desk, easing the weight on the chair. At the same time, his sizable forearms and substantial hands were within grasping distance of the hospital administrator's scrawny neck. "I have been hired by the widow, Theda Lazar Vogel, to investigate the mysterious circumstances of her husband's death."

"I am certain that Mrs. Vogel is distraught," Dankworth said. "Have her come into the hospital, and we can provide something for her frayed nerves, I'm sure."

"There are witnesses who claim that the two motorcars intentionally ran Dr. Vogel down, and then one of the drivers took something from his body." This was a bit of a stretch, but a small fib was better than wrapping his hands around the man's neck and wiping the smug look from his face. *Maybe.* Certainly not as satisfying.

"What is it that you want?"

8 wasn't sure what it was that he wanted. He just figured that if you poked the bear enough times, something would happen. "Can you think of anybody who would want Karl Vogel dead?"

"You are trying my patience, Mr. Ballo. It was but an accident."

"In my business, Dankworth, the process often involves crossing off possibilities until there is only one left."

"Imagine if we all did that," Dankworth said. "For instance, here at the hospital, if we were to treat every symptom but the correct one until the patient was dead."

Wrapping his hands around the man's neck was sounding better by the moment, 8 thought. Sometimes, it was best to not speak and wait patiently. It must've been a full minute before Dankworth cleared his throat and gave in.

"Dr. Vogel was a surgeon," he said. "And I'd imagine that at times his patients or next of kin were unhappy with the services provided."

"Could you get me a list of all the people who died on his operating table?" 8 asked.

Dankworth scoffed. "That is private information, Mr. Ballo; certainly you understand that."

"How about the other doctors and nurses," 8 said. "Did he have any enemies on staff?"

"Mr. Vogel was known for being a bit brusque with the nurses, but certainly that was not reason enough to kill the man." Dankworth made a production of opening a desk drawer, pulling a file out, and opening it. "I really must be getting back to work, Mr. Ballo, if that is all."

"Can you just tell me what Karl Vogel was like?" 8 settled back tentatively in the rickety chair and folded his arms, indicating he wasn't going anywhere.

Dankworth peered down his nose at him but must've realized that 8 would not be easy to remove from his office. "Dr. Vogel was a private man who kept to himself. He was very esteemed in his field. As a matter of fact, not only was he on the board of directors of the Department of Genetics for the Carnegie Institute of Washington, but he volunteered his time at Welfare Island."

"The Carnegie Institute of Washington? How often would he have to travel to the Capital?"

"The Capital? No, my good man, the offices of the Department of Genetics are just out Long Island in Cold Spring Harbor."

* * *

8 did his best thinking leaning back in his sturdy office chair with his feet up on the desk. Sometimes, this rumination overlapped

with napping, but quite often he woke from that slumber with an inkling or a notion, if not quite a solution.

Ronald Dankworth had proven to be an interesting, if unlikeable, character, 8 reflected. The man had been antagonistic in a passive aggressive manner that suggested he was covering something up. Or, he mused, just circling the wagons so nothing could sneak up and bite him or the hospital in the ass.

8 was starting to get a picture of Karl Vogel as an arrogant male who thought he was better than others merely because of his position, gender, wealth, and the color of his skin. What had Dottie said? That he believed in superior white European breeding and was opposed to those others of inferior genetic material who mated and had offspring. And Dankworth claiming that he might've been a bit brusque with the nurses sounded like a bit of an understatement. But nothing, it would seem, worth murdering him over.

Which, in turn, steered the suspicion of his slaying back to the purported theft of an incredibly valuable artifact. It seemed as if there had to be easier ways to relieve him of this Aquila. Theda had said that Karl was very much a creature of habit and took the same route, at the same time, every day for his morning walk. Thus, the assailants could've easily known his path and chosen their spot.

How would they've known that on this morning that Karl would be carrying the Aquila, if that theft from this person was indeed what happened? And why was he carrying it at all on that particular morning? 8 speculated that each question might hold the answer to the other. If Karl was transporting the Aquila for a reason, whether to hide, sell, or dispose of, it seemed to reason that the assassins knew he'd have it with him. How had they known?

It was possible that they'd been watching Karl, and then had learned at the last minute that Karl would have the Aquila with him. Hence, with little time to plan, those watching him had run him down on the street, relieved him of his package, and hoped that it hadn't been damaged as several thousand pounds of motorcar had rolled over him.

These musings on ancient artifacts taken from bandits during the Great War led 8 to drift into memories of his own time during that atrocious epoch. Memories that often arrived spun together in dreams and nightmares, a hazy, half-glimpsed reality.

8 had been a part of the 41st Division of the First Corps, mostly men from the Pacific Northwest, a replacement division fed piecemeal into wherever they were needed to replace the dead and wounded. He was put into the 77th Division just months before they would acquire the moniker that would brand them ever after— the Lost Battalion. He and Oliver Harvey, his former professor at Washington Square College and now friend, were transferred into this division because it was made up mostly of men from New York City.

When the Meuse Offensive began in September of 1918, he, Oliver, and the division pushed their way into the Argonne Forest. The first obstacles were the trenches and shell holes that they had to drive the Germans from. Then, their mission led them through woods strewn with barbed wire to slow the advance, some of it taller than 8's head if it wasn't lining the bottoms of streams and rivers.

The objective was Hill 198 which would give his division the high ground and be a major step in cutting off supplies shipped via rail car for the German Army. 8 and Oliver were part of Company 308 which reached the peak, but both flanks were driven back, leaving them stranded on the hill. The order came to dig in, creating a pocket, which was a strong defensive position, even if they were greatly outnumbered.

When Major Whittlesey asked for volunteers to try and break through and get word of their position to the command post, 8 and Oliver had proffered their services. They'd crawled out of the pocket that'd been dug into the hill at night, clouds obscuring the moon and stars and providing cover. It was a crisp night as they worked their way downward through the tangled barbed wire a foot at a time.

Part of the problem was that they weren't sure in which direction their command post was located, nor the positions of any of the other companies. Major Whittlesey had sent out homing pigeons with pleas for support, but it was unknown if they'd gotten through. What was known was that there'd been no sign of reinforcements. Food and water were low, their ammunition almost expended. The morale of the men was strangely buoyant for such a dire predicament. But how long could that last?

They came to a trench and slithered down into it to catch their breath and assess their next move. They'd no sooner arrived then the clouds parted, and the moon illuminated the crevice they'd crawled into. Not twenty feet from them was a group of soldiers, maybe seven or eight of them. They were grimy, their faces and uniforms mud splattered.

"Hallo," one of the soldiers said.

8 stared over his leveled Colt pistol, an M1917 given to him by an officer, as they'd left their rifles behind. The greeting had a German accent.

"*Amerikanisch?*" another soldier said. He, as did the others, had rifles leveled at the two of them.

The rim of the trench was four feet up. They'd never get back over the edge before being shot to pieces. There was no way they'd survive a shootout at that distance with that many soldiers.

"*Zigarette?*" A soldier asked.

Oliver slowly reached in his pocket and pulled out a tin in which he kept his pack of Lucky Strikes. He took two steps forward and tossed it to the man.

The man opened the tin and took out the green pack with the red circle on it with shaking hands. He looked back up at Oliver. "*Danke.*" The Germans huddled around him as he handed out the cigarettes. Luckily, there were just enough left for them all to get one.

"Water?" 8 asked.

One of the Germans, cigarette lit, hanging from his mouth, stepped forward and handed 8 a canteen. He and Oliver took generous sips but not so much as to be rude. "Thank you," 8 said. "*Danke.*"

The soldier nodded. 8 and Oliver waved and stepped across the trench to climb out.

"*Amerikanern,*" the soldier said and pointed the to the left of where they were headed. "That way."

"Wake up," Millie said. "Your client is here."

8 opened his eyes, not sure if he'd been dreaming or reflecting, the two states sometimes too similar in nature to know for sure when the subject was the war. Usually, his dreams held some sort of outlandish element, whereas these drifting memories had all been spot on, but at the same time, had held some mystical element that he couldn't quite place his finger on. It was as if he'd received a coded message that he didn't quite understand.

"Wars aren't fought between the likes of you and me, are they Millie?"

"What's that?"

"I mean, the recent Great War, which pitted Americans against Germans, that was the idea of politicians bent on power, the wealthy seeking more riches, and had nothing to do with us common folk."

"I suppose that is so… 8." Millie still hesitated to call him by his given name.

"I feel that we are always having our strings pulled by somebody above us with ulterior motives. It must be for more than power and money, isn't it?"

Millie shifted her feet. "The Übermensch."

"That's Nietzsche, right?

Into the doorway behind Millie stepped Theda Lazar Vogel. She was dressed in the Billy Burke beach pajama fashion, wearing, shockingly, flowing pants of a green satin material, a plain blouse, over which there was a colorful Asian kimono jacket that embraced her figure in a comfortable, yet alluring manner. Her cloche hat matched her wide-legged trousers.

"Good afternoon, Theda," 8 said, standing up with a nimble grace unusual for such a large man. "Come right in."

"Boss?" Millie hovered in the doorway. "Okay if I go ahead home?"

8 looked at his pocket watch, wondering where the afternoon had gone, noting that it was, indeed, five o'clock. "Absolutely. Don't worry about locking up, I'll take care of it." Perhaps he had been sleeping and dreaming rather than meditating and reflecting. He had, after all, been up quite late with Asta, and then down the road early to visit with that Dankworth fellow.

As Millie gathered herself to leave, 8 ushered Theda into his office to a seat across from his desk. He stepped to the door, said goodbye to Millie, and returned to sit across from Theda.

"And what brings you to Bushwick?" he asked, seeing no reason to beat about the bush.

"I was in the neighborhood and thought I'd stop and see if there was any progress in finding the stolen Aquila," she said tentatively.

8 didn't slightly believe she'd been in the area. There was something calculating about Theda's brown eyes that made him doubt she did anything by chance.

"I have descriptions of the two motorcars that struck your husband, a faint description of one of the men who went over to him and possibly took the eagle from him, and this morning spoke with a man at the Brooklyn Hospital who he worked for."

Theda sniffed. "Dankworth?"

"That'd be the gentleman."

"Have you located the automobiles that ran Karl down?"

"No. There is a Captain Archipoili investigating the incident, if not very convincingly, and I shared what I'd found with him. He said he'd look into it, but I got the impression that it was not at the top of his priority list."

"And what did the man look like? The one who ran my husband down."

There was a change of inflection when she asked this, just a slight change of pitch, but one that suggested to 8 that this was of great interest to Theda. "He was very tall and thin with a long and lean face, is about all the description I got. Do you know anybody who fits that description?"

"You don't happen to have a cup of gin lying around, do you?" she asked.

"Down in the basement is a juice joint," he said. There was a bottle of whiskey and gin up in his apartment on the third floor as well, but he had a feeling that going up there might be a dangerous proposition.

"Would you mind stepping down there?" Theda stood up in one flowing motion. "I could use some libation."

8 followed her out, locking up behind, and they went down the stairs to the tavern turned restaurant, through the coat room, and down the stairs to the basement. It was quiet on this Monday just after five o'clock, with only a smattering of patrons, mostly drinking alone and lost in their own thoughts, scattered about the room.

Theda ordered a Bees Knees, gin with honey syrup and lemon, while 8 went with the Old Fashioned. They sat at a corner table, a candle giving them a faint light, lost in the shadows for privacy.

"Do you know who killed your husband and stole the Aquila?" 8 asked.

"You're not married, are you, Mr. Ballo?" Theda took out a Lucky Strike.

8 pulled out his Ronson Wonderliter and lit it for her. He did like the occasional cigar and had also found it was beneficial to have the lighter handy. "No, no, I'm not."

"Ever been in love?"

8 thought about Camila, who he'd been engaged to before he went off to war, the woman who'd married another while he was over in Europe fighting Kaiser Bill. An image of Asta fluttered through the recesses of his thoughts, and even more faintly, of Velma. "Sure. I've been in love plenty of times." He wasn't sure that he believed that.

"Marriage is for better or worse, or so they say. Why don't they say for better or even worse, I wonder."

"Are you saying that you were having trouble with your marriage, Mrs. Vogel?"

"You must call me Theda and I will call you 8, sort of like we're old chums, don't you think?"

"Tell me about Karl, Theda."

She took a long drag on her cigarette through the extended holder. "Karl was a dashing man. He turned the heads of all the young ladies."

"Did you know him before the war?"

Theda snickered. "Karl was not in the war. If he'd been inclined to fight, it would've been a toss-up which side he fought for."

"But you said…my understanding was that Karl was part of the occupation forces after the armistice. Are you saying he didn't actually fight in the war, but arrived in Europe after the fact?"

"I'm saying, my lovely big six, or I supposed I should call you a big 8, that my husband was never in the military."

"Not three days ago you told me different."

"That story was… a fabrication."

8 stared at her, his mind whirling. "And the Aquila?"

"Oh, my, yes, the Aquila is quite real. It is just how Karl acquired the Aquila that was fiction."

"Why?"

"We all have secrets, darling, even from those we marry. I'm sure you've never told your lovers everything about yourself?"

"Are you saying that you kept secrets from your husband?"

"Oh, my, of course I kept secrets from Karl. He'd of never married me if he knew everything." Theda finished her drink and raised the glass, catching the bartender's eye. "How about a Tom Collins this time, my good man."

"How did Karl come to be in possession of this priceless Aquila?"

"It wasn't until after I married him that I learned who he really was, and not because he told me, but because I'm not a Dumb Dora, am I? I have ears and a mind and can put the pieces together when I do hear things."

8 took a sip of his Old Fashioned, just his second nip of the sweet concoction. "And what dots and dashes did you connect?"

"As all good lies, the story is based in truth." The bartender brought over the Tom Collins, and Theda waited for him to leave before resuming. "There really is a clandestine organization known as the *Rein Adler of the Batavi*. Or, in English, the Pure Aquila of the Batavi."

"And Karl was a member of this organization?"

"Yes. I believe he may've been spying on America during the war. They have people infiltrating every sector of the world. When it became apparent that Germany was going to lose the war, Karl was called upon to travel to the Netherlands where he was given the Aquila for safe keeping."

"And he told you this?"

Theda snickered. "Of course not. I've pieced it together, as I told you. He'd go out at strange times of the night. I found a letter he'd written to a man in Germany, and not yet sent, regarding the purity of the white European race, in which he talked of the Pure *Adler* of the Batavi, and how one day they'd rule the world."

8 finished his Old Fashioned in a gulp. This was quite a bit to take in. "That's a lot to piece together."

"Two more," Theda called, raising her empty glass and pointing her white-gloved finger at 8. "Well, now, I suppose one secret I kept form my husband is that I speak German much better than he thought I did."

"And therefore he—"

"Had conversations of a private nature in front of me, yes, it was very much to my advantage to keep him in the dark, don't you see?"

"Tell me about the Aquila," 8 said.

"Karl told me that he had to travel to the Netherlands on a matter of the utmost urgency regarding the war's end but would say no more. He tried to put it that he'd been called upon by his country to be of some great service."

"And by his country, you mean?"

"He wanted me to believe he meant America, but by this time, I knew better, of course." Theda scoffed. "After he came back, I found the Aquila, carefully wrapped, and in a bag, in the secret, or should I say, not so secret, space in the floorboards underneath the bed. It had the book that I told you about with it, that detailed its history, significance, and value."

The drinks came. 8's head was swimming. He didn't think it was from the alcohol. Theda's face was flushed. Her cheeks were infused with excitement, her eyes tinged with drink, and her lips suffused with promise.

"So you think your husband traveled to the Netherlands to be given the eagle symbol of the Pure Aquila of the Batavi to safeguard?" he asked.

"Yes." Theda licked her full lips, her tongue flicking over their glistening ripeness. She reached across the table and put her hand upon his.

"And who do you think killed him and stole the Aquila?"

Theda shook her head, loosening several locks of hair that sprang free of the cloche hat to cloak her cheeks. She was not stunningly beautiful by any stretch of the imagination, but there was a mysterious sexiness to the woman that was certainly intriguing. "I don't know."

"But you believe that your husband was part of this secret society that may well have been an important cog in the German war machine?"

"I do believe that he was part of the RAB, but I don't know what part they played in the German war machine. Or government. Karl has been in possession of the eagle for six years now, or was, until recently."

RAB, 8 thought, trying to untangle his tangled thoughts. What had the German been? *Rein Adler of the Batavia.* RAB. "Meaning that the Batavi could've been significantly weakened due to the war, or else, somebody would've come for the eagle, somebody before now."

"It was enemies that killed him, not friends," Theda said.

"And you've kept this secret all this time."

"He was my husband."

"Why are you sharing this now? With me?"

"I believe that my husband was a traitor to America. And now I need a hero to put things right."

Chapter 7

When Millie came into the office the next morning, 8 went out and sat across from her desk. "You are a constant surprise," he said.

Millie set her bag down and sat as well. "What did I do now?"

8 chuckled. "I mean, yesterday when you referenced Nietzsche and the *Übermensch.*"

"You think that I'm just some dumb woman receptionist?"

"No, not at all, I—"

Millie laughed out loud. It'd taken almost a year of working for him, but a confident and intelligent young woman was starting to emerge from the meek and mousy girl she'd been when she arrived. "Just teasing you. My papa used to read Nietzsche at the dinner table when I was a little girl."

8 saw the faraway look of diving into the past cross over her face. "Is your father still in Germany?"

Millie shook her head. "He died when I was twelve. The year after my mother did."

"Do you want to talk about it?"

"No."

8 nodded. "Okay. What do you know about the *Übermensch?*"

"It was a long time ago," Millie said. A smile tugged the corner of her lip. "I remember my papa reading about how the new man would rise from the ashes of a corrupt Christianity and a world of Nihilism to form a perfect human race of super men. The *Übermensch.*"

There was a knock at the open door, and a man stepped past her through the doorway wearing a skimmer, the straw boater hat a holdover from the summer.

"What can we do for you?" Millie asked.

8 didn't turn around, waiting to see what new surprise the morning of a PI might hold.

"I'm looking for a gent by the name of 8 Ballo." The voice was deep, rich, and husky.

"Fellow looking for you, boss," Millie said. "And he's almost as big as you are."

A wolfish whistle keened through the office. "That must be 8 Ballo, sweetheart. I heard he was a big six. But I bet he don't have arms like these, though, does he?" He held out his right arm, stepping past 8 and grasping Millie's hand with his other and placing it on his bicep.

"Not at all." Millie said, giving him a dazzling smile. "Not nearly as thin and flaccid as all that."

The man stared at her with a puzzled look, then smiled, whistled, and laughed loudly. "I like a woman with a bit of spirit." He turned back to 8. "Hello, Mr. Ballo." His skin was a rich ebony hue, his face boyish, even though 8 guessed the gent was older than him and might even be in his forties. When he took off the skimmer, his bald head gleamed.

8 stood and held out his hand. "8 Ballo. Private investigator."

The man eyed him carefully. "You is certainly a big enough palooka. You ever do any boxing?"

And then 8 knew who the man was. "No, sir, Mr. Jack Johnson. Never been in the ring, anyway, but might've got into a scrap here and there."

Jack Johnson had become the first Black heavyweight boxing champion some fifteen years ago or so, if 8 remembered correctly, having held the title for about seven years before relinquishing in a helluva fight back in 1915.

"Jack will do just fine," he said, holding out an enormous paw and shaking 8's hand. "And I bet you do okay when you scrap. You want to do some sparring, why, I wouldn't mind getting in the ring with you and seeing what you got."

The man's grip was firm but not trying too hard. 8 turned to the inner office and gestured. "Come into my ring, Jack." They went in and sat down. "I saw you fight Sailor Burke up to Bridgeport, Connecticut, back in... must've been 1907, because I remember I was just nineteen years old. You sure pack some power to your punches. I think you put him down more than ten times."

Jack flashed a wide smile. "Fourteen times I put the bum down. He didn't belong in the ring with me. I was awful hungry back then."

"Shame what they did to you with those trumped-up charges."

Jack's smile fell away to be replaced by a snarl. "Always trying to keep Black men down, they are. Don't like it when we rise up above the tidy little spots where they want us to remain. Hell with them. I'll not be intimidated."

8 nodded. Jack had been found guilty of transporting a woman across state lines for immoral purposes and sentenced to a year and a day in jail. He'd initially fled to Canada and lived abroad for some time before returning a few years back and serving his time.

"What can I do for you, Jack?"

"Hawk said you was good people. That you don't much care about what color a man's skin is or where he's from."

8 had run into Coleman Hawkins a few times the previous year in his search for the girl who'd gone awry, Velma. Maybe this favor coming was the reason for his invite to the Dog House the other night. "A fellow who can blow a saxophone like he can certainly gains all my respect."

"He sure can blow," Jack said.

8 waited. He figured that Jack Johnson would get to the reason of his visit when he was ready.

"You know the place up to Harlem called the Cotton Club?" Jack asked after a bit.

"Sure," 8 said. "Been up there a few times myself."

"You know I used to own it?"

"You used to own the Cotton Club?"

"Yeah, only it wasn't called that, and it wasn't such a production as now. Called it the Club De Luxe, a place couples could come and have an intimate dinner together. Was a real nice joint."

"What happened?"

"You ever hear of Owney Madden?"

8 contemplated that. "He ran with the Gophers in Hell's Kitchen. Was a top dog with them, but he got arrested quite a while back and sent off to Sing Sing."

"Not no more he ain't. Mr. Madden got out last year after serving nine. Made me an offer on my joint I couldn't refuse."

"Yeah? What was that?"

Jack held up a fist the size of a ham hock. "Funny thing that a little bit of lead could be more dangerous than this," he said. "But I took his point and went to work for him as the manager of the new Cotton Club. Didn't know he was going to turn it into some sort of recreation of plantation life. Jungle music he calls it, and girls baring their skin, not that that's all bad."

"You think about quitting?"

"Mr. Madden, he said I can leave when he says I can leave." Jack shrugged. "Pays me real decent, don't expect too much, and like I said, the ladies are mighty fine."

"They only employ Black dancers and staff up there, don't they?" 8 asked.

"You got that right. That the only way any Black folk can get through the door, is by working there. But it ain't the Black women got me in trouble. It's a white woman."

8 had a sneaking suspicion they were getting to the reason for this visit. "Go on," he said.

"This guy named Charlie Luciano been coming up to the club a lot lately. The talk is him and Owney knew each other when they was kids in the Five Points. Anyway, the last few weeks, he been bringing this blonde chippy in with him who can't stop looking at me. And she ain't a bad looking broad, not at all. Finally, I broke down, and asked her a few nights back if she might consider having a nibble with me and see what turned out, some night when she wasn't hanging around this Italian bloke, that is."

"You tried to make time with Charlie Luciano's moll?" 8 asked incredulously. Jack looked as close to sheepish as 8 figured the gregarious man ever got. "You're not telling me she went and blabbed to him, are you?"

"She sure enough did. Might've even made up a bit. The next day, Owney, he called me into his office, gave me my walking papers, which is what I wanted, so no big deal. But he told me that this Luciano was gunning for me, and I best disappear if I didn't want to be pushing up daisies."

"So you go away for a spell, let things cool down, and come on back." 8 figured the man could afford it.

"That's the thing. I got a couple dames in the wing in the city. One of them could be the next Mrs. Jack Johnson."

8 had heard all about the boxer's philandering ways, read some in the papers, too. "What do you want from me? To be your bodyguard?"

Jack scoffed. "Jack Johnson don't need no bodyguard. I thought you might go talk to that Luciano fellow, set him straight."

"You want me to tell Charlie Luciano to leave you alone?" 8 couldn't help but sound incredulous.

"Hawk, he said you knew those Jew boys down here in Brooklyn, ya know, Bugsy Siegel and Meyer Lansky."

"I wouldn't say I know them. They thought about killing me about a year back, if that's what you mean."

"And yet you're still alive. They must like you a boatload." Jack laughed, a boom like a cannon going off.

"I think I like my kneecaps the way there are," 8 said. "Unbroken."

"I'll give you fifty bills to get Charlie Luciano off my back."

8 chuckled. "Why don't you just go have a sit down with the man?"

"Because he's most likely to shoot me in the head before I can sit my ass in a chair after propositioning his woman," Jack said. "And me being Black—I ain't getting within a hundred feet of Mr. Charlie Luciano."

8 sighed. "Don't matter if you're white or Black. You don't ask his moll to make time with you unless you got a death wish."

"A hundred bills. Just to intercede on my behalf."

*　*　*

"This the car you're looking for?" McGee asked.

The Kissel Gold Bug Speedster was parked on a street lined with row houses in the newly booming neighborhood of Ridgewood in Queens, which was adjacent to Bushwick. Along the driver's side door there was a streak of red paint.

"Don't imagine there's too many Kissel Gold Bugs with that particular red streak," 8 said. "I'd say that's the one that ran down Karl Vogel."

"One of the roundsmen, lad by the name of Wally Horn, called the station and left me a message. I'd put out a request for them to keep eyes peeled and sure enough, here it is."

"Roundsman?" 8 asked.

"Sorry," McGee said. "They call 'em sergeants now. The lad who keeps an eye on all the other coppers in his unit."

"You know who the owner is?"

"Not yet."

As they spoke, a short man with a light-colored double-breasted mohair suit and a fedora with a black band came down the steps of a row house and made for the Gold Bug. 8 looked at McGee, shrugged, and moved closer. The man paused at the door, looked up, and spotted them approaching. His eyes grew wide under thick eyebrows as he froze for just a split-second, and then he turned and ran across the street.

8 sprinted after him, narrowly being missed by an automobile barreling down the road. Even though large, 8 was agile and fleet of foot, but the small man was fast as well as nimble, weaving in and around people and carts selling produce and other items as he fled. He went around a corner and down a side street, cut through an empty lot, and jumped a fence. 8 was almost upon him as he went over the white pickets with a single bound, impressive for such a short man, and not quite so easily accomplished by 8 as his foot caught the fence top, and he tumbled face-first into bushes on the other side.

The man hotfooted it across the lawn of the single-family home as 8 came to his feet and continued the pursuit. They went over the fence at the back, this time 8 clearing the obstacle easily and again cutting the distance between them. The fellow was looking back over his shoulder, the whites of his eyes showcasing his fear, when McGee hit him full in the chest with the broken limb of a tree.

It took 8 almost as long to recover his breath as it did the man. "What's your name, fellow," he gasped out, grasping the man by the shirtfront and pulling him to his feet.

The man's face was a mottled white and gray, his breath still coming in heaving gulps from the run and the limb to the chest. "What... do... you want?"

8 raised the man so his feet left the ground and slammed him into an oak tree. "What's your name?"

"Fred. Fred Peters."

8 set him back on the ground but wrapped one of his enormous hands around the minuscule man's neck, pinning him to the oak. "Why'd you run from us, Fred?"

"I'm going to pay, honest, it was just a tight month. I had some unforeseen bills and—"

"Pay for what?" 8 loosened his grip on Fred's neck.

"That's why you're here, right?"

"Why don't you tell me what you think this is about?"

"Me owing those Jewish boys money. I'm late on my insurance."

"What Jewish boys?"

Fred squirmed. "Meyer Lansky and Bugsy Siegel. On my juice joint up in Williamsburg. I'm sure glad you came instead of Bugsy. I like my knees fine just as they are."

"Look at me," McGee said. "Can't you see I'm a policeman?" He was, indeed, in full uniform, the four gold buttons on either side of his blue jacket with the badge over his heart and his police cap crooked on his head from the foot chase.

Fred scoffed. "You buttons are all on the payroll. Heck, I make my payment to an op wearing the tin."

"That's not why we're here," 8 said.

"Yeah? Why else you chase me down and bash me with a stick?" Fred was beginning to regain his composure, his anger and arrogance coming out.

"Is that Gold Bug your motorcar?"

"What's it to you?"

8 pulled the man forward and then slammed him back into the tree, his head whipsawing into the bark with a sharp crack.

"What the—"

8 backhanded him across the mouth with his free hand, splitting his lip.

"Sure, fellow, that's my car. Settle down." Fred spit a gob of blood on the ground.

"How'd you get that red streak on the side?" 8 released his hold of the man. "And the dents?"

"Some moron hit it parked on the street," Fred said. "Must've been about two weeks back. Came out about this time of day to go up to my joint in Williamsburg, and there it was."

8 took his pocket watch out. It was just before noontime. "What time do you get home at night, usually speaking?"

Fred shrugged. "A weeknight tends to be by two in the morning, no earlier than midnight."

Plenty of time, 8 mused, for somebody to swipe the man's car, run down Karl Vogel, and bring it back. "You notice anything out of the ordinary the day you realized somebody had hit your car?"

"Like what?"

"Like it was in a different spot then where you left it."

Fred scrunched his bushy eyebrows and pushed his upper lip out with his tongue. "Yeah," he snapped his fingers. "I was thinking it'd been moved but I figured I was just confused about where I left it. Same side of the street, but maybe half a block further down. How'd you know that?"

8 looked at McGee who gave an almost imperceptible shrug.

"Your car was used in a hit-and-run accident," 8 said. "You'll probably be a getting a call from a police detective named Archipoili. He'll have some questions for you."

"You're saying... was anybody hurt?"

"Yes. A fellow by the name of Karl Vogel was killed with your car, Mr. Peters."

Chapter 8

The Midnight Rose Candy Store had an awning over the nondescript brick and glass façade that said, CANDY-SODA-CIGARS. The owner, Rose Gold, was a wisp of an elderly lady with sharp eyes. The shop was open twenty-four hours a day, that being the midnight part of the name. 8 had first come here the previous year on a missing woman case. The second time he'd been there, a grain bag had been put over his head, and he'd thought his ticket was going to be punched.

Rosie gave them a no-nonsense stare when 8 asked to see Siegel and Lansky. He knew enough to not call him Bugsy, a name over which Siegel had reportedly broken several legs. There was a heavyset man with a head shaped like bowling pin to the rear of the shop sitting in a chair reading a paper next to a door. Rosie's eyes flickered in his direction. 8 knew the drill.

The man rapped on the door three times. A small panel at the top slid open. "That gumshoe, 8 Ballo, wants to see Mr. Lansky and Mr. Siegel," the man said through the small opening. The panel closed. About a minute later, the door opened, and a short fellow whose shoulders went up almost to his ears stepped out.

"You packing heat?" he asked.

"Nope," 8 said. It might be almost time to start carrying his .38, he thought, what with working a murder case and having to hobnob with gangsters.

The short fellow with shoulders that sprung up from his body like wings patted him down anyway before turning and gesturing 8 to follow him. They went through another small room past several men who cast them dark looks. In the next room, Bugsy Siegel and Meyer Lansky were sitting at a long table. There were no windows, and smoke swirled through the air of the dimly lit room.

Meyer Lansky stood and held out his hand. He was under five-feet tall and slight of frame. He'd just recently turned twenty-two years of age but had an old face, maybe due to his protruding ears. "My favorite gumshoe," he said. "Good to see you." He'd always been gracious and polite, even when he'd been threatening to kill 8.

"Mr. Lansky." 8 shook his hand.

"And to what do we owe the pleasure of this visit?" Benjamin "Bugsy" Siegel stood and shook 8's hand.

He had movie star good looks and a wide smile. Of course, when angry, which was often, his eyes bulged from his head like some violent monster from hell. This bug-eyed look had earned him his nickname. He also seemed no more than a boy, his face innocent of the touch of a razor. That might've been due to the fact that he'd just turned eighteen this past February.

"Please, have a seat," Lansky said, and the three men sat down, 8 next to Bugsy and across from Lansky.

"You're not poking your nose into our business again, are you?" Bugsy asked.

"Not at all," 8 said. "Well, just a tiny bit. I was hoping for an introduction to Salvatore Luciano." People had started calling the man Charlie, and sometimes, Lucky, as he'd been arrested so many times without anything ever sticking, but 8 thought it best to go with his given Italian name.

"And what business do you have with Lucky?" Bugsy asked.

"Actually," 8 said, "I've met the man once before. He delivered a note from Mr. Rothstein to me. I was hoping you might put me in contact with him." That didn't quite answer the question, 8 thought, but he was hoping to deflect his purpose without saying none of your business.

Bugsy's face blackened like a raincloud coming in hard and fast on the Texas plains. "Yeah, that was right before you shot up my crew."

"Now, now," Lansky said. "We've put that behind us, Ben. I do believe that 8 made that up to us in spades."

"I suppose he did," Bugsy said.

"And what exactly would we be telling Charlie that you'd like to see him about?" Lansky asked.

8 wondered if the man had a pile of books to sit on so he could see over the tabletop. "I'd like to ask him a favor."

Bugsy chortled. "Good luck with that."

8 waited. He'd never put his foot in his mouth when he'd said nothing. Plus, he liked his kneecaps just fine, and saw no sense in antagonizing the man-child next to him.

"I hear that your friend, Stephen McGee, is a sergeant for the 83rd Precinct now," Lansky said.

8 nodded. He knew where this was going. It paid to know your enemies as well as your friends, especially when that designation could switch on a dime. Meyer didn't ever miss a beat, always had another play, and thought like a chess player, nine moves ahead. After the last interaction that 8 had had with the man, he'd done some background research, making sure he knew what there was to know about the budding gangster.

Maier Suchowljansky was born on July 4, 1902, in the Russian Empire, even if he claimed it was Poland. He'd come to the U.S. in 1911 with his mother and brother to join his father and grew up on the Lower East Side. The word on the street was that this Jew from Russia was one of the most brilliant minds of all the gangsters and was going places. So, 8 waited for the shoe to drop.

"The brass up there to Bushwick have rebuffed our entreaties to work together," Lansky continued. "I suppose it has something to do with them not liking Jews."

This might, or might not be true, 8 thought, trying to keep a wry grin form his lips. It might also have to do with what had happened to the last man who'd been paying them off, and who'd done what to him. While Bushwick was largely a German and Hungarian neighborhood, there were plenty enough Jews who'd emigrated from those countries to the shores of the New York and found homes in Bushwick.

Lansky cleared his throat. "If we were to set up a get-together with Charlie, I'd want you to do the same for us. With Sergeant McGee."

8 had an inkling that it wouldn't be long before this tiny man would reach a stature that didn't involve him meeting with lowly sergeants. But, as of yet, he was growing his fiefdom and was interested in Bushwick.

"He's not on the take," 8 said. "Won't do you no good."

"Everybody's on the take," Bugsy said. "But for starters, we just want him to put his elephant ears to work, you know? He hears something, he passes it along."

8 knew he was on very thin ice here. But he never saw much sense in skirting an issue when straight across was where he was going. "No."

Bugsy leaned forward, his eyes beginning to protrude, always a bad sign for whoever they were popping out at. "No?"

"I won't set up a meeting for you."

Bugsy pulled a pistol from a holster under his suit jacket. It looked to be a Walker Colt, not as efficient as some of the more modern guns, but certainly intimidating, most likely why the man carried it. He pointed the long barrel into the side of 8's head.

"I don't much like the word no," Bugsy breathed.

8 knew that the man-child gangster wasn't beyond pulling the trigger. He turned his head so that the barrel was at his forehead. "You got three seconds to pull that trigger or put that gat away before I stick it up your ass,' he said.

Bugsy smiled wickedly and cocked the gun.

8 figured the man's eyes would tighten slightly before he pulled the trigger. That would be the time to act.

"Ben, Ben, put the gun away," Lansky said. "Mr. Ballo has proven very helpful to us in the past."

8 had the thought that it might be tough to tell if Bugsy's eyes tightened as they were fully extended from the sockets like some demented tree frog.

"Bang," Bugsy said. He tilted the pistol upward, uncocked it, and put it back underneath his jacket. "That easy and you're dead, no matter how big you are."

"It might be easy to kill elderly shopkeepers behind on their insurance," 8 said. "But don't mistake me for one of 'em."

* * *

Bettie Young took a deep breath and knocked on the alleyway door of *Tom Thumb*, a speakeasy in Bedford. Sometimes, the best things in life happened at the worst times. "Ain't that the truth," she said softly to herself.

She'd finally made it to the free clinic this morning, standing in line for four hours with an assorted and bedraggled group, all poor, all ailing. If there wasn't something wrong with her when she arrived, Bettie was fairly certain that there would be by the time she left.

People hacked, coughed, sneezed, and spit around her, globs of mucous, sometimes blood. Others were covered in rashes, and one man dragged himself forward each time the line moved on what was an obviously broken leg, so awkward was the bend of the knee. Several people passed out before reaching the front of the line, whether from exhaustion, sickness, alcohol, or drugs, it was hard to tell.

When she finally got inside the building and into a room, the doctor palpated her abdomen where the pain was, asked a few questions, and told her that her appendix was inflamed and would have to be taken out. He was a nice enough sort of man, Bettie thought, with kind eyes that didn't leer at her as he pressed his hands into her flesh.

The lady at the desk gave her a piece of paper that told her to be at the Brooklyn Hospital on Monday morning, or so that's what she told Bettie it said. If the pain were to increase drastically, she should get herself right down to the hospital, as that would most likely mean that the appendix had burst. And that wouldn't be good.

Bettie was about a block from the clinic when she ran into Peaches. He was a thin and grizzled fellow who'd played the piano at the brothel where Bettie used to work. Peaches was the one who'd recognized her voice, and encouraged her to sing, allowing her momentary reprieve from being a Jane for rag-a-muffins. For a time, there'd been no swells for her, not at Madame Johnson's, nicknamed Dirty Johnson's brothel by the regulars.

Peaches latched onto her like she was his lost sister or love, she couldn't quite tell which, hugging her so tightly that her lower stomach growled in pain. The appendix is what the doctor called it, some sort of thing down in there that had to be taken out. Apparently, it had no real purpose other than to cause pain.

It turned out that Peaches was in a bind, as he'd scored a gig at Tom Thumb for him and his band, but the singer had come down with the robber of youth, or tuberculosis as people were calling it now, and he was in a pinch.

That is why she now found herself knocking on a door in an alleyway. A panel opened to reveal two dark eyes looking out at her. "P.T. Barnum," Bettie said.

The door opened, and she left the eerie quiet of the alley into a tsunami of sound. Four men with horns, a trombone, a trumpet, a bugle, and an enormous saxophone marched their way in a weaving pattern across the floor between the patrons blowing on their instruments for all they were worth. The all-Black audience danced, cheered, drank, and celebrated like it was their last night on earth. It was not that large of a space, dimly lit by two chandeliers, small tables around the outside crammed into the walls, a bar at the front four deep with people trying to get drinks, and a crazed dance floor in the center.

Bettie was swept into the room as if caught in a riptide, stumbling, tumbling, and helpless. Her abdomen hurt. Sweat popped out on her brow. She could feel the panic rising in her with insidious intensity. She had to get out of here, a voice screamed in her head. Where was the door she'd come through? It was impossible to see more than a few feet as she was jostled, bumped, and knocked around the dance floor.

A hand grabbed her elbow, and Bettie turned to see Peaches at her side. He guided her smoothly through the melee to a table in the corner where four men sprawled on chairs. Peaches placed her in a chair and introduced the others, names that didn't register, so it wasn't really that she forgot them, but she never knew them at all. They were the band.

Peaches handed her his handkerchief, and Bettie wiped her face of sweat, handing it back embarrassingly damp. A glass of water was put in front of her, and Peaches told her they would be onstage in twenty minutes, as soon as this other band finished up. When a glass of gin followed behind the water, she gulped it down greedily, hoping to soothe her frayed nerves. It was of little help, but the second one put her on the right path.

Before Bettie knew it, she was on stage standing at a microphone with Peaches and four men she didn't know behind her, and a sea of strangers writhing in front of her. A few faces stared up at her, but mostly the crowd yelled conversation back and forth that made little sense out of context, and maybe less in context.

A drum behind Bettie began a slow and steady beat. After a bit, Peaches began trickling notes out of the piano. The man on the bass began strumming. When the horns kicked in, the crowd started to calm as faces turned toward the music.

Bessie cleared her throat. Thought of her life. Changed that to her dreams. A house. Her two children. A man. Two more children. Flowers out front on the porch. She opened her mouth, licked her lips, and began to sing.

> *There ain't nothing I can do, or nothing I can say*
> *That folks don't criticize me*
> *But I'm goin' to do just as I want to anyway*
> *And don't care if they all despise me*
>
> *If I should take a notion*
> *To jump into the ocean*
> *'Tain't nobody's bizness if I do, do, do, do*
>
> *If I go to church on Sunday*
> *Then just shimmy down on Monday*
> *Ain't nobody's bizness if I do, if I do*

By the time this third stanza was complete, you could hear a pin drop in Tom Thumb, but Bettie had no comprehension of that as she was in her dream and lost in her passion. She wasn't even aware of the hooting and hollering as the last note died away.

> *I swear I won't call no copper*
> *If I'm beat up by my papa*
> *'Tain't nobody's bizness if I do, if I do*

It was a two-hour set, and the time passed, dreamlike, each moment as fleeting as the beat of a hummingbird's wing. Bettie started and ended with songs made famous by Bessie Smith.

To the milkman I heard Mary scream
Said she wanted a lots of cream
You've gotta give me some, oh gimme some
Catch it when you come sir, you gotta give me some

Hear my cryin' on my bended knees
If you wanna put my soul at ease
You've gotta give me some, please gimme some
Can't stand it any longer, you gotta give me some

Sheeper called to camel, sugar lump
Said I'm going crazy about your hump
You've got to give me some, please gimme some
I can't wait eight days, you gotta give me some

Jay bird said to the peckerwood
I'd like to peck like a pecker should
But gimme some, yes gimme some
I'm crazy about them worms, you've gotta give me some

The speakeasy called Tom Thumb came unglued as the last notes died away. As Bettie returned to the world, the cheering caressed her soul, and she felt happiness, perhaps for the first time. Or that she could remember. Oh, sure, there'd been little nuggets, but nothing like this. Her soul expanded to where she thought it would burst out of her chest.

A man jumped up on the stage as if carried by the crescendo of applause behind him. "Bravo! Bravo!" he said. "What is your name, my dear?"

"Bettie. Bettie Young." It was as if she'd used up her voice in singing as the words leaked out in a barely audible whisper.

"My name is Fletcher Henderson. My friends call me Smack. I hope you'll do the same." He took her hand in his and smiled broadly.

Bettie Young focused in on the dainty man with the long fingers and the boyish face. He had a pencil-thin mustache, a receding hairline, and a black bow tie. He was also one of the most famous arrangers and bandleaders in the country and a damn fine piano player to boot.

"Hello, Mr. Hend... Smack." Bettie smiled shyly as the man's nickname left her lips. Did this mean they were friends, she wondered?

"I've never heard you sing with these hombres."

"One time deal filling in." Bettie realized her hand was still in his and blushed.

"Outstanding. I got a gig with a few friends at the Back Room of Ratner's two nights from now. Thursday night. Do you think you could be there?"

"What for?" Bettie figured she couldn't afford the price of admission of this Back Room of Ratner's place.

"To sing, my dear Bettie, to sing to the heavens and allow the mere mortals on earth an opportunity to hear your voice."

"You want me to sing with you?"

"Me, Coleman Hawkins, and a fellow by the name of Louis Armstrong. Our regular lady is out of town."

"What?" Bettie almost fainted, and Smack stepped closer to support her.

"You have a talent, Bettie. A true blessing from God. Please tell me you'll do it."

"I can be there."

Smack must've been able to read lips because he smiled broadly and hugged her. "That'll just be a step on your journey, my dear Bettie."

"My journey?"

"We'll let you refine your talent, and then I'll want you to join my orchestra at the Roseland Ballroom up on Broadway and 51st Street."

Bettie did faint at that point.

Chapter 9

On Thursday evening, Pearle picked up 8 in front of his place at just past nine. That morning, a message had arrived for 8, summoning him to a meeting with Salvatore Charlie Lucky Luciano. Bugsy and Lansky had come through. 8 had some trepidation about the visit, as why would a gangster such as Luciano who was rising to the top of the criminal underworld agree to see him? Thus, he invited Pearle to go along. If things went south, there was nobody else in the world he'd rather have watching his back.

8 was sitting on the stoop when Pearle arrived, not wanting his pal to draw attention by laying on the horn of the Nash. He knew someone would probably call the police department if they saw a Black man driving the expensive and gaudy automobile in their neighborhood. The purple and white exterior with orange rims on the white-wall tires had grown on 8, but he could see where some people might be slightly shocked.

It was in 1898 that Brooklyn became part of New York City, when 8 was ten years old, that he first met Pearle Hill. That summer, 8 had fallen in love with baseball, and like most boys his age of the time, would play stickball from morning until dark if allowed. Unfortunately, his father had made it clear that baseball players were of a lower social status, mere entertainers who played the game for the amusement of others and that no self-respecting Ballo would consort with them.

Thus, 8 had taken to wandering outside of his own block to find a game so that Ballo, Sr., wouldn't catch him playing stickball. On that day in the summer of 1898, 8 had found a game in nearby Bedford, asked to join, and had been accepted, perhaps because there was an odd number playing, and they needed one more. It had never crossed his mind that all the other boys were Black. It wasn't until he brought Pearle home one day several weeks later that this difference in skin color was pointed out to him by the back of his father's hand and the lash of his belt.

None of this had stopped 8 and Pearle from becoming the closest of friends. They both had a love for stickball. That bond grew into a shared disregard for injustice. This, and the fact that 8 was white and Pearle was Black, led them into many fights over the years. By the time 8 was fifteen, he was larger and stronger than most men with Pearle not far behind, earning them a reputation as a pair to steer clear of, as Pearle could hand out the chin music with the best of them as well.

Pearle had always proven to be a savvy entrepreneur and grew his business empire while 8 had gone off to Washington Square College up in Manhattan. Their lives, as much of the world's, were interrupted by Kaiser Bill's War. They fought in different units, often not more than ten miles apart. Upon their return, 8 became a PI, and Pearle's business interests flourished. So, ever since 8 had been ten years old, when in a pinch, Pearle had had his back, and vice versa.

"Getting involved with German and Jewish gangsters isn't enough for you," Pearle said by way of greeting, "but now you feel the need to add the Italian mob to the list?"

8 chuckled. "I did get us in a bit of muck with those Italians up to Williamsburg last year already, just saying."

Pearle pulled the car out onto Bushwick Avenue with a squeal of tires. He drove like he lived life, fast. "Them was Sicilians. They like to keep to themselves. Keep their heads low and don't try to draw attention. Your new friend, Luciano, he wants to take over the whole goddamn world, even if he has to walk across piles of dead people to do it."

"We'll make sure to not get in his way," 8 said.

"We're going up to the Back Room at Ratner's?"

"The back of the Back Room as a matter of fact," 8 said somewhat mysteriously.

"What's this all about?"

"Jack Johnson came to see me the other day."

Pearle turned his head to look at 8. "The boxer? Wow. I saw him fight a few times. That man is a bull. Wait, that's right, we saw him fight Sailor Burke together. What'd ole Jack want?"

"Seems he made a play for Lucky Luciano's moll, and she blabbed."

Pearle whistled. "Surprised he's still alive."

"He thought I might intercede. Coleman Hawkins recommended my services."

"Good man, Hawk. As long as he can keep his eyes off my woman. Not sure why he's pulling you into the mess, though."

"Frankly, I'm surprised Luciano agreed to see me. I thought I'd reach out, be rebuffed, and report back to Johnson that I'd been unsuccessful. But here we are."

And there they were, Pearle pulling to the side of the road. Neither one had been to Ratner's before, certainly not to the Back Room, but the message had included instructions for entrance. They went through a gate, down a flight of stairs into a dark alleyway, shadows dancing around them from the flicker of streetlamps behind them. They went up a few short steps.

At the top there were two thugs at the door who were almost as big as 8, even if with significantly less neck. One was bald and the other had a comb-over. It must be something about their beefiness that led to hair loss, 8 figured, or maybe it was the other way around.

"We're here to see Mr. Luciano," 8 said.

Comb-over stepped in front of Pearle. "White patrons only," he said.

"I said we are here to see Mr. Luciano," 8 said. "This is business. We're headed to the back of the Back Room. I don't suppose you wanna explain to him that you turned us away."

"You 8 Ballo?" Comb-over asked.

"That's me."

"Mr. Luciano didn't say there'd be two of you."

"Just one of me," 8 said with a straight face. "This other gent is Mr. Pearle Hill."

"Funny guy, huh?" Baldy said. "How about we tear your tongue out of your mouth and see how funny you is then."

8 chuckled. "Not a good idea. If we have to crunch you two Daises into the cobblestone, who's gonna let us in? And if we don't get in, Mr. Luciano is going to be mad. Do you want to make Mr. Luciano mad?"

"Just you. Not the Black fella," Comb-over said.

"Tell Mr. Luciano we stopped by," 8 said. "Let's get out of here, Pearle." He turned and went back down the four steps with Pearle behind him.

"Wait," Baldy said. "I suppose you can both go in. You packin' heat?"

"No," they both said. 8 thought there was a chance that Pearle was lying.

"Pat 'em down," Baldy said to Comb-over. He did not find a gun on Pearle, but that didn't mean the man didn't have one. "Come with me."

The place was jammed to the gills with human flesh. There was a bar on the left with people vying for a variety of cocktails. Across the room in the far corner there was a small stage with a quartet playing. 8 recognized Smack Henderson on piano, the sight raising his ire, as the man had been sending Asta letters ever since meeting her at the Nest a bit back. With him was Coleman Hawkins blowing the saxophone like a tropical storm and that new fellow, Louis Armstrong, blowing a trumpet sweet as he'd ever heard. He didn't recognize the fourth man.

"This way." Baldy was like an ocean liner moving through the room as people parted like the water in front of him.

They went up a few steps to an upper level, and just as 8 reached the top, a voice in song trembled its way up behind him.

Gee, but it's hard to love someone
when that someone don't love you!
I'm so disgusted, heart-broken, too;
I've got those down-hearted blues;

Once I was crazy 'bout a man;
he mistreated me all the time
The next man I get has got to promise me
to be mine, all mine!

He turned back to look over at the stage. A heavyset Black woman had joined the quartet on stage, her voice beautiful and haunting and provocative all at the same time.

"Who in heck is that?" Pearle asked at his side.

"C'mon," Baldy said. "They's waiting for you."

8 turned and followed the man across the room to a back corner where there was a bookcase. He pushed on a spot to the right, and then swung the entire bookcase inward to another room. "C'mon," Baldy said. "Move it."

They followed him through the opening into another space set up like a room of leisure. The walls were brick, with blue fabric draped here and there, matching the covers on the furniture. A man stood over a bar trolley with various liquors. He had a lean, hatchet face and dark flashing eyes. 8 was pretty sure he was a gentleman by the name of Jack 'Legs' Diamond.

There was a stiff-looking couch shared by Bugsy and Lansky. Across from them, sitting behind a desk, was Salvatore "Charlie Lucky" Luciano. Underneath the wavy curls of his hair was a face that looked like it'd been smashed repeatedly with a two-by-four until it'd been permanently set in a flattened grimace. He was a rising star in the bootleg liquor, brothel, and narcotics business of lower Manhattan.

"Good evening, Mr. Luciano," 8 said.

"Call me Lucky." Luciano stood up and extended his hand. "Who'd you bring with you?"

8 shook the man's hand. The grip was strong and brief. "This is my associate, Pearle Hill."

"Mind if I call you 8 and Pearle?" Luciano asked.

When they nodded it was fine, he waved them to another stiff-looking couch that didn't look like it'd hold their combined weight. 8 perched his bulk gently on the edge. It was solid, and he relaxed a bit.

"The Brain said you were a big fellow," Luciano said, sitting down across the desk. "He sure enough was right."

8 knew that The Brain was Arnold Rothstein, fixer of the 1919 world series, and the top of the organized crime ladder in New York City. "Thank you for agreeing to see us. But we met once before."

"Yeah, I remember. I brought you a message from The Brain." When your face was as flat and craggy as Lucky's, a deadpan look was an easy act to achieve. "I heard about how you helped out Meyer and Bugsy last year. I'd like to thank you for that. It opened up Bushwick for business."

That was the problem with eliminating one criminal, 8 thought with chagrin, as it just opened the door for another one to come through. "It was a matter of self-preservation," he said.

"Whatever." Lucky waved his hand in a twirling motion. "What is it I can do for you?"

"I'd like you to leave Jack Johnson on this side of the ground," 8 said. He saw no reason to beat around the bush. "He is extremely sorry for his actions and will keep himself far away from you and your lady friend."

Luciano scowled. "What's your connection to Johnson?"

8 shook his head. "Never met him before he showed up to my office the other day. But the man sure could fight."

Luciano nodded. "That he could. Why'd he come to you?"

"Coleman Hawkins sent him down to me."

"That Black fellow out there blowing on the saxophone?" Luciano said.

"That'd be the one," 8 said. "What do you say to overlooking a moment of weakness by Mr. Johnson, a mistake of epic proportions, and let him keep breathing the air?"

"I might be able to overlook his transgression, on account of his work in the ring, and more importantly, you asking me." Luciano leaned forward on his arms and gave 8 a piercing and intense stare. "If you think you might be able to do me a favor, that is."

8 sensed that the trap was being laid in plain sight, but he was still going to be unable to avoid it. "What's that?"

"Meyer tells me you got a head on your shoulders."

"What can I help you with... Lucky?"

"I want to hire you to dig us up some dirt on a gent," Luciano said.

"Don't you have plenty of people for that sort of thing?"

"Thing is, I don't think an Italian or a Jew would have very much luck poking around in this gent's suitcase, if you know what I mean."

"No, I don't know what you mean."

Luciano sighed. Sat forward. "On account of him being a racist pig who don't like Italians and Jews, is why. A fellow like you, on account of your white skin and being from the north of the European continent, why you should be able to open more doors than my boys could."

"You'll have to narrow it down as racist pig describes about half of our fair city."

Lucky stared at him, a slightest grin creasing his stony visage. "The one I'm speaking of is a gent called Herman Wall. You heard of him?"

"Sounds familiar, but I can't quite place him."

"He's a schoolteacher who fancies himself a scientist and expert on immigration. He works for the Carnegie Institute of Washington out in Cold Spring Harbor. His testimony to Congress that we Italians are undesirable as citizens helped pass that Johnson-Reed Immigration Act this year. That law drastically reduced the number of my countrymen who can enter the United States."

The Carnegie Institute, 8 thought, keeping his face impassive, the same place that Karl Vogel was on the board of. A small world, indeed. "If I recall, it put a ban on *all* Asians as well."

Lucky waved his hand dismissively. "Yeah, yeah, and a whole bunch more. Seems the only pure people are those from Western Europe. The rest of us are all *pezzi di merda* to be wiped off the shoe before entering the United States."

"But your concern is the Italians?"

"And the Jews. It was Arnie's idea to come speak with you. He's got it in his mind that he can get that racist act rescinded. The Brain, he's got connections in the government, and he's started the wheels moving."

"I'm sorry," 8 said, "but I still don't understand my part in all of this."

Pearle cleared his throat. "He wants you to dig up some dirt on this Wall fellow. Take away his credibility."

Luciano slapped the desk. "Bingo, my man Pearle, you hit that one right on the head. Now I see why the big man brought you along. Credibility! Love that."

8 nodded slowly as he processed this information. "And you think that discrediting the expert testimony of Herman Wall will help that cause?"

"That's about it. You know they based their quotas for us on the 1890 population census? On account so many Italians and Jews came here in the years between then and now. If they used a more recent census, there wouldn't be nearly so many restrictions on our immigration status. Using that number has gotta be illegal or something."

"What if I can't find any dirt on the man?"

"Then you ain't looking hard enough. The man is as dirty as they come. You poke around, you'll find some stuff, trust me."

"What is it that Herman Wall is an expert in?" 8 asked.

"Some sort of notion that certain races of people are superior to others, just due to their genes," Luciano said. "What was it that you called it, Meyer?"

Lansky crossed one leg over another and cleared his throat. "Eugenics," he said.

Chapter 10

The voice of Graham McNamee poured from the radio, his low, sonorous voice overcoming the less-than-ideal reception. *"We have one out here in the bottom of the fourth inning in this scoreless baseball game coming to you from Griffin Stadium in Washington D.C. The pitchers are the story of the day thus far, but Bucky Harris has other things in mind as he digs in at home plate, a glint in his eye as he tries to stare down Vergil Barnes on the mound. Here comes the windup, and there's the pitch. Harris swings his lumber at the ball and makes solid contact. The ball is heading toward the fence and over it. Home run! Bucky Harris has hit a solo home run here in the bottom of the 4th inning to give the Washington Senators a 1-0 lead in this final game of the 1924 World Series."*

The gang had convened again at Pearle's house for the seventh game of what had so far proven to be a historic world series as the Giants and Senators battled it out for the championship. 8, Pearle, Marty, and McGee sat around a table playing poker as they listened to the game. The largest pile of chips was in front of Pearle. They all had drinks in front of them and cigars lit.

"I told you the Giants don't have it in them," Pearle said. "You boys might want to call it a day and hand over the cash."

"It's only the fourth inning there, me lad," McGee said. "Don't be counting your money yet." His pile of chips, as so often was the case, was the smallest.

"I was counting your money as soon as you placed the wager,"

Pearle said as he raked in yet another pot. "As a matter of fact, I've already gotten it spent."

"What's going on with that hit-and-run you been investigating?" McGee ignored Pearle and turned his head toward 8. "Any progress?"

8 shook his head. "Pretty much a dead end so far. Although, I did find out a bit more from the widow. Theda tells me that she thinks her husband may've been targeted for the Aquila, you know, that eagle thing, that he had from the war. Except that he didn't relieve bandits of this priceless Roman heirloom like she told me first. Seems he was part of this secret society tasked with protecting it."

"Secret society?" Marty asked. "I mean, from what you told me at the deli, the Batavi were already a kind of clandestine group, right?"

"Seems that after the Batavi rose up in revolt and wiped out the Roman Legion, capturing the Aquila, that the Romans came back and kicked some ass. A core group of the Batavi went into hiding with the Aquila in their possession. They've existed ever since, but under a different name. As a matter of fact, over the past hundred years or so, they have flourished. Karl Vogel was a Batavi."

"Holy shit," Marty said.

"Game is five card stud," McGee said.

"You're telling me that Vogel was hiding the Aquila in Brooklyn for safekeeping?" Marty picked up his hole card and looked at it.

"He went over to Amsterdam during the war and smuggled it back when things were looking bleak for Kaiser Bill," 8 said. "The organization he belonged to was known as the *Rein Adler of the Batavia,* or RAB for short."

"The Pure Eagle of the Batavia," Marty interpreted. German was just one of several languages he was fluent in.

"Yes."

"What do you know of them?" Marty asked.

"Not much." 8 shrugged. "That's where you come into play."

"Do you know what this...RAB wants to accomplish?" Marty asked.

8 shook his head. "Nope." He pushed a pile of chips into the center of the table. "Two bucks," he said.

"Bullshit," McGee said and matched him.

Marty and Pearle threw their cards down.

"How about you?" 8 looked at Marty "You find out anything more about the Batavi and their rebellion?"

Marty shook his head. "No, but this could be a whole new angle. Clandestine operation hiding a priceless antique. For what purpose? Hm. I'll keep digging. But I did find some connections between that *shmendrik* in Germany, Hitler, and the politics here in the US. I came across an article where Hitler praises America as the one state that has made progress toward a primarily racial conception of citizenship, by excluding certain races from naturalization."

"Meaning what?"

"That Reed Johnson Immigration Bill this year that limits immigrants from certain countries, for one."

"Hm." 8 said. He decided to keep mum about his conversation with Lucky Luciano for the moment. "You think this fellow Hitler has something to do with all this?"

Marty shrugged. "A German-American is killed and has the priceless Aquila stolen from his body. He has something to do with an ancient secret German organization that, as far as I can tell, is based on views similar to those expressed by our dear Herr Hitler…"

"Pretty thin," 8 said.

"Gotta start somewhere," Marty said. "That is the plight of the journalist. Starting thin and growing fat."

"Fat like my bankroll." 8 turned his hole card over revealing a pair of queens.

McGee threw his cards on the table in disgust revealing a pair of jacks. "Jack shit," he said.

8 raked the pot in. "Any more on that fellow's stolen car? The one that ran Vogel down?"

McGee scowled at him. "No. Not that I've been looking. I got my own job to do other than being your errand boy."

"The game is five card draw with deuces wild and the jackpot rule." 8 moved the conversation on as he shuffled the cards. He probably should've let McGee win the last hand, he thought, a wry grin hidden behind a poker face.

"Wild cards?" Pearle said. "Really? That's like honest cheating."

"You just called jacks or better to get my goat," McGee said. "Seeing as I had them last time."

8 dealt the cards around the table. "Anybody heard of the Carnegie Institute of Washington?"

"Some place for science research in the hometown of the baseball team currently winning the world series," Marty said.

"Me and Pearle were chatting with Lucky Luciano yesterday and—"

"You was chatting with Lucky Luciano?" McGee said.

"Yeah, well, we were interceding on behalf of Jack Johnson—"

"The boxer?"

"Would you let the man tell what he's going to tell," Pearle said.

"Whatever," McGee said. "Go ahead."

"Lucky was asking, on account of him doing a favor for me, that I might do one for him. Namely, see if I can dig up some dirt on the assistant director out there, Herman Wall."

"In Washington?" McGee blurted out.

"They got a branch in Cold Spring Harbor called the Station for Experimental Evolution," 8 said. "Which Karl Vogel was on the board of directors of said institute, according to Vogel's boss at the Brooklyn Hospital, a fellow by the name of Dankworth."

Marty whistled. "That Vogel got around. Hospital surgeon and on the board of the Carnegie Institute by day, secret society at night."

"That's what this Dankworth fellow said. Seems they believe in this thing called eugenics. I stopped by the library and started reading up on it, but it was like reading German."

"Marty knows how to speak German," McGee said, missing the

true gist of the statement, a smile creasing his face as he looked at his cards.

Marty sighed. "I'll see what I can dig up on this, what'd you say it was called?"

"The Station for Experimental Evolution at Cold Spring Harbor on Long Island."

"But don't be getting my name mixed up with Lucky Luciano."

McGee held up a finger and turned toward the radio where the announcer, McNamee, was suddenly speaking animatedly.

"And here in the top of the 6th inning, the Giants have something going. Ross Youngs led off with a walk, Kelly singled to center, and Meusel is at bat. Here's the pitch and a crack to right field. Rice settles under it and makes the catch, but Youngs tags up and heads for home. Tie game folks. This game is tied."

"We got us a new game now, me lads. Maybe tonight's the night that Stephen McGee wins the money."

8 chuckled. He, too, had bet on the Giants, as had Marty. He bumped his glass with McGee's as the Giants went on to score two more runs in the inning to take a 3-1 lead.

In the bottom of the 8th inning, the Senators came back and tied the game 3-3 much to the delight of Pearle and chagrin of the others. They'd moved to playing darts, a game that McGee was currently winning.

"You want to take a ride out Long Island on Monday morning?" 8 asked Pearle as McGee went about whipping Marty at darts.

"Sure. What's the name of that place again?"

"The Station for Experimental Evolution."

"Is that another name for some sort of kinky whorehouse?"

8 chuckled. "Tell you the truth, I've no idea what it is. Your guess is as good as mine."

"Sounds good," Pearle said blowing out cigar smoke, his eyes half-closed in the relaxed warmth a few glasses of good hooch will bring.

Here we are in the bottom of the 12th inning with one out and Ruel at the plate. The game is deadlocked 3-3. Here's the pitch, the swing, and it's a pop foul behind the plate. Gowdy flips his mask off and has a bead on the ball. He circles under it...wait, he just tripped on his mask and missed the ball. He missed the ball. Ruel has new life.

"Ugh. Brutal." McGee went and poured a glass of Jameson from the bar.

"You should know better than to bet against me." Pearle chuckled. "The gambling gods shine bright upon me."

With his newfound life, Ruel rips one into the outfield. The ball is in there safely for a hit, wait, he's rounding first and digging for second. He's safe with a double.

"It was sure painful to bet on the Giants after they cheated the Dodgers out of the pennant," McGee said, taking a dollar from Marty and coming back to sit down with Pearle and 8. "But I figured the *cute hoors* they are, they'd figure a way to win this game, not give it away."

And Jackson misses the easy ground ball and the pitcher, Walter Johnson, is safe at first. Ruel stays at second. We have one out and McNeely coming to the plate with two runners on base.

"What a *gobshite*," McGee said. "Just so you know, if the Senators win this game, I'm staying and drinking that entire bottle of Jameson."

"Welcome to it, my friend," Pearle said. "I'm not going anywhere."

'And McNeely hits a ground ball to Lindstrom at third base. This could be a double play ball if—the ball bounces over his head! Ruel rounds third base and crosses home for the win. The Washington Senators win the world series. This game is over!'

Chapter 11

The four men once again met in Fort Green Park. Again, the rotund German and the American sporting a cowboy hat again doing the talking. The other two men, both quite thin, appeared to be bodyguards of some sort for the talkers. They wore long overcoats even though the day was unseasonably warm for late October.

Across the way was a gang of children, about ten to twelve years old, playing skully, a game with thirteen marked spaces, the object being to flick bottle caps into the spaces, starting with number one, and finishing with number thirteen, or the skull.

To their right, a group of younger children played punchball, being too poor to own a proper bat or stick. Older boys and girls strolled around the park, sometimes as a couple, sometimes just eyeballing each other with wistful longing eyes and burning loins.

Men and women paraded along, either courting, married, or just watching the children play, sometimes their own, sometimes not. Through the throngs walked prostitutes, women unattached to any of the brothels in the city such as The Flea Bag, Scottie Lavelle's, Paddy Mullins', or Little Jumbo's.

These women were more prone to be beaten and abused, even worse than in the brothels where a blind eye was usually turned. They were also more likely to be arrested, as they had no benefactor paying off the police, and the Committee of Fourteen was pushing hard to abolish the sex trade in the city. This organization, founded almost twenty years prior by members of the New York Anti-Saloon

League to abolish the practice of saloons acting as brothels, was still a powerful force during Prohibition.

"We have made contact with the men you have asked us to," Rotund German said. "They have heard of the work you do and would be happy to meet with you."

"They will come to New York?" Cowboy Hat asked.

"They will. Most of them are here already." Rotund German took a pinch of snuff between his index finger and thumb and held it to his nose, snorting, and then sneezing, a sing-song sound from such a large man. "What of the item you have promised us?"

"The widow of Karl Vogel has hired a man to investigate his death and search for the Aquila," Cowboy Hat said. "We have hidden it for the time being."

"That is not the agreement." Rotund German's cheeks grew red as he bit off each word. "We have done our part, now it's up to you to turn over the Aquila."

"I hear tell that they will let Herr Hitler out from prison early." Cowboy Hat ignored the demand. "I believe he will be very interested in the work we are doing."

"The *Führer* has spent his time wisely. There is rumor that he has penned a book about his struggle that will change the world, *Mein Kampf*. In it, he marks out the steps to be taken to return Germany to the greatness it deserves."

"A greatness, that I have suggested, lies within the realm of possibility only if the United States and Germany combine their resources. The Bolsheviks to the east, the Italian Fascists to the south, the uptight Brits to the north..." Cowboy Hat stood up, his accomplice rising in one flowing motion at his side.

"It is the United States who has humiliated Germany, what with their *bösartig*, their utterly vicious and humiliating terms of peace at Versailles."

Cowboy Hat took a fat cigar from the inner pocket of his jacket. He made a production of cutting the end, lighting it, and blowing several puffs of smoke. "There is a new wind blowing in America, my friend, and it is fanning the flames of a revolution, a new world order. One of genetic purity, undiluted by inferior races."

Rotund German and sidekick stood as well. "The new Prime Minister of Italy could be that friend to Germany. The *Führer* has made overtures to this Benito Mussolini, and he seems of similar mind."

Cowboy Hat spit to the side. "An Italian? You would ally yourselves with an Italian?" He scoffed, puffed on his cigar. "I am offering you an olive branch between two genetically superior races that we might rule the world unmixed, unblended, pure in every gene, and you speak of some bastardized mongrelisation of the human race?"

Rotund German sneered. "America is the very definition of a mongrel. A mix of Blacks, Jews, Irish, Slavs, and inferior immigrants from all over."

"We are working on that," Cowboy Hat said. "By the time you get your home in order, so too will ours be. But when the time comes, we will not ally with the Italians."

"Sometimes, you must hook the mutt to the sled to get where you are going." Rotund German stepped closer to Cowboy Hat. "And when you reach your destination, then you can make a nice stew."

* * *

8 was feeling on top of the world. Sitting next to him in a splendid red dress was Asta. Jack Johnson had secured them a table right up front at the Cotton Club in appreciation for 8 getting Lucky Luciano to give him a pass on his faux pas.

Edith Wilson and Johnny Dunn's Jazz Hounds were on stage ripping through a set. Light-skinned dancers gyrated onstage as well as off, wearing shockingly little. Waiters wove through them and the throngs of people with drinks and food. Cigarette girls with high top hats hawked their tobacco from boxes slung around their neck in front of them.

I know a gal, got a daddy named Razor Jim
Pistol Pete, Two-Gun Sam, take their hats off to him
He's got a graveyard of his own,
always cuttin' on somebody's bone

Edith Wilson stood onstage like she owned the entire club. Her hair was swept across her forehead from right to left, thick, lustrous, almost like a helmet shined to perfection. At first, she'd stood up with a shy smile, the look of a southern country girl in the big city, but then the music started, and she transformed into a diva, her voice soaring high above and around the mere mortals below her.

Got a gal named Tiger Lil,
he always wants to kill
He has got him her way,
and every day you can hear her say

"He's a mean, mean man, but he's so good to me
When he's around, he's my easy devil as can be"

An all-white mass of couples swayed and surged on the dance floor, men in tuxedos and suits, women in ball gowns and scandalous flapper dresses that hugged the body and stopped short of the knees. Cigarette smoke filled the air, rising into thick clouds above.

When he starts to love, I must confess
That his love is different from the rest
I must tell you, he stands the best
He's got another gal, and they call her Sal

He always pawn her clothes, and kept her in the bow
Girls don't like me 'cause I speak my mind

But he's crazy about me 'cause I take my time
He's a mean, mean man, but he's so good to me

I got myself a razor, also a gun
Cut him if he stands still, and shoot him if he run
He's a mean, mean man, but he's so good to me

"This is marvelous," Asta said, her blue eyes wide and deep, her cheeks glowing to match her red-tasseled dress that hung modestly just past her knees. "If you can get past the way the Black folk are treated here. Can you imagine? They can dance nearly naked, entertain with fine music, wait upon us—but not sit at a table? There's something askew with America."

8 nodded. He agreed. "Jack Johnson said something about plantation entertainment. A show for us white folks to glory in the antebellum period of slavery."

"How very erudite of him." Asta delicately used a fork to eat one of the Oysters Rockefeller that Jack had brought personally to their table.

8 finished his #1 Beer, Owney Madden's own particular brand, thinking it was fine but not a whiskey, and that had to be soon remedied. "I might've filled in a few blanks," he said.

"That Edith Wilson is sure something," Asta said. "But the band isn't bad. I especially like the trombone player."

"I believe his name is Dope Andrews," 8 said. "And that's Edith's husband on the piano."

The waiter delivered a Waldorf salad for Asta and mignon of spring lamb for 8. He ordered a red wine, not being much of wine drinker, he wasn't sure if that paired well with lamb or not, and she got a white.

They'd just finished eating and were contemplating leaving, the mood dampened by the realization of the undisguised bigotry of the Cotton Club, when Jack Johnson appeared with two bottles and three snifter glasses. He wore a white tuxedo and bow tie.

"Brandy for the lady," he said, "but I figured you for more of a whiskey kind of gent, Mr. Ballo."

"You got that right," 8 said, a warm anticipation radiating throughout his body. "Please, join us for a nip?"

Jack poured two whiskeys and a brandy before pulling a chair over and sitting at their table. He raised his glass. "Here's to no more looking over my shoulder, thanks to you, 8 Ballo."

They tapped glasses and drank.

"I've been asked to do a favor for Mr. Luciano," 8 said. "In return for you staying on this side of the ground."

"Anything that I can help with?" Jack asked.

"I'll keep you in mind." 8 took another nip of the fine whiskey.

"Is it hard for you to work here, Mr. Johnson?" Asta asked. "I mean, being treated so poorly and all, on account of the color of your skin."

"Rich people need to feel superior," Jack said. "As long as you smile and say yes sir, no sir, well then, everything is just fine."

"Better than down south, at least, I imagine," 8 said.

"I was born and raised in Galveston, Texas." Jack poured more whiskey for 8. "But it was the poor section, and their ain't no racism with the poor. As long as we're all poor, we in the same boat. I ran with a gang of mostly white boys growing up and never felt they looked down on me or treated me like I was trash." He laughed. "We were all trash, truth be told!"

"That's some truth," 8 said. "My best pal since I was a youngster is Black. I used to play stickball over to Bed-Stuy every day with a bunch of Black kids, and nobody thought much of it, not until we crossed over certain lines."

"It wasn't until I started fighting in front of rich white people that I really got an idea that anything at all was wrong with the color of my skin," Jack said. "It took some time to unlearn that."

"Yeah, well, that's the sort of thing that Luciano asked me to help out with," 8 said.

"Yeah? What sort of thing is that?"

"Seems that there's a fellow out to Cold Spring Harbor who has given expert testimony to Congress on the deficiency of certain people."

Jack leaned forward, his massive forearms bulging, a look to his face that had most likely terrified many a boxer. "What you talking about?"

"This fellow says he has proof that the Italians are predisposed to personal violence, the Irish have considerable mental defectiveness, and the Jews and Blacks are even worse."

"And what are you? Ballo. What's that?"

"I guess maybe a thousand or more years ago I was Italian, but since then, my family lived in Hungary until my parents came over when they were young."

"Germanic, basically."

"According to the fellow out to Cold Spring Harbor, us Germans are thrifty, intelligent, and honest."

Jack's face tightened and his glare increased. Then a flicker of a smile was followed by a huge guffaw. "What's the name of this fellow who thinks so highly of you and so low of me."

8 finished the whiskey and stood up, holding out his hand to Asta, who joined him. "Wall. Herman Wall."

Chapter 12

8 was in his typical position resting his feet on the desk in the back office, but he was reading instead of sleeping. He'd stopped at the Bushwick Public Library, just down the street of the avenue of the same name, where he'd picked up a book on eugenics. The irony of the fact that he got the book from a Carnegie Library to research the Carnegie Institute was not lost on him.

It seemed that the concept of eugenics had its roots in Darwinism and had evolved over time into a powerful social movement in the US, Britain, and Germany. It was no real surprise that these majority white populated countries thought themselves superior based upon the genes that apparently gave their skin its color. Or lack of color. The money for the Eugenics Records Office of the Carnegie Institute had come from John Harvey Kellogg, the inventor of a corn flake cereal, and apparently, also a true believer in superior and inferior genes.

The big chief of the ERO was Charles Davenport who'd been quoted as saying, "Can we build a wall high enough around this country, so as to keep out these cheaper races, or will it be a feeble dam … leaving it to our descendants to abandon the country to the blacks, browns and yellows and seek asylum in New Zealand." Before becoming the head of the ERO, he'd been an instructor of zoology at Harvard.

Davenport's right-hand man was Herman Wall, a former schoolteacher who was an expert on breeding flowers, which for some reason had been considered sufficient qualification for fine-tuning human breeding patterns. They'd started off researching prisoners at Sing Sing, mentally handicapped patients at Gowanda State Hospital, and the freak shows at Coney Island to determine undesirable traits. It seemed that Wall had come a long way, 8 mused, from high school teacher, to interacting with freaks, criminals, and the insane, all the way to influencing Congress to pass restrictive immigration acts.

A banging on the door brought 8 out of his reading and reverie. He slid his feet to the floor and crossed through the outer office to the door, which he yanked open.

A newsboy stood there, a thin ragamuffin of about ten years of age, hat pulled low over his eyes, hair bristling out from underneath, and suspenders over his dark shirt holding his britches up.

"Got a delivery for 8 Ballos, whatever that is," the boy said.

"You got him. I was the 8th Ballo." 8 looked at the shoulder satchel that the boy carried, which was overflowing with newspapers. "This from a Martin Hoffman?"

"Yessir," the boy said. He strode past and into the office, dumping the stack of newspapers on the desk with the confidence of a mature adult who feared little. He pulled an envelope from his pocket, folded and crumpled, and handed it to 8. "And this here note."

8 gave the boy a quarter, thought better of it, and gave him another. It'd been a heavy load to carry. After the newsboy left, 8 looked at the note from Marty Hoffman.

Plenty of material on Cold Spring Harbor, Davenport, Wall, Eugenics. -M

Curt and straight to the point, 8 thought with a wry smile, vintage Marty. He picked up the top newspaper. Marty had circled the headline.

Eugenics—Fad or Function by The Rev. L.O. Rotenbach

8 sifted through the papers, reading just the headlines as he went.

Eugenics or Money to Rule in Marriage

Treating Insanity by Studies of Heredity

Eugenics Propose Laws, Would Use Sterilization, Family Pedigrees

All Men are not born free and equal

Eugenics research Association hears immigration report

Malaga Island in Maine proves Blacks Deficient

8 perused the article under this latest headline. The state of Maine had forcibly removed the citizens of an island off the coast, many of them Black and all of them poor, placing most in an institution for the feeble minded in New Gloucester, going so far as to dig up the dead and rebury them elsewhere to discourage anybody from returning. On its face, the article espoused the degeneracy of the island inhabitants. Reading between the lines, 8 read a portrayal of a Black community that threatened a white population merely because of its mere existence.

He thought of the book he'd just been reading called *The Golden Rule of the Eugenics* by Dr. Albert Edward Wiggam, in which the man had stated that if Jesus were still alive today, he would've been the first president of the Eugenics Congress. 8 wondered if the good doctor thought that meant Jesus would be cleaning up the mess that his father had made with the human race. He grinned, sighed, and sat down at Millie's desk, choosing the article on sterilization and family pedigrees to begin reading.

Charles Davenport had opened the Station for Experimental Evolution in 1904, changing the name to the Eugenics Records Office in 1910 when Mrs. S.E. Harriman had donated a bundle of money to buy an 80-acre tract of land and buildings in Cold Spring Harbor. It was during this period that they'd sent people out into the immigrant neighborhoods, and to hospitals, foundling homes, penal institutions, and asylums to gather records of the insane, those imprisoned, deemed feeble minded, or of loose morals.

The ERO promised to do family pedigrees to get the participation of those suspected of inferior genetic makeup in their record gathering. As the movement gathered force, the organization began recommending sterilization of groups of people, almost entirely women, who were thought to have deficient genes. Over time, the ERO had been assimilated into the Carnegie Institute of Washington at Cold Spring Harbor under its current name, The Department of Genetics.

8 was jarred from his reading by the ringing of the phone. It was Dottie Parker, inviting him to a Sunday afternoon cocktail party being hosted by Theda Lazar Vogel. So much for the grieving period of the widow, 8 thought. Dottie also asked him to meet her that afternoon, in Brooklyn Heights, at a juice joint across from where Theda lived.

One hour later, 8 met Dottie at the basement speakeasy. She was working on a gin drink and deep in conversation with a woman with short wavy hair and a wide smile that appeared only half convinced to be there.

"My dear 8, what took you so long?" Dottie asked. "Never mind, I ran into Eleanor, do you know her? The niece of Teddy Roosevelt and married to that chap named Franklin?"

"It'd probably be best if you didn't associate me with Teddy," Eleanor said, "as I've been campaigning against my cousin, his son with the same first name, in the governor's race. Alfred is just such a better candidate than young Teddy, don't you think?"

Dottie chortled. "Well, if he's handsome, ruthless, and stupid, then he's my kind of man."

Eleanor snickered back. "We all create the person we become by our choices as we go through life. In a real sense, by the time we are adults, we are the sum total of the choices we have made."

"I, of course, know of Mrs. Roosevelt," 8 said. "And the marvelous social work she performs, especially in the Black communities."

Eleanor stood up and held out her hand to shake. She was extremely tall, almost as tall as 8, with broad shoulders and sparkling blue eyes. "Why thank you. Dottie has told me about you, and explained your unique moniker."

"Funny," Dottie said. "I was just telling Eleanor that we were soon to be going across the street to a cocktail party given by Theda Vogel this weekend, and she was saying that our lovely Theda is no friend to the Black community."

The bartender came by and 8 ordered a whiskey as Eleanor sat back down. A scowl blew across her face when he ordered, quickly disappearing behind the challenging half-smile.

"Or the Jews, Asians, or Italians for that matter," she said.

"I've heard that her late husband was on the board of directors at the Department of Genetics out to Cold Spring Harbor," 8 said. "Part of the Carnegie Institute of Washington."

Eleanor snorted. "Quacks, they are. So-called scientists and doctors twisting facts to get a rise. No better than yellow journalism if you ask me."

"What are they after?" 8 asked. "I mean, why?"

"Rich bigotry," Eleanor said. "They are backed by the wealthiest members of our country, to do just one thing, prove that white Europeans are superior to all other races."

"And I thought we were a melting pot here," 8 said. "Accepting all who chose to come."

"Give me your tired, your poor," Dottie recited, "your huddled masses yearning to breathe free, the wretched refuse of your teeming shore. Send these, the homeless, tempest-tost to me, I lift my lamp beside the golden door."

"As long as they are industrious, rich, and white," Eleanor said.

"I thought all that hatred was bottled up back in Europe," 8 said. "Perhaps with that fellow in Germany, Adolf Hitler."

"What do *you* know of Hitler?" Eleanor asked.

8 shrugged. "Got a buddy down to the Eagle who was talking about him some."

"Hate and force cannot be in just one part of the world without having an effect on the rest of it." Eleanor set her empty glass on the bar. "I have to get back on the campaign trail."

8 watched the woman leave, striding through the speakeasy like it was her living room. "I thought she was against the consumption of alcohol."

Dorothy smiled her quirky smile. "She had a lemonade, I believe. Although, you ask me, she's probably going to report this place to the commissioner as soon as she gets a chance. We should split before the coppers arrive."

Theda Vogel lived in an apartment on Pierpont Street in Brooklyn Village, formerly known as Clover Hill, with a catty-corner view of the East River and Manhattan across the way. It was on the top floor, and they took the lift, 8 thinking that it surely must be bad luck to live on the 13th floor.

They were let in by a young man in a tuxedo who sported a thick mustache and had mournful eyes. 8 wondered if he was the butler or just one of the guests. About twenty people milled about the sitting room, a cloud of smoke wafting above them.

Dottie must not have told Theda she was bringing 8 as her escort, for her face momentarily registered shock before carefully tucking itself back into a welcoming and warm smile. The grieving period most certainly seemed to be over as Theda wore a low-cut dress, even if it was black, with an embroidered pattern in gold, as well as beads and sequins. A red boa was wrapped around her neck, and there was a feather in a band upon her head.

"Dottie, so lovely of you to come, and to bring my PI along as well, how darling," Theda said.

Dottie tittered. "I was afraid if I came alone, I'd leave with somebody's husband."

8 blushed, thinking that it was not so long that Theda's husband had been run down on the street and killed. "I hope it's okay that I came," he said.

Theda cast a glare in Dottie's direction before turning and enveloping 8 with a smile. "On the contrary, I am quite glad that you came. I've come across something that I wanted to share with you." She turned back to Dottie, her eyes calculating. "Do you mind if I steal your escort for a bit? I promise to return him in one piece. Perhaps you could go speak with somebody's husband?"

"Oh, I will find myself a gin and some handsome young man to drool over," Dottie said. "You make sure to show my dear 8 a good time. He looks rather gloomy today."

Theda led 8 to her bedroom, closing the door behind them. He was glad to see a drink cart that had a bottle of Bowmore scotch on it with several tumblers. Theda poured him one without asking, handing the glass over, before spilling a nip into another glass for herself.

"Do you have an update for me?" she asked, stepping in close so that he caught a whiff of the vanilla scent wafting from her body, as well as a view down the front of her dress.

"I found the car that hit and killed your husband," 8 said. "Unfortunately, I believe it was...borrowed without the owner's knowledge." As he said these things, he wondered if that was entirely true. Maybe the fellow in Bushwick who owned it had *let* somebody use his car and was just covering his tracks.

Theda shuddered. "You must think me awful. Throwing a soirée like this with my husband so recently dead."

"Not my job to judge." He shrugged. "I leave that to others."

She put her hand on his chest, eyelashes flickering as she looked up at him, her upturned face just below his. "I told you that my marriage was…well, a shambles. It is hard to love and care for a man who deceives you about everything and is a traitor to his country. To my country."

"What did you want to speak with me about?" 8 took a step back, away from the intoxicating temptation before him. Feature by feature, 8 thought, she was no beauty, but somehow all the pieces put together created quite a mysterious and sexy bombshell. He took a drink to steady his senses, clear his head, dampen the tingle that vibrated through his body. "I'm sure it wasn't just that your marriage had difficulties."

Theda giggled. "No, but I hope that you believe me and don't think me awful." She stepped tentatively toward him, crowding his back to the side of the bed.

"What is it, then?" 8 felt the blood surging through his body, which was electric with a delicious torment. Her lips were red, glistening, inviting.

"I remembered that I saw Karl arguing with two men the day before he was murdered. A heavyset man with greasy hair underneath a beret that matched his oiled mustache. And the other fellow was tall and thin. You said that the man who struck Karl, and then went over to his body, fit that description, didn't you?"

"You didn't think to tell me before now that you saw your husband arguing with two men the day before he died?"

"Oh, I'm such a ditz, but it really has been quite a whirlwind, and my thoughts have gotten themselves all muddled like the sugar in an Old Fashioned."

8 didn't believe that at all but held his tongue.

Theda put her hands around his shoulders, her breasts pressed to his stomach as she looked up at him. "Don't think harshly of me, please, 8, for that I couldn't bear."

"What did they argue about?" 8's voice didn't sound like his own. Or, if it was, as if it were echoing through a cavern.

"I don't know. I saw them out the window. They were waving their arms, and I'd thought I'd go down and see what it was all about, not that I'm a busybody, mind you, but because I was beginning to piece together that my husband was not who he said he was."

"Did you go down?"

"Yes. My husband was no longer there, but I saw these two fellows ambling down the street, so I followed them over to the Hotel Bossert. They were staying in adjoining rooms on the fourth floor. Rooms 5 and 6."

8's mind raced with this information, and he didn't realize that Theda was pulling him down while standing up on tiptoes at the same time, her lips inches from his, her scent bewitching, her body firm and ripe and pressed against his.

The door opened. "Oh, there you are my dear 8," Dottie said. "Nothing but bores out there. Do come save me. You don't mind, my lovely Theda, do you, if I steal my date back?"

Chapter 13

8 put Dottie in a yellow cab down on Pierpont Street. He was still reeling from the bewitching seduction that he'd almost succumbed to. Theda Lazar Vogel was quite the woman.

Dottie reached up and put her palm flat against his cheek before he was able to close the door. "Be careful of that one, my dear 8. Theda can speak eighteen different languages but is unable to say no in any of them."

8 chuckled and wondered about his own seeming lack of ability to say no. "I think it was me struggling to say no, to be honest, so thank you for the intrusion."

"Just because the fruit is hanging ripe on the tree doesn't mean you have to pick it." She pulled the door shut and the cab lurched into the street, teeming with late afternoon automobiles, wagons, carriages, and even several bicycles.

8 watched until the cab went around the corner on its way to the Brooklyn Bridge and back to Manhattan. He looked up at the outside of the building in which Theda lived and flirted with the possibility of going back inside.

She was a client. Her intentions were murky at best. He thought of Asta.

He and Asta had a good relationship, but it was not one that appeared to be either serious or meant for longevity. They had a good time together, enjoyed each other's company, laughed together, and the lovemaking was enjoyable. Perhaps that was enough, 8 mused, wondering about that spark of burning intensity that people and poets spoke of when one fell in love. Maybe that was all just a pipe dream.

Before he knew it, his feet were in motion, taking him down the street, away from the intoxicating Theda, toward the Bossert Hotel. He thought of Velma as he walked, a young lady he'd met the previous year, and one who'd also been staying at this particular hotel. It was from the rooftop restaurant, *The Marine*, that the man Mouse had taken her. Even though 8 was dating a blonde-haired, blue-eyed, Dutch woman, it seemed that he might have a weakness for slender women with dark hair and eyes. Rapport, love, lust, and infatuation. So hard to distinguish between them.

It wasn't far to the Hotel Bossert. 8 went through the lobby to the stairs, knowing right where they were, avoiding the elevator and prying questions from its operator. 8 wasn't a man to shy away from doing what needed to be done. Sometimes you had to take the bull by the horns. He went up to Room 5 on the fourth floor and knocked.

There was a bit of rustling and then the door opened. The man who opened the door had on a rumpled white shirt, his extra flesh bulging out of it. His jawline had missed the razor this morning, and his hair was carefully patterned in a cowlick fashion to cover up bald spots on his head. And he had an oiled mustache.

"What do you want?" He had a thick German accent.

"Do you mind if I come in?" 8 crowded the man backward and into the apartment-style hotel room.

"Who are you?"

"My name is 8 Ballo."

The man's eyes tightened in recognition at the words. "What do you want with me?"

"Do…did you know Karl Vogel?"

"Karl? No, I know of no Karl. Please leave my room."

There was a bottle in an ice bucket with a label that said *Obstbrand* next to two silver jiggers. 8 went over and poured the clear liquid smelling of fruit and spirits, turning and handing one to the German. "*Schnappen*," he said, and tossed the brandy drink back.

The German stared with narrow eyes at 8, gave an almost imperceptible shrug, and poured the cold liquor down his throat. "Now I must ask you to go."

8 took the jigger back, poured two more, handed one back, and again knocked back the fruity spirit. It was ice-cold and refreshing. "What is your name?" he asked.

"I am Heinrich Funk. Now please tell me your business."

"Let's have a seat." There was a small round table pushed into the corner with two wooden chairs.

Funk stood still without moving, and 8 stepped into his space, looking down on the man who was no more than four inches over five-feet tall. He put one hand on the man's shoulder and gave a squeeze. 8 could be very persuasive in a very subtle manner when necessary.

"Please," 8 said. "Have a seat."

Funk allowed himself to be guided over and seated at the table.

"Now," 8 said, "tell me how you know Karl Vogel."

"I told you. I do not know this man."

"His wife told me that she saw you, and another man, arguing with Karl the day before he was run down on the street and killed."

"She is mistaken. I know of no such man."

"She followed you and a tall, thin man back to this very room afterward."

"Women get very easily confused. I think she mixed me up with somebody else."

8 reached over and took the man's elbow. Squeezed firmly. He'd once broken a man's elbow in this fashion. Funk squirmed. Sweat popped out on his face giving him a sweaty look as if he'd been laboring.

8 smiled and loosened his grip. "The day after Theda witnessed

your altercation with Karl Vogel, he was killed. He was struck by an automobile driven by a tall thin man. This man stole something form his body."

"What does any of this have to do with me?"

"I believe that what was taken from him was an Aquila. A relic of the *Rein Adler of the Batavi*. What do you know of them?"

The fat man's jowls bulged and sweat ran freely down his face. That was when the tall, thin man stepped into the room with an ugly pistol pointed at 8. He thought it was a Mauser, of which he'd seen plenty of back in Kaiser Bill's War.

The man hadn't immediately shot him, which meant that he didn't intend to unless he had to. It was unlikely that these two Germans wanted to draw attention to themselves, much less be discovered with a dead man in their hotel apartment.

"I appreciate your hospitality." 8 stood. "But I think it is time for me to go." He took two steps toward the man with pistol who didn't waver. "My, you *are* a tall fellow, aren't you? And thin, too."

"What are you doing here?" the man asked.

"I just came over for a friendly chat with Funk, here."

"What do you know?"

8 sensed a rustle of movement behind him and then something crashed into the back of his head. He stumbled forward, fighting the shadows, and the thin man struck him in the side of the head with his pistol. Then the shadows went to night.

Chapter 14

Pearle didn't say a word for the first fifteen minutes after he picked up 8 the next morning for the trip out to Cold Spring Harbor. Finally, he cracked. "You gonna tell me what happened to you?"

8's eyes were still blurry from the blow to the back of his head, which he was thinking may've been the base of a lamp that struck him, from the size of the lump. Or maybe it was the pistol blow to the side of the head. He wasn't sure if he'd fallen on his face or if they'd kicked him around some more, but when he came to, his right eye was swollen almost shut and dried blood caked his mouth and chin.

The two Germans had packed and scrammed. Through a fog, 8 had made inquiries at the desk. The manager had ended up calling the police, whether due to the insistent nature of 8's questions or his blood-splattered visage, it was tough to say. Luckily, it was Captain Archipoili with another officer who finally showed up to get to the bottom of the matter.

After telling Archipoili what he knew, which was precious little, he'd allowed himself to be shooed away to care for his injuries. It was suggested he might want to stop over to the Brooklyn Hospital to get his noggin checked out, but thoughts of Dankworth and hospitals in general made that a no go. They'd brought along a paddy wagon, most likely because the manager had exaggerated the ruckus, but he refused a ride in that as well, choosing to walk and clear his murky melon.

Pearle listened carefully, quietly, his hands grasping the steering wheel of the Nash in a death grip. "You think it was them two gents who killed Vogel and stole his eagle?" he asked when 8 was done.

"Hard to say for sure but there's certainly a plethora of circumstantial evidence pointing its accusatory finger at Heinrich Funk and his tall and thin gunslinger."

Pearle guffawed. "Man, you must've really taken a wallop to the ole' melon. What, when you start throwing plethora, circumstantial, and accusatory all into one sentence like that."

8 groaned and closed his eyes. "But the question is, why are they still here? If they came from Germany to steal the Aquila, why haven't they left and gone back?"

Pearle paused before putting words to his thoughts. "Let me get this straight. The story according to the lady who keeps changing it, is that Karl Vogel was part of some sort of secret society based in Germany called the Batavi, or some such thing. As Germany is losing the war, and they are worried about looters finding their... mascot? They contact Vogel to come smuggle this eagle out of the country."

"That's about it," 8 said. "I believe she tried to seduce me last night before I went over and got whacked by Jerry and his pal Fritz."

"She? Theda Vogel? You mean the grieving widow tried to barneymug you?" Pearle laughed loudly. "Why do all these women think you PIs are all sheiks? How many clients have you slept with since you hung your shingle out?"

The thirty miles took them almost two hours to traverse. It was not long before they moved on from the case and 8's battered face to other things. They talked a bit of politics but mostly of sports. They argued the outcome of the World Series before moving onto the upcoming season in the Metropolitan Basketball League. The Brooklyn Visitations had won the championship the year before and were projected to do so again this year. As long as they didn't have to play the Celtics, that barnstorming team from Boston, who pretty much trounced everybody they played. Good thing they didn't belong to the league.

The complex at Cold Spring Harbor was nestled on the water. Foliage season had arrived, and hardwood trees partly hid the buildings with their beautiful array of colorful leaves. They asked for the Eugenics Records Office, were told politely it was now called the Department of Genetics, and were directed toward a building that looked like it'd been converted from a home into a business office. They went across a grassy lawn, up onto a porch, and into the repurposed Cape.

It took some haggling and waiting, but eventually they found themselves sitting across a massive maple desk from Herman Wall, the assistant director of the facility. He wore what looked to be a large fedora or a small cowboy hat, suggesting that he rarely took the topper off, appeared to have a receding hairline, a stiff jaw, squinty eyes, and small ears. He wore an oak-brown tweed wool suit over a starched white shirt and a snug tie. Another man, very tall and very thin, sat in the corner.

"I am a very busy man," Wall said by way of greeting. "What can I do for you?"

"My name is 8 Ballo, and this is Pearle Hill. I understand that you are Herman Wall?"

Wall coughed. "Yes. Maybe it'd be best if your chauffeur waited in the car, Mr. Ballo."

8 felt the ire emanate from Pearle next to him and spoke before his friend could. "Mr. Hill is my associate."

Wall never took his eyes from 8. "Is that so?"

"That is so. We are looking into the death of one of your board of directors."

"Is that so?" Wall said again. "You are with the police?" His tone suggested that he knew this was *not* so.

"I am a private investigator."

"Is that so?"

"I understand that Karl Vogel was on the board of directors here at the Eugenics Records Office."

"The Department of Genetics of the Carnegie Institution of Washington," he corrected, his voice officious.

"That has a much more polished scientific ring to it, for sure," Pearle observed primly.

Wall looked at him with disdain.

"What can you tell me about Karl Vogel?" 8 asked. He figured it best to try and get some essential information before Pearle hauled the man across the desk and taught him some manners.

Wall steepled his fingers in front of him and appeared to be thinking. "I didn't know him very well at all. I knew his wife, Theda, much better. She was a record collector for us fresh out of college with a biology degree. That is, until she met Karl. Then, she stopped working and became a housewife. We lost her but gained him."

There was a lot to disassemble here, 8 thought. "Theda worked for you?"

"Yes, I believe she started back in 1911 or 12."

"And what is the job of a *record collector*?"

"To collect records, Mr. Ballo."

8 felt himself bridle but took a deep breath. "Tell me what it is you do here, Mr. Wall."

"We collect information." Wall took his hat off and placed it on the desk, running his hand back over his mostly bald top, thin hair circling his bare dome. "Our purpose is to improve the human race and make it the best it can possibly be. To that end, we collect data through questionnaires."

"And what data is that? 8 asked.

"The characteristics of individuals and their extended family, ranging from physical to temperamental properties."

"To what purpose?" Pearle asked.

Wall looked at him with narrow eyes. "I've already said. To improve humanity."

"How, exactly, is asking some questions going to make people better?" Pearle's eyes were flashing dangerously.

"We are in the process of locating deficient genes and weeding them out," Wall said. "It is no different than breeding horses, really, when you think about it. Take the Kentucky Derby champion, Black Gold," he scoffed. "Unfortunate name, really, but his breeding is impeccable, and that is why he is the fastest horse in the world. It is not training but genetics. If he in turn was bred with a zebra from Africa, do you think that the resulting offspring would be equally fast? No, of course not."

8 could sense the explosion rippling up through Pearle. He thought, trying to hide the smirk, of asking Pearle to go wait at the motorcar. "So, Mr. Wall, the ERO, or whatever it is you call it now, collects data for the purpose of ensuring that thoroughbreds don't breed with zebras? So to speak, of course."

"Thoroughbreds breeding with zebras has only one outcome," Wall said. "The end of the civilized world."

Okay, 8 thought, time to bring the man back onto topic before Pearle stepped across the desk and ripped the smug smile from his face. "What was Karl Vogel's...area of expertise for the ERO?" he asked.

"The Department of Genetics, Mr. Ballo."

"What did Karl Vogel do for the Department of Genetics?"

"You are Hungarian, Mr. Ballo?" Wall said.

"Yes." 8 sat forward and drummed his fingers on the desk. "Why do I get the feeling that you're avoiding my questions?"

Wall leaned back and laced his fingers over his stomach. "There is not much to tell you, Mr. Ballo. Karl Vogel was a doctor and a student, a student of the work of Gregor Mendel. Nothing more than that."

"He was the fellow who did breeding experiments with pea plants?"

8 asked. He had, after all, done some research on the subject.

"Yes."

"Was Vogel on any special committees?"

Wall leaned forward, opened a desk drawer, and took out a folder. He skimmed through the papers within before looking up. "He was on the committee of feeble mindedness."

"You mean the committee was feeble minded?" Pearle asked.

Wall looked down his nose with scorn. "It is a committee tasked with finding and understanding those who are deficient in mental capacity."

"And is that also what he consulted about?" 8 asked.

"No, his consult work relied upon his medical knowledge as a doctor."

"What, specifically?" 8 asked.

Wall pulled up a pocket watch from his vest pocket. "I am sorry, but I have another meeting that I must be getting to. Luther, will you see these... men out?"

Luther stood up from his perch in the corner, the angles of his body straightening, forever it seemed. 8 guessed that the man was close to seven-feet tall but weighed less than his own 240 pounds. His face reminded 8 of a vulture, with a hooked beak for a nose and beady eyes.

*　*　*

Bettie took a deep breath, squared her shoulders, and opened the door of the Brooklyn Hospital. Thursday night she'd been singing with Smack Henderson, Coleman Hawkins, and Louis Armstrong. At a real clip joint. Swanky with rich patrons. This coming Friday she was going out to dinner with Smack, presumably to talk about her singing with his orchestra at the Roseland Ballroom. But the way he'd asked, well, it had sounded more like a date. A romantic evening. As if the man was interested in her. Bettie Young.

Today, she was going to get her appendix out, get rid of that burning in her abdomen. Smack had paid her twenty dollars for singing at the Back Room the other night, and that money had bought good will with her aunt, gained a stay of expulsion by a few more weeks for her and her children. If this thing with Smack worked out, the orchestra, for she couldn't even allow herself to consider more, well then, she'd be able to get her own place. There'd be no more begging her aunt, no more pleasuring strangers in the park, no more going hungry.

She went up several steps. There was a woman at a desk with square, black glasses, her hair tied severely back. Bettie had to wait in a line of three people, but soon enough, found herself facing the stern woman.

"Bettie Young. I, uh, I have an appointment."

The woman shuffled through some papers. "I don't see your name."

A skinny, balding man stepped up behind her. "I'll take care of this."

"What?" The stern woman turned her head. "Mr. Dankworth? I don't have any record of this woman."

"I said I would take care of this." Dankworth spoke curtly, and then with difficulty, pasted a smile on his face as he looked up. "Bettie, is it? Please come with me."

"I'm here for a, uh, a medical procedure," Bettie said. "I'm supposed to get my appendix out."

"Yes, I know," Dankworth said. "Please. Come with me." He gestured down the hallway with a wide smile enveloping his face. "We'll get you taken right care of."

* * *

Asta Holm had worked the noon to eight shift at the telephone operator office and was on her way home. It was a dark night, shifting clouds above only occasionally allowing a glimpse of the moon, looking like a muffin broken in half, before again disappearing. It was a mile from her work to her home in the top corner of Bushwick where she shared an apartment with another woman.

The city was quiet, or as calm as it ever was, on this Monday evening. It was as if the beast had paused to take a breath, resting before lurching onward. Connecting people on the blowers was not a bad gig, as jobs went. Of course, there were the occasional mugs who treated her poorly, likely thugs and dope fiends, but for the most part it was the bee's knees. She was friends with most of the other girls, and the big cheese was a nice enough fella.

What she really wanted, though, was to work with 8. Even though it was not her ambition to be his secretary, answering the phone and typing up things, she'd been severely disappointed when he'd hired that Millicent Winter without even asking her. A girl had to start somewhere, and at the front desk at least got her foot in the door. What she really wanted was to be a gumshoe, investigating crimes, looking for missing persons, and solving murders. Asta knew that many of 8's cases were of a more mundane sort, but a girl could dream, couldn't she?

Not that she'd ever told 8 she was interested in working with him, in his office, side by side, solving crime. But she was. Badly. She'd fallen for the big lug of a Hungarian from the first time she set eyes on him, but it wasn't until last October, just over a year ago, that she'd realized that she wanted to be a gumshoe. That was when she had come across the magazine called the *Black Mask* and read the first installment of a serial by a fella called Dashiell Hammett. *The Continental Op*. Asta had hungrily gobbled up that and every installment since.

As she came to a section where several streetlights were out, she glanced over her shoulder. The tall man who'd been on the corner, just outside of the telephone office, was about a block behind her. It could be a coincidence. The man might just be going in the same direction as her, at the same pace. But 8 had told her many a time that coincidences were unlikely events. And betting your safety on an unlikely event, especially when you were a woman, was not a very smart move to make.

An old man was sitting on his stoop, and Asta thought about joining him. But if this flagpole of a man was targeting her, the old man would be only an innocent victim on the thug's way to ravishing her. No, better to keep moving. There was a restaurant a couple of hundred yards up the street that she could duck into. Asta quickened her pace.

The footsteps behind her seemed to come faster, louder in her ears. She turned to look again and realized the man had increased his speed, his long legs chewing up the gap between them like a wolf devouring its prey. Asta realized she'd reached the darkest spot on the street, an empty lot overgrown with weeds to her left, still too far to reach the lights of the restaurant.

Two shadows emerged in front of her from the gloom, a couple walking arm in arm, weaving slightly. The footsteps were right behind her now, but they'd slowed, matched her pace. Asta reached into her purse, her hand grasping the knife that had been a gift from 8, a Schrade two-blade pushbutton automatic. The longer blade was just under four inches, plenty enough to dissuade a man if plunged into his neck.

She passed by the couple, took two steps, and turned around. "What do you want?" The knife was in her hand, the blade sprung, but hard to even see in the darkness.

The couple stopped, the man looking back around, first at Asta, and then at the tall, thin man behind her.

"Hey pal, you bothering the lady?" he said.

The tall, thin man had a fedora pulled low over his face. All that Asta could make out was that his nose was hooked, his cheeks lean.

"Mind your business," the thin man said. His voice was gravelly, like the jagged edge of a rocky coastline.

"He's been chasing after me," Asta said.

The man grasped the arm of the thin man who punched him in the jaw, the sound cracking out like a gunshot, the man crumpling to the ground without a sound.

Asta turned and ran.

Chapter 15

8 woke in the morning before the first light of the day crept over the horizon. He had a sense of unease. This hit and run, potential murder, possible theft, had morphed into something entirely more complicated. It'd been less than two weeks since Theda Lazur Vogel had shown up in his office. She'd proven to be less than straightforward, of questionable moral values, and possessed an intangible sexiness.

What was this secret society of the Batavi all about? And if the story of the "stolen" Aquila were indeed true, what were these shadowy figures really doing in the US?

Ronald Dankworth, Vice-President at the Brooklyn Hospital, had seemed to be covering something up. Damage control. What did he have to hide?

Then, Jack Johnson comes into 8's office and gets him tangled up with Lucky Luciano, who wants him to investigate the assistant director at the Department of Genetics at Cold Spring Harbor, a place where Karl Vogel was on the board of directors. Herman Wall had been equally unhelpful, not that people were inclined to open up to a gumshoe. Everybody has secrets they don't want revealed.

Of course, his client, Theda, had out of the blue remembered her husband arguing with two Germans. What's more, she'd conveniently followed them, and so knew where they were staying. And when 8 paid them a visit, he got clunked in the head for his troubles.

Last night he'd been poring through the newspapers Marty had delivered to his office when the telephone had jingled. On the other end of the line was a very distressed and frantic Asta Holm.

8 had taken a yellow cab to the restaurant she'd taken refuge in from the lanky man who'd threatened her. He badly had wanted to go in search of this fellow, but Asta had needed him by her side rather than out on the streets looking for a phantom.

They'd eventually retreated to the bed, where Asta wiggled her way closer into his spoon. He put his arm around her body, pulling her tight. She sighed. He kneaded her shoulder, first one, then the other, and then ran his fingers up underneath her nightshirt to scratch her back.

Asta wiggled her bottom into him contentedly, reaching her hand back around to rest on his thigh. He continued to rub and scratch gently, and her hand dropped lower. And then they were one.

Later, he made them buckwheat pancakes with a slice of ham on the side, and a strong cup of coffee. Asta agreed to call in sick to the telephone company. She offered to help in the office. 8 thought about the piles of yet unread newspaper articles gathered by Marty and readily agreed.

Morning sex, shared breakfast, and working together in the office. Had he envisioned this a year earlier? No. But he found himself content. He thought that maybe, just maybe, he could get used to this comfortable domesticity. Asta was a fantastic woman. Sexy, witty, and smart. But then the thought of spending so much time together made him pause, and he felt a sneaking tendril of panic creeping through his being.

When Millicent came into the office at nine, Asta was set up across from 8 at his desk going through the newspapers.

"What exactly are we looking for?" Millicent asked as she hung up her coat and stuck her head into the inner doorway.

"Anything, pretty much," 8 said. "But first, I wanted to ask you more about that Hitler fellow and how he connects with the *Übermensch*."

Millie's eyes darkened, and she grew very still. So soon after the Great War, it wasn't always wise to be too German. "What about them?"

"Why would you put them together?"

"Nietzsche is the building block upon which much of German education is based," Millie said. "He is revered, almost like a god, in certain circles, such as over in Murray Hill in lower Manhattan or over to Park Slope, and most certainly, in Germany."

"And the word is that this fellow, Hitler, is Nietzsche's *Übermensch*, or his Superman?"

Millie shook her head. "There are whispers amongst some of the more radical Germans, those angry with the treaty, that a new race of Germans is being spawned, one comprised of an army of supermen and led by the *Übermensch*."

"And that person is Adolph Hitler?"

Millie shrugged. "I can't say for sure. It is a twisted logic to begin with."

"Can you look more into that, maybe talk to some recent arrivals who might know more about what Germans are thinking now? Buy them a cup of coffee and sound them out?"

"Sure. Anything else? What do you want me to look for in all these papers that Marty sent over?"

"I suppose any connections between Karl Vogel and that Carnegie Institute Department of Genetics at Cold Spring Harbor might shed light on why he was killed," 8 said. "And anything that might suggest that Herman Wall is a bit sketchy."

"Sketchy?"

"Criminal. Steals money from the Boy Scouts. Visits brothels. Kicks his dog. Has close ties to a fanatic in Germany who thinks he is replacing God and is the fulfillment of Nietzsche's *Übermensch*

Philosophy."

"Gotcha. That should be easy enough." There was a stack of newspapers still on her desk, and she went and sat and dug into them.

8 was fairly certain that her reply was sarcastic in nature, but wasn't quite sure, as she usually delivered her mockery and derision with a completely Germanic deadpan expression.

A few hours later, with no significant discoveries, McGee came through the door, his Irish brogue bouncing back to the inner office. "Millie, me lass, top of the morning to you."

"Good morning, Officer McGee."

"You look especially fetching today. A sight for sore eyes for sure."

"Thank you. And how are your wife and kids?"

"Aine is a right proper queen, she is. The *scuts* are getting along fine if their aim is to fight, fart, and get filthy dirty."

McGee came through the doorway, pausing as he did so. "Looks to me that you got yourself a new associate. Gonna have to change the door to read 8 Ballo and Asta Holm. Gots a ring to it, that does."

"Some fellow chased after her last night after she got out of work." 8 leaned back in his chair. "Right here in Bushwick. I can only imagine that all the police were keeping an eye on the juice joints and brothels."

McGee ignored the barb. "Chased after ya?"

"A tall, thin man with a face like a straight line." Asta wrinkled her nose as if she had a bad taste in her mouth.

"Any idea what for?"

"More than likely he wanted to get to know me better," Asta said.

"Or it might be the beanpole who ran down Vogel and stole the Aquila," 8 said. "Looking to send a message to lay off looking for him."

"Seems to be a bit... thin." McGee guffawed, and then sobered quickly. "Whoever it was, we'll find him and give him a thrashing, we will."

"Thank you, Stephen," Asta said. "I thought about marking him with a knife but chose to run instead."

"Aye, and good that you did." McGee smiled and then turned his gaze toward 8. "And what of your face? Did you get fresh with this lass?"

8 chuckled. "I'd look worse than this if I got on the wrong side of Asta. No, this was the work of a short fat German and *his* tall, thin friend."

"Jeez. Tall, thin friend, eh?"

8 told him about the run-in at the Hotel Bossert. "Could've been him, I suppose, that was after Asta to send me a message."

"You make him as the lad who ran over Vogel? Two Germans viciously running people down on the streets of Brooklyn."

"It all seems to be getting in a straight line pointing that way," 8 said.

"Well, I got another point to add to the line." McGee plopped himself into a chair. "You know that lad who owns the motorcar that ran down Vogel? Well, I been keeping an eye on him like you asked."

"You find out something?"

"We went to a meeting in the woods the other day out to Ridgewood."

"Yeah?" 8 gave McGee an exasperated look. "You gonna tell me about it or just sit there grinning like a fool?"

"Maybe you don't want to hear about all the lads dressed up in white sheets around a fire pissing and moaning about the Jews, Blacks, and Catholics." McGee shifted as if to stand up.

"You went with Fred Peters to a Ku Klux Klan meeting?" 8 asked.

"Well, not exactly together. I followed him over and lurked back in the trees because I hadn't thought to bring my sheet."

"Interesting, but quite a few of our white Protestant population are involved with the Klan," 8 said. "Something about feeling threatened."

McGee scoffed. "According to one lad who was speaking, the Catholics control the government, the Jews got all the money, and the Blacks have taken all the good jobs."

"Well, there you have it," Asta said. "It's one big conspiracy against you white boys, it is."

"Well, seeing as us Irish are mostly Catholic, we are part of the conspiracy," McGee said. "That just leaves the Hungarian lad here that is being persecuted."

8 chuckled. "Us white Germanic people have had a rough go of it, that's for sure."

"I was thinking," McGee said, "that Vogel and that group he belonged to, the Batavi, probably have a lot of similar beliefs to the Klan. You know, racial purity and all that. And it was in Germany that that lad, Martin Luther, started the initial protest against the Pope, the Catholics, the corruption of Rome and all that."

"Some four-hundred years ago, that was," 8 said.

"History goes in cycles," McGee said.

"The Batavi and the Klan," 8 said. "Interesting."

"Mix in the eugenics movement, and you get quite an ugly recipe," Asta said.

Chapter 16

8 met with Marty at Kaan's deli, where he assumed he'd be paying again. It was small price to pay for access to the brilliant mind of the journalist with his finger on the pulse of Brooklyn. He idly wondered if his friend did favors for others, and if he ever had to pay for his own lunch.

"Trouble with the razor again?" Marty asked by way of greeting. "Or did you fall down the stairs?"

8 chuckled as he sat down at the outdoor table. He liked the brisk weather but wondered at Marty's choice as the man didn't much like the cold. "My barber thought a pistol barrel would be the best way to trim my sideburns."

"Have anything to do with what you got me into? Because, you know, I don't much care for putting my mug in harm's way."

8 thought of lying to appease his friend, but then thought of the man who'd chased Asta. It could be that everybody 8 knew was in danger, especially those helping him on the case. "Might want to be careful."

"Yeah? Of who?"

"A short, round German and a tall, thin one." 8 told him of his altercation with the two men.

"Great. It wasn't long ago you had me standing on a street corner outside some gangster's house. That fellow was German, too, wasn't he."

8 chuckled. "You, too, my friend, are German."

"I'm a Jew. From Germany. Big difference. My mother always used to say…"

8 knew his friend was covering his anxiety with words and allowed him to drone on for a bit before interrupting and redirecting him. "You find out anything on that Carnegie Institute place in Cold Spring Harbor? Other than what was in the newspapers you sent over yesterday?"

"What do you want to know?"

"I suppose tell me what you found out, and I'll see if it fills in any of the holes in what I know."

Marty sighed. "The Carnegie Institute of Washington also known as the Carnegie Institute of Science came about as the result of Andrew Carnegie growing a heart back in 1895 and giving much of the fortune he'd made on the backs of the poor to the government to create institutions bearing his name. Soon after, they opened their own doors, the Science Institute opening the Station for Experimental Evolution, or SEE, in Cold Spring Harbor out on Long Island. The purpose was to study heredity and evolution through breeding experiments with plants and animals. The head of this station was, and still is, a man by the name of Charles Davenport."

"That fellow hasn't got back to me," 8 said. "His secretary said he was down in Washington on business, but me and Pearle got in to speak with his assistant, Herman Wall. Real charmer, that one. Tell me what you found out about what, exactly, they study."

"The thinking out to Cold Spring Harbor is that if breeding works with plants and animals, why not with humans? That's where your pal, Herman Wall, comes in. He's a bit of an expert on breeding plants and believes that the same general principles hold true in humans."

8 nodded at the table which had a flowerpot with a purple flower in it. "Like purple is the dominant color over white. Does that make it superior?"

"Hard to say. They seem to think that the inferior genes are going to taint the superior genes, weakening the organism, and making it less, well, superior."

The waiter came and delivered two sandwiches with potato salad and beans.

"And have they been at it for long?"

"They opened their doors twenty years ago," Marty said. "But back in 1910, Davenport got the wealthy widow, Mrs. E.H. Harriman, to establish the Eugenics Record Office, or ERO, at Cold Harbor, for him to head as well. He operated that independently for eight years before it was turned over to the Carnegie Institute of Washington as well."

"And what in hell is the Eugenics Record Office?"

"Do you even know what eugenics is?"

"Sure. That much I got," 8 said. "It's the belief that character in a human being is determined solely by genetics, and has nothing to do with other factors, such as education or living conditions."

"That's about it," Marty said. "A few years back, the old Station of Experimental Evolution merged with the Brooklyn Institute of Arts and Science's Biological Lab, known as BIAS, which Charles Davenport also was the director of, as well as the ERO, putting them all under one roof."

"What they now call the Department of Genetics," 8 said. "And their purpose is to purify America by keeping *inferior* immigrants from coming to our shores? The point of that law, the Johnson-Reed Act that got passed earlier this year. That's what Luciano was upset about."

"Charlie Luciano might be one terrible human being, but at least he likes us Jews just fine," Marty said.

"He's pretty tight with Bugsy and Lansky," 8 agreed.

"But it goes way past immigration acts," Marty said. "What of the inferior people already here? They're going to have sex and reproduce, and every time that happens, the racial purity of America becomes more diluted."

8 shook his head. "So, what? They want to stop people from having sex?"

Marty scoffed. "Good luck with that. No, they want to stop certain people from reproducing. Stamp the inferior genes out for good."

"That sounds like the talk of that fellow in Germany you told me about, Adolph Hitler. Did you find out anything more about him?"

"Only that the people he hates the most is us Jews."

"Why is that?"

"I read some of his comments just this morning. Seems he got a lot of his rhetoric from Henry Ford."

"The motorcar manufacturer?"

"That'd be the one. He just published an autobiography that Hitler read in prison and spoke highly of. Seems Ford talks about a Jewish conspiracy to take over the world. Something about Jewish lack of civilization, religion, and lack of power, yet we are taking over, some such *schmegegge*, baloney, as that."

"Do the eugenics people and Hitler also share ideas about what to do with inferior people, Jews, and what have you??"

"Davenport and Wall are pushing for mandatory sterilizations."

"Bullshit," 8 said. "No way that will ever be allowed."

Marty looked at 8, a sad look on his face. "Thirty-two states have already passed legislation allowing it."

"What? Not here in New York, I trust?"

"Apparently they were already sterilizing women here up until '18 when the state Supreme Court threw it out the window."

"Can't believe I haven't heard of this. Who's getting sterilized?"

Marty wiped his hands, showcasing that he'd finished eating. "They started off with the feeble-minded, those with mental deficiencies, and have thrown in a couple of prisoners, almost all women."

"And you don't think they're going to stop there, do you?"

"Nope. If I was to guess, the Blacks are next, then us Jews, or maybe the Asians, before they get to the Italians and Irish."

"You think they're still performing illegal sterilizations in the city?" 8 asked.

Marty shrugged. Finished his sandwich. Stood up. "If they are, it'd be out to Damnation Island." He turned and walked off.

8 sat finishing his sandwich, pondering these last words. The famous Lunatic Asylum on Welfare Island had closed years ago after Nelly Bly went undercover as a patient there and then wrote an exposé on the horrible corruption, abuse, and conditions there. It still was home to the penitentiary, the Metropolitan Hospital, and almshouses. Most New Yorkers knew nothing about it as it was hiding in plain sight, secreted on a spit of land in the East River.

8 knew of the place, and also what others actually called it. Damnation Island. A place that imprisoned the poor, abused those with mental deficiencies, and provided medical care to those nobody cared about. A place where, likely if anywhere, forced sterilizations might occur. 8 was more of a mover and a talker than one to burrow his nose in research. He always got a better, more complete picture of a place by talking to real people and seeing real things.

8 put a buck on the table under his plate and went down the street to the trolley stop. Damnation Island was a bit too far to walk. He wasn't even sure how one got out to the island. The Queensboro Bridge had been built a few years back going right over it, but as far as he knew, there was no access. There must be a ferry of some sort. With forethought, he would've lined up Pearle, who owned a boat, or at least had access to one, but it might be bad form to float up to an island housing a penitentiary on a private boat anyway.

The trolley map showed a stop for the Elevator Storehouse, Welfare Island, on the Queensboro Bridge. He had to change trolleys in Queens, but before long, he felt the car going up the bridge, the Manhattan skyline in front of him, and Welfare Island coming into view below. It was a two-mile long piece of land in the East River that was only 800 feet at its widest point.

The trolley car jostled to a grinding stop with screeching brakes, rocking back and forth as it braked in the middle of the bridge. 8 stood and stepped tentatively out of the open door, joining seven or eight other people. Three looked to be doctors, a couple others most likely prison guards, and a few administrative sorts. To the left, on the far tip of the island, a large stone lighthouse warned boats of the land mass in the river.

There was a large building attached to the side of the bridge that 8 didn't remember seeing before, not that he got over this way much, but a fellow on the trolley had told him it'd been constructed about five years back. There was a walkway to the building as well as a ramp from the bridge for motorcars. Six elevator bays, large enough for automobiles, descended shafts in the building to the island below.

8 peered over the edge, taking in the numerous structures littering the enclave below. The largest and most prominent structure was a massive octagon, directly below, next to the Elevator Storehouse. He remembered reading about this architectural wonder. It used to be the entrance to the famed Lunatic Asylum that Nelly Bly's reporting had closed.

With a loud, grinding noise, an elevator car came to a shuddering halt, and 8 clambered through the open door with the others. He felt a bit as if he were on the elevator to Hades or Hell as the descent to Damnation Island began, grim-faced men and women around him as they went down. He wondered if this short trip was like crossing the River Styx, and the emotion was so powerful, he checked his mouth to make sure there was no coin in it to pay his toll to Hades.

8 emerged from the elevator with no clear thought of what he might actually do here. Coupling the new information from Marty with what he'd read, his experience out at Cold Spring Harbor, and interaction with Ronald Dankworth at the Brooklyn Hospital— all that had pointed him distinctly in this direction. If forced sterilizations were occurring anywhere in New York, Welfare Island would be the place. He just needed proof, and a link to how it connected to the death of Karl Vogel, the stolen Aquila, and the

anti-immigration legislation being pushed by the Department of Genetics.

There were stone steps leading up to the Octagon and a sign that said Metropolitan Hospital. This seemed to be a good place to start, 8 thought, shrugging his shoulders and starting up the steps. Nothing ventured, nothing gained. At the top of the stairs, he looked off to the right where a group of women shuffled along, hobbled and chained together, all dressed in shapeless dresses with black and white stripes. These would be the more serious offenders, whereas those sentenced to Damnation Island for the crime of merely being poor would be at the Workhouse, paying for their incarceration with their labor.

Inside, in the center of a lobby with soaring ceilings, sat a solitary woman behind a desk. She was dressed all in white, a puffy hat like a pastry perched on dark hair that was pulled severely back from her face revealing thick black spectacles. 8 thought that she might be trying very hard to not look pretty. So, this was Cerberus, guardian of the underworld, 8 thought, a wry grin creasing his features.

"Can I help you?" Her voice was stern, and her eyes flashed, as if in displeasure at his smile.

"Yes, I'm looking for the person in charge of this joint."

"And who are you?"

8 considered telling her he was Odysseus but didn't think she'd find the humor in it. "My name is Zack Wheat and I'm running an investigation into the practices here at the Metropolitan Hospital. On behalf of Mayor Hylan." 8 sincerely hoped that she was not a baseball fan as he'd plucked the name out of the jumble of his brain, Zack Wheat being one of the best players on the Brooklyn baseball team.

"I've heard nothing of that."

"I'm telling you now."

8 held her gaze until her eyes flickered away. She looked down, shuffled some papers, before looking back up. "Dr. Bacon is not here

today. He had a meeting with the War Department."

"You mean to tell me that he is directly ignoring a meeting set up by Mayor Hyland? This is not going to go down very well. Believe me, Dr. Bacon will be looking for a new job by tomorrow morning."

"Perhaps you can see his assistant, Dr. Bedford?"

She must've pushed a button, for on cue, an orderly appeared behind her, a slender fellow, also in a white uniform.

"Thomas, take Mr. Wheat to Dr. Bedford's office," she said. Again, she was in control, dismissing him as if he'd never existed.

The pristine serenity of the outer lobby continued as they went through the doors into a hallway that looked to be lined with administrative offices. 8 doubted that the actual hospital, a charity hospital for the poor, was as clean and, above all, quiet.

Dr. Bedford sat behind a desk even more imposing than that of the receptionist in the lobby. 8 wondered about the modest size of his own desk. Maybe he should be getting a new and larger one?

"Yes? What can I do for you?"

"Dr. Bedford? My name is Mr. Wheat. I am the head of Mayor Hylan's special investigation looking into the treatment of patients in the state institutions and hospitals."

"Sit down, Mr. Wheat." Dr. Bedford motioned to a plush armchair across from him. He was a shortish fellow with dark hair that puffed out from his ears and swirled upward atop of his head. "I have heard of no such investigation."

8 settled into the chair indicated. "I can assure you that this is not some tabloid rich witch story, Mr. Bedford. Mayor Hylan merely wants a report that showcases the stunning successes that have gone on here, ever since that terrible Nellie Bly incident."

"That was indeed many years ago, and much has changed for sure." Bedford steepled his fingers under his tightly trimmed goatee. "The Lunatic Asylum has, in fact, been mostly closed for going on thirty years now."

8 removed a pad of paper and a Parker Duofold Ink Pen that had

been a gift from Asta from his jacket pocket. "Mostly closed? Our office records suggested that all patients have been removed and that no such facility exists here."

"Just the very dregs, my dear sir. The homeless, those guilty of crimes, but unable to exist in either our workhouse or prison." Bedford shrugged. "The hospital has a ward for those who need treatment but also restraint and guards."

8 nodded and wrote on the paper. This was more for show than anything else, as his mind was adept at remembering, often word for word, and any questions he had would burn brightly in his head until answered. "Was the Metropolitan Hospital involved in any sterilizations of patients, either from the prison, the mental asylum, or the poor house?"

"What?"

"Oh, of course I mean before the courts outlawed it," 8 said. "That period up until 1918, I believe it was."

"I don't know."

"How long have you been here, Mr. Bedford?"

"Fifteen years. What does the sterilization of patients have to do with Mayor Hylan putting together a report of the successes of Welfare Island, Mr. Wheat?"

8 leaned forward across the desk, staring directly into the man's eyes behind his round and rimless spectacles. "Don't you believe that rendering criminals, homeless, and lunatics unable to reproduce is a stunning victory for our city, our state, and our country? Heck, for the world?"

Bedford leaned back, his eyes flickering away from 8's to the door, and then left and right, as if looking for an escape route. "Well, yes, I suppose that is true, but it's been illegal for six years now, so I don't see how it is pertinent."

"It's coming back, Dr. Bedford. It's only a matter of time before the powers that be establish this proscriptive policy at a national level, and it won't just stop at the derelicts." 8 sat back, particularly proud of that "proscriptive" he'd thrown in.

"What are you suggesting?"

8 smiled broadly and leaned backward. "How many homeless people fill out the population of the almshouses, hospitals, and prisons here on Welfare Island? Do you service the Jews, the Blacks, the Asians, and the Italians, or is it just good white folk?" The smile covered up the dirtiness he felt just uttering these words. "You see, Dr. Bedford, we are planning ahead, and want to know where the institutions of Welfare Island stand."

Chapter 17

"What'd your pal, Dr. Bedford, have to say when you asked him that?" Pearle asked with a grin creasing his round face. "Do you service the Jews, Blacks, Asians, and Italians, or is it just the good white folk?" He guffawed loudly, a laughter that didn't reach his eyes.

"He said that the majority of the patients and prisoners were white, but that some *inferior* bloodlines were occasionally incarcerated or operated on, depending on the circumstances."

"We might pay him a visit, cut him up, and see what color his blood is," Pearle said.

They were at a speakeasy around the corner from Pearle's home, drinking Laphroaig, a scotch whiskey from the isle of Islay. The price tag for the brown liquor was hefty, but Pearle was paying. The joint was far more highbrow than 8 was used to. The light was gentle, and they reposed in cushy armchairs in a corner with a bit of privacy and a platter of cheese, olives, and mixed nuts on a small table in front of them.

"This is a mighty fine scotch," 8 said, attempting to change the subject and settle the smoldering anger never far below his best friend's smiling exterior.

"Been around since 1815, just not outside of Scotland," Pearle said. "But the owner here at this joint, his father was from Islay, so he has connections."

Pearle had introduced him to the owner, who's skin was blacker than Pearle's, matching most of the clientele other than 8.

"You suppose they have cigars here?"

Pearle pulled a case from his pocket, first cutting the tip of one for 8 and handing it along with his Clark lighter over, before cutting his own then taking the lighter back. Once they were again settled, puffing the Cubanos, sipping the Laphroaig from Scotland, 8 got to the reason for the get-together.

"If you're not too busy for work these days, I'd like to engage your services," he said.

Pearle chuckled. "The normal rate, I suppose?"

The going rate that 8 paid Pearle for his services was a dollar a day. In truth, he'd never even paid him that. 8 did some mental calculations and realized that this nominal daily fee had most likely grown over time to a number of some significance. "If you mean pulling you from the tedium of a business mogul's humdrum existence into the exciting world of private investigations, then yes, the normal rate applies, thank you very much."

"The excitement you refer to generally takes on two very different guises." Pearle took a nip of the scotch. "It is generally me sitting in the front seat of my Nash bored out of my mind or having my life threatened by Brunos with knives, axes, pistols, and Tommy guns. Which particular excitement can I expect this time?"

"Axes? Can't say that I ever got you involved in something where you were imperiled by an axe."

"Humph. Maybe that one wasn't you. Never mind the axes, then. What do you want?"

"That fellow we paid a visit to down in Cold Spring Harbor?"

"Yeah, the one who thought I was your chauffeur. What of him?"

"Thought maybe you could keep an eye on him. Find out what he does in his spare time."

Pearle nodded his head. "That could be interesting. What does a fellow who spends his days keeping America pure and white and Protestant do for fun?"

"According to Marty, he was well involved in the forced sterilization of the feeble minded, criminals, and the hopelessly poor."

"But that's all done with, you said?"

"Yeah, the Supreme Court of New York outlawed it back in '18."

"So, now he's putting his efforts toward passing legislation preventing, what'd you say? *Inferior* bloodlines from coming to our friendly shores."

"I thought that you might like this diversion in your life," 8 said. "You never were one much who liked to be thought of as weak."

Pearle glared, sneered, and then chortled. "We sure beat some asses in our time, didn't we?"

8 chuckled. "Yes. Yes, we did."

Best friends since a young age, one white, one Black, they'd run into their share of bullies. Quickly, boys their own age realized the futility of challenging them. Older boys had taken longer, but it'd been some time since any group of hooligans had bested them in a fight.

After a few seconds, Pearle's face sobered. "That Wall fellow, he seems like he might need himself a good beat-down."

"Let's wait on that until we gather some dirt on him." 8 had worried about sending Pearle on this task, knowing the man's impatience might lead to an altercation. "Something that would be more damaging than a busted nose."

"Oh, it'll be far worse than a busted nose," Pearle said grimly. "But I can wait until the time is appropriate."

"Good. Follow him. Find where he lives. What organizations he frequents. Is he a Mason, that sort of thing. Who are his friends. You know the rigmarole."

"Don't expect he has a lot of Black people in his orbit," Pearle said. "Sure I'm the right man for the job?"

"The whole point in surveillance work is to not be seen." 8 grinned wickedly. "So don't be seen. Plus, I'm sure his neighborhood has a whole bunch of hired Black help. Put on a suit and say you're someone's driver."

* * *

It was a short walk from the speakeasy to 8's office in Bushwick. There were three black Packard automobiles parked in front of his office. In the middle one there was a solitary woman in the back seat applying lipstick with a hand mirror. Six men loitered at the bottom of the steps up to his entryway. They were carbon copies of each other. Lean men with hatchet faces wearing black overcoats and fedoras. Not the sort of men strangers asked for a light.

"You fellows are scaring the neighbors," 8 said. "Why don't you climb back into your motorcars and wait there?"

A man, distinguished from the others by a scar on his right cheek, cleared his throat and stepped forward. "Limousines, Mr. Ballo. These here are the finest automobile made."

"Am I lucky enough a man..." 8 paused to see if anybody caught onto his word usage but there was no flicker of acknowledgment, "that I'm being paid a visit by Salvatore Luciano?"

"He goes by Charlie Luciano now," Scar said. "Or Lucky Luciano, to his friends."

"Why don't I just pop up there and see what he wants." 8 shouldered his way through the men who made way grudgingly.

Two men stood on either side of his open door on the second floor. As opposed to the chopper squad of gunmen downstairs, these two were the beef, the same bald fellow with his buddy, Comb-over, who had escorted him into the back of the Back Room last week.

Lucky Luciano was sitting on the corner of Millie's desk speaking quietly with her. Her face seemed caught between a smile and fear.

"The PI returns," Luciano said, looking up with a broad smile crossing his pockmarked face. "I was just about to give up on you."

"Helps to call ahead." 8 hung his jacket and hat. "That way you don't get stuck waiting."

Luciano waved his hand. "Ah, not a problem. I was in the neighborhood, well, on my way back from Brownsville to see our mutual friends, and I thought to myself, hey, why not stop in and see the gumshoe."

The Candy Store in Brownsville was Bugsy and Lansky's hangout, 8 knew. Did that mean that now, those two gangsters were their mutual friends?

"Well, let's leave Millie to her work and go back into my office." 8 waved the suave thug with the expensive suit into his inner office.

"Very pretty eyes on that *la ragazza* you got out there," Luciano said. "I don't recall that bombshell being here last time I stopped by with the message from the Brain."

8 had never really thought of Millie in terms of being a bombshell. He gestured to a seat and went behind the desk and sat down. "She used to work for Hartmann. Seems she was out of a job, and I hired her."

Luciano snorted. "That she was. Always tough when your boss gets whacked,"

"What can I do for you, Mr. Luciano."

"Meyer, he tells me that you have a *buon amico*, a buddy who works as a copper here in Bushwick at the 83rd Precinct."

8 didn't reply. Or, at least, he let his deadpan stare be his response.

Luciano cleared his throat. "It would be nice if we had a friend in the police department."

"No."

Luciano laughed harshly. "I don't much like that word, Ballo."

"That's what Bugsy said. Do you guys get a script in gangster school or something that tells you what to say in certain situations?"

Luciano leaned forward. His droopy eyes gave him the look of a hound dog. "You come to me and ask a favor. Then I come to you, and you are rude?"

"No disrespect meant, Mr. Luciano. But I won't be intimidated. The morals of my friends are not on the table here. I have, though, agreed to repay your favor to me by looking into Herman Wall."

Luciano licked his lips and sat back. "Well, at least tell me that you have uncovered something on that pig fucker who has the ears of congressmen."

"I have gone out to Cold Spring Harbor and met with the man. I have some leads on things that might cast him in a bad light, a very bad light, and am having him watched."

"I expect results, Ballo. If you cannot deliver, then perhaps we'll have to work out another arrangement, such as Stephen McGee."

"If there is anything to be found on Herman Wall, I will find it. If there is nothing..." 8 shrugged his shoulders.

"In my world, failure means death," Luciano said.

"Are you threatening me?" 8 leaned forward so that his hands were close enough to grasp the gangster around the neck if necessary.

Baldy and Comb-over stepped into the room with pistols that looked like toys in their huge hands.

Luciano leaned forward so that his face was just inches from 8's. "What's the name of that pretty little Dutch telephone operator you play house with sometimes?"

8 clenched his fists. He could wrap the Italian gangster into a headlock, and the two goons at the door would be fearful of taking a shot. But that would only create a war, and his resources were much thinner than Lucky Luciano's.

"I will hold up my end of the bargain," 8 said. "Now, if you'd let me get to it, I have work to do."

*　*　*

The four men met in a blind pig in the area that used to be called Cobble Hill, now just part of the 6th Ward and Brooklyn Heights. The American with a cowboy hat looked around with distaste.

This place represented all that was wrong with America. He looked for telltale signs of Jews, Blacks, Asians, or Italians in the features of the poor and downtrodden drunks who populated this sleazy speakeasy.

It was possible that the genetic waters had been muddied here, he thought, looking at one man with a prominent nose, and another so stumpy and pinch-faced it was tough to tell around the bedraggled clothes and dirty face if it were man or woman. The fact just may be, he mused, that an occasional mutant gene barged into the purity of the blood. Maybe it was a throwback from when the Romans were marauding their way across the countryside and raping the local women with wanton disregard. Or that Asian Hun, Attila, who'd laid waste to large swaths of Eastern and Western Europe back in his day.

No mind, Cowboy Hat thought, these dregs of genetic rejects could be pinpointed as easily as all of the others. Mental impairments. Criminal behavior. Impertinent women. Sickly and broken. Just like those darker-skinned, with their bulging greedy eyes and kinky hair. They would be stamped out of existence along with all the other undesirables.

From the ashes would emerge the Phoenix, the Master Race, those of pure blood, and he would be singled out as the father of racial purity. It was time for the birth of a *new* nation, he liked to say, and thought that would most likely become the slogan as they emerged into the public view to present their new vision for America. The symbol of the Phoenix and the Eagle would intertwine, representing a United States based upon Germanic ideals.

"That man came to our hotel room and accosted us," the rotund German who was called Heinrich Funk was saying.

"What man?" Cowboy Hat asked.

As always, the tall German and the even taller American were silent, standing quietly by the table as the other two spoke.

Funk wiped his brow with a handkerchief. "My people tell me

that he is called 8 Ballo and that he is a private investigator hired by the widow, Theda Lazur Vogel, to investigate the death of her husband and the theft of the Aquila."

Cowboy Hat nodded. "I know of this man. He is of no account. A fool."

"This fool attacked me. He was asking me about Vogel. Accusing me of killing him."

"How did he connect you to Vogel?"

"He said that Theda saw us arguing."

Cowboy Hat eyed the German coldly. How was it possible that the obese slob represented the pure bloodline of the chosen. "How did he find you?"

"He knew about the Aquila. About the *Rein Adler of the Batavi.* The Pure Eagle of the Batavi. How could this American fool know of us?" Funk was now sopping the sweat from his face.

Cowboy Hat pondered this. Maybe this gumshoe was not quite as thick as his body suggested. "There is nothing he can do. I have the full backing of the wealthiest men in America. Once we introduce your Herr Hitler to my people, there will be nothing stopping us. An alliance of Germany and the United States will surpass the former British Empire in power and control the world."

"Herr Hitler is a big fan of your Henry Ford."

"Ford is but one of many. The wealthy in America are all for racial purity."

"But what of the man? This 8 Ballo?"

Cowboy Hat scoffed. "One man? You think one man can stop the Pure Blood Master Race of America and Germany rising from the ashes? I suppose if this 8 Ballo worries you, well then, you should kill him."

Chapter 18

Her life had been one big shamble, Bettie thought, mostly due to the poor moral character of men. And now, here she was, going to another man to sort out her problems. Where had that ever gotten her before?

It was a long walk, but Bettie had walked long distances before. It was as simple as putting one foot in front of the other. And then again. With the amount of walking she did, Bettie though that she'd at least lose some weight. That and the meager food that was her daily diet. Yet, no matter what, she was big, heavy, and labored to walk.

It wasn't supposed to be like this. Not at twenty-three years old. Bettie supposed that the first man who'd screwed her over had been her father. He'd ruined any chance of happiness for her mother or herself by leaving before Bettie was born.

Momma had told Bettie about the promises that he'd made, assurances that had dissipated like the cake after a church social once Momma became pregnant with Bettie. Gone. The man decamped one day and had never been heard from since.

Bettie wondered what it would be like to just up and leave. Here one day, absent the next. All responsibilities vanished. Her past erased. To start anew. But that was the reality for men and not for women.

Women didn't have that convenience. Where men could sleep in a flophouse, piled in with other men, the choice for women was a brothel, earning their keep in the oldest profession known to womankind.

Looking back, Bettie understood that Momma had resented her. Just like Bettie sometimes resented her children. If it hadn't been for getting pregnant with Grace, perhaps she could've ridden her singing voice out of the tenements, out of the slums, away from her hateful aunt, onto a stage and fame and money.

But she had gotten pregnant, and there was no way under God's good grace that she was going to get rid of the child and go to Hell. So, seven years ago, when Bettie was just fifteen, she'd given birth to a baby girl. And she resented the heck out of her. And loved her more than life itself. The emotions were too strong to reconcile and raged within her even to this moment.

Bettie had been forced to leave the brothel where she'd moved from servicing men all the time to occasionally singing as Peaches played the piano, entertaining the men waiting their turn, filling the house of ill-repute with beauty and music. She'd gone from there to work in a glue factory, forced to perform favors on her shift manager to keep her job, treated as something with no more value than one of the horses that had been killed and ground up to make the glue.

Of course, when Grace was born, she'd lost that job, and it wasn't long after that her aunt kicked her out of the house for the first time. Her and her recently born baby had slept in the park for a month until Bettie had given enough blow jobs to get them back into her aunt's house and all had been good for a bit. One of her cousins would watch Grace at night so that Bettie could work in a brothel, not the same one, not singing, but providing for the physical pleasure of men.

And she began to save up some money, hidden from her aunt, with dreams to get her own place, maybe get a respectable job, and leave her sinful past behind. Then Abel was born. He was such a sweet child. One of God's creatures for sure. But another burden for

Bettie, another source of conflicting emotion, and another source of irritation to her aunt. It seemed that every time she started to get ahead, her way forward was blocked by what some man had done to her.

The seventh time Bettie was kicked out was when her aunt's boyfriend forced himself on her and, when her aunt walked in on them, baldly lied, saying that Bettie had come onto him. She'd been busted by a policeman for prostitution in the park, but her punishment was not jail. No, instead she had a weekly rendezvous to pleasure the man for as long as she lived, it seemed. This was how Bettie got by. This was her life. Torn askew by men. And here she was, on her way to get help from yet another man.

Running into Peaches had been a miracle. God had finally smiled upon her and thrown her a rope. Singing on stage at Tom Thumb had melted the years of pain and suffering away, if not completely, at least enough for a breath of warmth to reach her heart, a feeling she'd not felt in eight long years, and then, only briefly.

The music, the applause, the love—was surpassed when Fletcher 'Smack' Henderson had bounded onto the stage and invited her to sing with his quartet at the Back Room. Bettie truly thought she'd died and finally gone to heaven when she walked on stage.

She'd never heard music as pure and beautiful as what Smack's quartet played. He was on the piano, Louis Armstrong on the trumpet, Coleman Hawkins on the saxophone, and that fellow George on the drums. Smack had started off tickling the ivories with a quiet yet delicious tune that caressed the cockles of her heart, and then George came in with a steady, low, deep beat, and Bettie could feel her spirit rising.

Then, Hawk, as he told her to call him, rippled in with the sax, and Louis kicked in on the trumpet, the sound rising and falling like the ocean. Bettie could feel herself riding the wave, rising higher and higher. She couldn't even remember opening her mouth to sing, or what she'd sung, the emotion was too deep.

Smack had given her two sawbucks for that night's performance, money that had warded off an eleventh eviction from her aunt, bought her another month. And her dreams for that time were bigger than any she'd ever before considered. What she wanted was modest. A roof over the head for her and Grace and Abel. Food on the table. Clothes on their backs. This would be the culmination of all her dreams.

The means of accomplishing those modest dreams, incredible as it sometimes seemed, was happening already. After that first night's performance, she was going to sing several more times with Smack Henderson before joining his orchestra at the Roseland Ballroom. The thought thrilled and terrified her all at the same time.

There was that matter of the searing pain in her guts. That involved seeing another man, which is what she'd done four days prior, on Monday. The pain still sluiced through her body like writhing electric eels cavorting in her abdomen. That was to be expected, the doctor told her, after the operations that she'd experienced. It was that word operations that shocked her. And why she was on the way to see yet another man to help fix the problems caused by that man.

With a start, Bettie looked up, and realized she was here, at the address Smack had given her. One foot in front of the other and just keep going. There was a sign over the door and one inside that told her to go to the second floor. An open door at the end of the hallway bore the same inscription, and Bettie shuffled her way inside where a woman sat at a desk reading a newspaper.

"Can I help you?" the woman asked.

"I'm here to see a fella by the name of 8 Ballo," Bettie said.

"I am Millicent Winters, but you can call me Millie," the woman said. "Can I get your name?"

"Bettie. Bettie Young."

The woman rose and stepped to another door, poking her head inside and saying something that Bettie couldn't hear.

"Right this way, Bettie." Millie waved her forward to the open doorway.

Bettie stepped past her into the inner office. A man was coming unfolded from his chair, his body rising smoothly on and on. He was awful tall, she thought, several inches over six feet she'd guess, but she'd never seen a man as large as this big six. His shoulders were as wide as most doorways and his chest looked like two barrels glued together.

"Hello. I'm 8 Ballo." His face was smoothly shaven, his eyes a sparkling blue, and he exuded a comforting aura of serenity. "Please, come in, sit down."

Bettie shuffled forward and eased into one of the seats in front of the desk as 8 Ballo followed suit once she was seated.

"What can I do for you Miss Young?" he asked.

"Fletcher Henderson sent me. Said maybe you could help me out."

"Ha. First Hawkins and now Smack. What did he say that I might help you out with?"

Bettie cringed slightly at his tone. Perhaps it'd been wrong to come here, she wondered. Men. White men at that. Why had Smack suggested she come here? He was, after all, just another man.

"Sorry," 8 said. "That chagrin was for Hawk and Smack. Do you also know Coleman Hawkins?"

"Yea. I sung with him last week."

8's eyebrows raised. "Was that you at the Back Room last Thursday night?"

Bettie gave a short nod. "Uh huh."

"I only caught a smidgen of your performance but your voice, well, ma'am, that was something else. There aren't words for the miracle that is your crooning."

"Thank you."

"Sorry I was short about Smack sending you over. Just last week, Hawk, he done the same thing. Not that it's a problem, mind you, but I seem to be the go-to PI for those two musicians."

Bettie liked how the man talked to her and not at her or over her or around her. His blue eyes were friendly without strings. His suit was a bit too tight, but then again, she wondered, how would he ever find one that fit?

"Well, anyhow, what can I help you with Miss Young?" 8 asked.

Bettie smiled shyly. "Well, for starters, what is the meaning of chagrin?"

8 chuckled. "A slight irritation, I suppose. But not really, for anybody that can make music like those two fellows is never going to be in my doghouse for long."

"Smack, he said I should come tell you my story, and that you'd know what to do."

8 nodded. "Go ahead."

"I been feeling these pains down in my gut, you know, twisting and agonizing. I went down to the free clinic across from the Brooklyn Hospital, and the doctor said my appendix was inflamed, that it'd have to come out. He said it didn't do anything, anyway, other than get infected. Well, he set me up with an appointment for this past Monday morning at the hospital to get the operation. Said it was no big deal, he did."

8 nodded. "Go on."

Bettie sniffled, fighting back the tears. She wiped at her eyes with her hand, willing away the weakness. The man, 8 Ballo, leaned forward with his handkerchief. She took it, wiped her eyes, but not her nose, as he wouldn't much like having her snot on his hankie.

"When I showed up Monday morning," Bettie said, sniffed, wiped her eyes. "A man in a suit came out to the reception where I was checking in. Told me to come with him, that he had my paperwork in his office."

"An administrator came out and called you into his office to check you in for an appendectomy?" 8 asked. "That is awful strange indeed."

"That is what I thought as well, but who am I to say anything to a doctor?"

"Was he a doctor, as well as an administrator?"

"I didn't get his name when he first introduced himself, on account of being all too frazzled, first with having to get an operation, and then with being summoned back to his office. But afterward I remembered seeing his name on his desk in one of those holders, what do you call them?"

8 shrugged. "Name plate, or some such thing, I imagine."

"That sounds about right. Well, I remembered it afterward, like a vision engraved in my soul, you know?" Bettie looked at 8 and saw understanding in his eyes. He said nothing. "The name on the name plate was Dr. Ronald Dankworth." She saw a flicker of recognition, starting with his eyes, quickly flitting across his stoic face.

"Dr. Ronald Dankworth," he said.

"That was his name. He asked me how I planned on paying for this operation, only he said procedure, not operation, like it was akin to getting a tooth pulled or something."

8 nodded. Said nothing.

"I told the man what the doctor had said. That there'd be no charge, on account of my having no money." Bettie sniffled, choked, cried. "The day you saw me up on stage was the second time in my life, Mr. Ballo. I been just scraping by, trying to feed my children, keep a roof over our heads, not always successful at that."

"You have children, Miss Young?"

Bettie nodded. Sniffled. "That's what he said as he read from a piece of paper. No job, two kids, is what he said. We can't treat you here, he said. I'd have to go over to the Charity Hospital, he said. You know the one I mean?"

8 nodded. "Out to Welfare Island. The real name is Metropolitan Hospital, but people call it Charity Hospital."

"They put me on a meat wagon and took me out there." Bettie thought about climbing into the back of the ambulance and sobbed again. "Next thing I knew, I was waking up on an operating table out there. A doctor came in and said that everything had gone perfectly, and I'd be able to leave the next day."

"But?" 8 looked puzzled. "What's the problem?"

"The doctor, he said, on account of how I had no job, and already enough children, that he took care of something else for me while he took the appendix thing out. Said something about tying up my tubes. He made it so I can't have no more babies. He sterilized me. Ain't that something I should have a say in?"

Chapter 19

After Bettie left, 8 sat at his desk, strumming his fingers lightly as he looked out the window seeing nothing. Forced sterilizations. Wow. He was having quite the time wrapping his head around it. He wasn't sure what he thought. When he'd learned that legislation had been passed, since repealed in New York, that allowed for the forced sterilization of criminals and those of feeble mind, truth be told, he hadn't thought it to be such a crazy idea.

Now? Now that he learned this had been done to Bettie Young without her consent, well this touched off a round of soul searching for him. When, if ever, should a woman lose the power to decide if she were going to have children or not, 8 wondered? Should the feeble minded be prevented from having children? His mind swirled with multiple scenarios, and he slowly came to the conclusion that nobody ever had the right to determine whether or not a woman should be allowed to have babies.

It seemed that the powers that be had determined that Bettie Young should have her right to become pregnant taken away because... because why? She was poor? She already had two children? Because she was a woman? Those might be factors in the decision, but 8 knew that the real reason was that she was Black. And this was the crossing of the line that raised his ire to an explosive point. Women shouldn't be sterilized for the color of their skin, nor for any other reason he could think of. Wrong was wrong.

The founding fathers hadn't suggested that only certain people were included in the right to life, liberty, and the pursuit of happiness. Okay, he thought, smiling wryly, criminals did forfeit their rights to liberty and in some circumstances, their right to life. And certainly had their right to pursue happiness infringed upon.

That was the problem, 8 thought, with starting down this particular road splitting moral hairs. If you allow for the forced sterilization of criminals, it's a short leap to people with mental retardation, and then the hopelessly poor, which leads to Blacks, and more than likely from there to Jews, Asians, and Italians if allowed. Who would be next? Where did it stop?

Lucky Luciano had engaged 8's services because he was concerned about the Reed-Johnson Immigration Act being passed curtailing immigration in America for certain people from certain places in the world, most particularly the Italians and the Jews, but meanwhile, something much more sinister was afoot. The active elimination of genes that the elite white people of Western European descent deemed unfit to live on.

Was it all connected, 8 wondered? The death of Karl Vogel. The theft of the Aquila. Jack Johnson. The Reed-Johnson Immigration Act. The stalking of Asta. The sterilization of Bettie Young. His mind whirled, each of these things leaping forth to be replaced by another, as if underlined in bold on the page. Murder. The secret order of the Batavi. A Roman Legion Standard. Lucky Luciano. Herman Wall. Ronald Dankworth.

Enough thinking, 8 breathed aloud. There was a time for thinking and a time for action. Dankworth was the key that could possibly lead him to the answers that he needed. Everybody else, everything else, was conjecture. Ronald Dankworth had sent Bettie Young to Damnation Island to be sterilized without giving her any choice in the matter. He gave a nod to Millie as he grabbed his jacket and hat and went out the door.

Four hours later, 8 was on his third afternoon coffee of the day, sitting on a bench across the street from the Brooklyn Hospital. The coffee was from Kelley's Irish Pot. It wasn't a bad cup of joe at all. 8 had gone to the front desk of the hospital to ascertain that Dankworth was there. He was. 8 had then walked the perimeter of the medical buildings to establish where the employees exited the building. It was right across from where he now sat.

8 figured that an administrator like Ronald Dankworth was a man of routine and would be leaving the hospital promptly at five o'clock. Still, he'd arrived early to make sure to not miss his man and to further ruminate on the recent revelations from Bettie Young and how it might tie together with everything else he'd discovered.

His cerebrations led him to the man who'd put a scare into Asta. A tall, thin man with a jagged face. Was this connected to the case or was it just a random incident? Either way, the result had been that Asta had been staying with 8 all week. There were perks to this arrangement, that was for sure, a wry grin popping onto his face as he thought of the sweet rewards of spending the entire week together.

At the same time, 8 had grown used to living alone, and this new situation was starting to feel crowded. Asta was working the noon to eight shift, meaning that she was mostly still asleep when he slipped out the doorway in the morning to go get breakfast. 8 had made dinner for her when she got home twice, and twice they'd gone down to the first floor to the tavern. So, he wasn't complaining, but it was certainly a change.

Right on time, at five minutes past five, Dankworth came down the ramp that the hospital staff arrived and departed from. For a tall man, his steps were like that of a small bird, punchy and jerky and rapid. He turned and walked up Ashland, away from 8, who stood and followed him.

Bettie Young told 8 that what she most wanted was for the people who'd stolen her ability to have babies to be punished. Not just the doctor who performed the operation but those mysterious men behind the scenes who'd ordered it done. The way she said *men* made 8 wince a bit, to be grouped into that hateful category.

"I'll tell you who is behind it all," Bettie had said, a bite slicing the edges of her words. "It's the rich folks. People with too much money and too much time that get off on fucking with people. Telling women what to do, how to do it, be seen and not heard, and go around hanging our heads because we wasn't born with a goddamn hot dog hanging down between our legs." 8 had stayed silent while she gave in to a searing anger that appeared to have been pent up for some time now. "Rich. White. Men. With nothing better to do than shame women, insult Black people, and lord it around like the world is their castle. They think all women is their whores and Black people their goddamn slaves. Didn't they hear of that there Civil War that ended…" Her voice choked up and she took a gasping breath. "That's who I want to pay for what's been done to me."

It wasn't something that you took to the police, 8 thought, strolling along about fifty feet behind Dankworth. He'd run it by McGee of course, but he was fairly certain that he'd be laughed out of the building if he and Bettie Young went to the men with badges. Some poor Black woman got her tubes tied to prevent her from having any more babies, and they were supposed to arrest the doctor who did it? They were more likely to go buy the fellow a beer and slap him on the back for a job well done.

Bettie hadn't even got the name of the doctor who'd performed the operation. She was hazy from morphine when originally told about the procedure, and then the man hadn't come back to check on her until after she checked herself out the next day. 8 thought about Bettie riding up the elevator to the Queensboro Bridge and then trudging the five plus miles back to her crowded tenement after having her insides sliced and diced like that. She was one tough lady, that he knew, even after having known her for but a few hours.

8 looked up in surprise as Dankworth turned into the Bossert Hotel, which was in Brooklyn Heights, about a mile from the hospital. The same place that the Germans had been staying. Coincidence? 8 didn't much believe in coincidences. 8 watched as the man went to the counter in the lobby, got a key, and went to the elevator and took it up to the second floor. Interesting.

8 went to a corner of the lobby and sat down in a plush armchair to devise a strategy for his next move. He hadn't really got very far when he saw Theda Vogel come through the front door. She was dressed in an off-the-shoulder black dress that hugged her curves very tightly and was covered in an array of dazzling sequins. As she breezed past 8, who tried, the best a man his size could, to be inconspicuous, he was somewhat shocked that her entire back was bare.

Theda, bent on a mission, didn't notice him as she went straight to the elevator. 8 slipped through a doorway to the stairs, knowing their location well, and bounded up to the second floor. He watched through the cracked open door as Theda got off the elevator and went down and knocked on a door. Almost immediately, the door was opened, and in she went. 8 walked past to get the room number and then went back to the lobby to try and make some sense of this.

Of course, Theda's husband had worked at the hospital where Dankworth was the vice president. So, she knew the man, perhaps well. Maybe very close friends? Meeting in a hotel room and not at one of their residences suggested that perhaps they were very close friends. It seemed that Dankworth had most certainly been covering something up when 8 had spoken to him. But it'd been Theda who'd hired him. And now they were meeting in a hotel room. 8 shook his head to clear the confusion, but it didn't help.

An hour later, Theda came back through the lobby, and 8 decided to confront her. He rose and joined her side as she stepped out the door into the dusk of approaching evening in Brooklyn, looking across the East River, to Manhattan.

"Theda!" He turned and looked at her with what he hoped was a surprise. "What are you doing here at the Bossert?"

She swung her head to look at him, a flush spreading across the extremely white skin of her face. "8, why hello, funny you being here, too."

He noticed that she'd avoided answering his question. "Are you on your way home? I'd be happy to walk with you."

"Uh, I was... that'd be fine and very gentlemanly of you. I wanted to apologize for the other night. I just get so lonely, you know, and you are so ruggedly handsome." They turned to the right and began walking.

Lonely, 8 thought, was a bit of a stretch as her husband had only been dead a few weeks. With Karl Vogel's body still warm in the ground, she'd tried to seduce 8 and was now leaving the hotel room of a man her husband had worked with. "No worries," he said. "This is where you sent me off to that night, remember, right here to the Bossert Hotel, as you'd followed two men here that you'd seen arguing with your husband the day before he was killed."

Theda shivered, and 8 wondered that she had no sort of jacket or shawl on a chill night with such a flimsy dress. "Would you like my jacket?" He took his suit jacket off and hung it around her shoulders. It almost reached her feet and enveloped her like a blanket.

"Thank you. Did you find those men?"

"Briefly," he said. "But do tell what brought you here this afternoon?"

"I have a friend visiting from out of town who is staying here," Theda said. "I was just visiting with her."

"Is she in town for long?"

"Just a few days. But what brought you here? Were you looking for those men who argued with Karl? What did you mean by briefly?"

"No, I'm sure that they checked out and moved on to greener pastures. I'd actually followed Ronald Dankworth here." 8 watched her chin jerk as if struck.

"Ronald… Dankworth? You mean the man who my husband worked for at the hospital? Whyever would you be following him."

8 shrugged. "How well do you know him?"

"We've had dinner with him and his wife on several occasions. We saw him at cocktail parties and medical functions, I suppose, but I can't say that I know him very well. Why do you ask?"

"When I spoke with him at the hospital, it seemed like he was trying to hide something. It probably was nothing, but then his name came up again, so I decided to tail him."

"He and Karl were very good friends. I don't believe that he could possibly have anything to do with his death."

"You're probably right."

They reached the front door of her apartment building. "Thank you for walking me home, Mr. Ballo. I'll be fine from here." And Theda Vogel handed him his jacket then breezed through the door and left him standing on the sidewalk.

Chapter 20

8 was in the basement of his building nursing a whiskey when Pearle sat down next to him. The place was bathed in a soft light, the brown liquor was tasty, and it was the sort of place somebody could think without being bothered.

"How'd you find me?" 8 asked.

Pearle shrugged. "You weren't in your office, and you weren't in your room, and you weren't eating in the tavern. Only one more floor to check."

8 chuckled. "You saying I don't leave my building?"

"Not unless you have to. Why would you?" Pearle raised his hand to the bartender, pointed at 8's drink and raised two fingers. "Especially since you settled down into domestic bliss, taking up house with one Asta Holm."

"She's just staying with me until all this gets resolved," 8 said. "For her safety."

Pearle nodded. "Sure. Sure thing. I like Asta. She's a nice dame."

"Seriously. This is not a permanent situation."

"Okay. Whatever you say, Bo." Pearle's drink slid in front of him. He picked up the glass. "To pretty ladies with a good sense of humor."

8 clicked the tumbler with his own and took a nip. Pearle usually had a few different women on the line, ready to be reeled in when desired. There was one, 8 was guessing, who he might've grown partial to. Clarissa. But that remained to be seen.

"What brings you to my *building*?' 8 asked.

"You'll never guess who came out to Cold Spring Harbor to pay our friend Herman Wall a visit today." Pearle took out a cigar, clipped it, lit it, and puffed.

8 eyed him without answering.

"I was sitting there reading a book by that British dame, Agatha Christie, *Murder on the Links*, about that Hercule Poirot fellow, when this Kissel Gold Bug Speedster parks right next to me."

"With a red streak of paint on the door," 8 said.

Pearle nodded. "This short dude wearing pretty expensive clothes gets out and goes into the building."

"Fred Peters. Who claims his car was stolen. Visiting with Herman Wall."

"You got it," Pearle said. "About ten minutes later, he comes back out with that tall fellow who didn't say a word when we were there the other day, just stood and glared at us. They looked like Mutt and Jeff, the two of them did."

"That gent by the name of Axel something or other said that the man driving the Gold Bug was tall and thin."

"This fellow barely fit in the car. Had to fold himself all up just to get in."

"You follow them?"

Pearle gave him a look. "Seemed like the thing to do."

"Where'd they go?"

"They parked right across the street from here," Pearle said. "Sat there for maybe twenty minutes. Then they drove off. I would've followed them, but I thought it might be best to pass on the word to you that you seem to have attracted somebody's attention. Not that I'm all that fretful about your safety, big man, but that pretty lady you hanging around with? I wouldn't want to see any harm come to our Asta."

8 took out his pocket watch. Almost time to go walk her home, a task he'd been performing all week. Not that it was much of a chore.

It was quite pleasant to walk alongside Asta on their way back to his apartment. There was something comforting about it. And scary.

"Anything else out of the ordinary with Wall?"

"So far, this week, I've counted three senators, seven house members, and three millionaires who I know of having visited him. Wall has a more prestigious guest list than Silent Cal."

8 chuckled. "President Coolidge isn't much at socializing, but he will welcome delegates coming in for a visit. His frugality is what we need in these heady times."

"How long you been hitting this hootch?" Pearle asked.

"Seen any Germans coming by?"

"I'm not sure I could tell a German from an American, at least the good Western European stock that visits with Wall. I can tell you there wasn't a single Black, Asian, or Italian stopping by all week."

"Had a visit earlier today," 8 said. "Got a new client. Young Black woman. Actually, you've seen her. Remember that lady singing on stage when we went out to the Back Room?"

"Hard to forget a lady with pipes like that," Pearle said. "What'd she hire you for."

"Smack Henderson recommended me." 8 finished his drink and shook his head no when the bartender went to refill it. "Seems that she went to the hospital to have her appendix removed, and they took the liberty of sterilizing her at the same time. For her own good."

"Son-of-a-bitch," Pearle said.

"Seems that Dankworth fellow out to Brooklyn Hospital personally arranged for her to be delivered to Damnation Island for the procedure."

"We going to go over and tie his tubes up?"

8 grinned. "No. But I did follow him today, and he had a rendezvous at the Bossert Hotel with Theda Vogel."

"Rendezvous?"

"She went up to his room for about an hour. I happened to run into her just outside the hotel, and she lied about her reason for being there."

"I suppose a recent widow doesn't want to go around sharing that she's bopping her late husband's boss."

8 stood up. "You want to drop me off at the telephone company? I got to go walk Asta home."

"I can pick up and drop off as well, if you like, big man."

"I kind of like walking home with her," 8 said. "Something to look forward to at the end of the day."

Pearle snickered. "I'm betting that's not all you're looking forward to at the end of each day with young Miss Holm."

* * *

8 watched the women spill out of the front of the telephone office. In the middle of the pack was Asta, her blonde hair recently cut short, her blue eyes sparkling, and her well-proportioned figure stirring something inside of him. Love or lust? He certainly liked being with her, in all the different ways, but how did you know if she was the one?

He'd thought he was in love, back before the Great War. Camila Morales. A young lady with dark eyes and a wicked wit. But their relationship had been interrupted by Kaiser Bill and by the time he got back from overseas, Camila had married a banker. And of course, more recently, Velma, who'd twisted him all up in knots.

"Hey there, my handsome and sexy man," she said, bouncing over to him and kissing him on the lips in front of the whole world.

"Mm. Hey there yourself."

"You got plans for the night?" Asta took his hand as they started to walk down the sidewalk. "I'm famished."

"I have plans for you," 8 said. "But we can eat first if you want."

Asta giggled. "You're wicked."

"Wicked for you."

"How'd your day turn out?"

8 told her about the visit from Bettie Young, tailing Dankworth, who'd met with Theda, and the conversation with her.

"Is Theda Vogel a good-looking woman?" Asta paused and looked at 8's eyes. "You call her the Widow Vogel, and I picture an old crone dressed all in black with wrinkles and saggy body parts."

8 wondered how one was supposed to answer that question. He wasn't one for lying, but he also wasn't interested in getting Asta angry with him. "She, uh, is certainly no old crone. She's, um, quite a bit more vibrant than that."

"In other words, she's a real Sheba." Asta giggled and continued walking, pulling him along with her. "And willing to shack up so recently after her husband's death with a gent by the name of Dankworth."

"I'm not certain that her visit…was of a sexual nature."

"Has the horrible Widow Vogel come on to you?" 8 didn't answer, causing Asta to pause again. "She has, hasn't she. I don't think I like her very much. And tell me, did you succumb to her wiles?'

"That would be ridiculous of me, when I have you waiting at home, now wouldn't it?"

"That's not really an answer, now, is it?"

"No. I have not, nor do I intend to, have anything other than a professional relationship with Theda Vogel."

Asta stared him in the eyes, smiled, stood on tiptoes, and kissed him. "What say we eat at *Emil's*?" She nodded across the street.

"Sure." 8 realized that his reply had been accepted, and a reprieve had been granted. "Will you be seeing Jill Grady at work tomorrow, do you suppose?" He took her hand and crossed the street.

"Jill?"

"Yeah, the lady who was having a bit of trouble with her husband, Joseph. The fellow I went and had a chat with suggesting that he stop smacking her around when he had too much to drink."

"Why?"

"Well, he's a janitor at the Brooklyn Hospital, and I thought it might be helpful if he got me in there some night. I imagine he's got access to every room in the whole place."

"Probably even get you into the office of that gent, Ronald Dankworth, who may or may not be sleeping with his former employee's widow."

"Especially that fellow," 8 agreed, holding the door open for her. "I'd like to find out more about him."

They got a table for two in the front window. 8 got the pot roast and potato dumplings. Asta had the sauerkraut soup. The waiter brought them each a glass of red wine in a teacup without asking. Asta was off the following day and wondered if there were some things she could help out with in the PI business. They did not talk about how long Asta would be staying with 8 at his place. They had a small plate of *pfeffernuesse* for dessert, the German molasses and honey cookies tinged with cinnamon, nutmeg, and ginger.

As they came out the door, a tall, thin man stepped from the lamppost and pointed a pistol at 8's head from five feet away and pulled the trigger. 8 wasn't sure if he ducked, twitched, or if the man just missed. He did know that the bullet fanned his ear as it went by, exploding the window in the door.

In one motion, 8 pushed Asta to the side, knocking her from her feet to a crumpled heap on the ground as he stepped forward, his arm sweeping up just as the man pulled the trigger again, the bullet digging a hole in the beam over the door as 8 crashed his fist into the man's lean face knocking him backward into a parked motorcar.

The man held onto the gun, bringing it once more to bear as 8 charged into him, slamming him against the door of the automobile. He grasped the wrist of the hand holding the pistol and banged it against the window, smashing through it in an exploding spray of glass. Still, the man clung to the weapon, his free hand grasping at 8's face, his thumb digging for 8's eye.

8 leaned back slightly, and then snapped the top of his skull

into the man's nose. A spray of blood splattered forth as the man wrestled his arm free of 8's grasp and turned the gun again toward 8 who brought his forearm upward, clubbing the gun back just as the man pulled the trigger again.

The bullet went in under his own chin, rattled around in his brain, and came to rest somewhere within his skull. 8 stepped back as the tall, thin German tumbled to the ground in a heap. He twitched, made some sort of whistling sound, gurgled, and died.

Chapter 21

8 was back in the Great War, in the trenches, fighting the Germans in Kaiser Bill's War. It'd been raining for days, and everything was one big muddy, sloppy, mess. Barbed wire snaked its way through the goop that was the no-man's land between them and the Heinies, a stretch of land that was no more than 500 yards at this point. The flashes of rifle fire could be picked up at night, a bit further back the larger flashes of artillery fire, and during the day, smoke curling lazily upward, mixing with the mist, creating clouds of rain and sulfur.

The man on his right suffered from trench foot and had cut his boots free and was now barefoot. His feet were almost unrecognizable, swollen attachments to his legs, distorted and distended, the flesh of various mottled colors. The man to his right had trench mouth, displaying rotting gums when he opened his mouth, a small collection of his own teeth cached away in his pocket.

It was hard to tell day from night when the black clouds clung to the earth like a blanket enveloping the soldiers of both sides in a discordant embrace. 8 was not sure when he'd last eaten. Slept. Shot a man. The war had become a blur, a disconnection from reality, and he swam through the murk in slow motion, just trying to survive minute to minute, second to second.

Down the line, rifle fire erupted, and screams echoed. Pain. Anger. Fear. It was difficult to tell. They were all the same. 8 risked a look over the top of the trench, across the way to where the Heinies lay in *their trenches. He wondered if their conditions were any better or worse than their own and if they suffered from the same ills.*

A tall, thin German with a pistol in his hand was skimming across the top of the ooze, skipping over the wire, his feet like that of Jesus walking on the water. He looked to be eight feet tall, his stride gobbling up space like some hungry dragon, and yes, he was breathing fire. 8 realized with horror that his chin was missing and the gaping hole in his face belched flames. 8 checked to see if his fellow soldiers saw what he saw and found that next to him was a very naked Asta, fast asleep, small snores rippling from her lips, unaware of the approaching danger.

8 brought his rifle to bear, resting it comfortably in the crook of his shoulder. He pulled the trigger. One. Twice. Three times. The tall, thin German somehow smiled without a mouth or any teeth and kept coming. 8 looked at the rifle in confusion. Shrugged. Fired off three more shots. Now he could hear the enormous feet of the German slapping the mud as he ran. They made a booming sound. Boom. Boom. Boom—

"8, me lad, wake yourself, and answer your door."

He opened his eyes. Looked to his right. It was not the soldier with trench foot but rather, Asta, albeit not naked. She was softly snoring, unphased by the banging at the door. They were in bed, in his bed, in his apartment, not in a trench. It was 1924 and not 1918.

8 slid from bed, pulled on a pair of trousers and a shirt, and padded his way to the door, grabbing socks and shoes on the way. He opened the door, shoes in hand.

"Top of the morning to you, me lad," McGee said.

"Let's go downstairs to my office," 8 said.

"What for? You got company?"

"Asta is sleeping," 8 said, stepping past the Irishman and pulling the door shut. He walked down the stairs barefoot, the policeman following along behind.

"I would've called ahead but you still haven't gotten yourself a phone for your home, I take it, have you?"

"Got one in my office. Why do I need one upstairs?"

"You got any whiskey down here?" McGee asked as 8 opened the door and led him into the inner office. "I'm parched, I is, and could use a wee dram."

8 went behind his desk, opened a drawer, pulled a flask out and tossed it to McGee. He tucked in his shirt, sat, pulled his socks and shoes on, and wondered if a nip of the brown would be a fair substitute for a cup of joe.

McGee smacked his lips. "Elixir of the gods, right there." He did not hand the flask back.

"What can I do for you this morning?" 8 risked a look at the window. Light was seeping through, suggesting that morning must have indeed arrived.

He'd been up half the night, first with the two elephant ears who'd shown up at the scene, one Irish and one German policemen, who'd been convinced to roust McGee from other duties and come on down to the scene while the meat wagon took the tall, thin, and very dead German to the morgue. Unlike the German from the dream, this German still had his jaw, the bullet having traveled cleanly up into the skull where it pinged around a bit before coming to rest.

McGee tipped the flask back and took another snort of the whisky. "Managed to get Captain Archipoili from downtown to go find that lad. You know, the one who saw Karl Vogel get run down in the street. Well, he brought him down to the morgue to see if the guy you shot was the same man as who killed Vogel."

8 nodded. "Axel Theisen."

McGee snapped his fingers. "That's the name of the lad."

"And? Did he identify them as the same?"

"Said he didn't get a real good look at the guy who killed Vogel. Just that he was tall and thin. And this lad's face was all swollen and discolored, making it hard to be sure. But he did identify his coat."

"His coat?" 8 asked.

"Said that it was the same coat. Aquascutum, or some *shite* like that."

"Any idea what the dead German's name is yet?"

McGee shook his head. "No identification on him. We checked the records at the Bossert Hotel for when you had a run-in with him and that fat guy. The room was under the name of Heinrich Funk, which is the name the heavyset German fellow gave to you. We're looking that up as well, but nothing so far."

"Sounds like we got our man," 8 said. But it did not feel right. "But if he'd come from Germany to get the Aquila, one would think he would've been long gone. Why were he and the other fellow hanging around? Something more than some former Roman Standard, now symbol of the Batavi. We need to find out more about this clandestine organization."

McGee stood up, handing over the flask. "That cloak and dagger *shite* is all yours, me lad. This is where us coppers wash our hands, close the case, and let you private dicks dig deeper if you want."

8 went down to the corner store and got himself a cup of coffee. He had some eggs, ham, and bread upstairs that he'd cook up to share with Asta a bit later, but for now, he needed some caffeine to chase away the cobwebs. He bought a paper as well and sat at a table in the corner to look through it. He didn't imagine that his shooting of the German would make the paper, probably not until the next day.

They'd moved that fellow who the Tongs had tried to kill, Wing Wing, from the Holy Family Hospital, as they'd received information that he was being targeted for murder. Things had been pretty tense in Chinatown lately as the Ong Leong and Hip Sing Tongs had recently declared war on each other.

The Army-Navy football game was slated to be played today. Some fellow had opened fire in a Broadway Dance Club last night. Three rum runners were captured in the Narrows. A Black man who stole a purse and bit the ear off a policeman was shot and killed. There was a rodeo at Madison Square Garden that might be a hoot to go to. But nothing about a man being shot in Bushwick outside of a restaurant.

8 folded the paper, put it under his arm, took the last sip of coffee, and left with a much better outlook than he'd claimed before coffee. It was Saturday, so Millicent had the day off, and he had the office to himself for the time being. He read through more of the back issues of the *Brooklyn Eagle*, looking for connections between the Department of Genetics at Cold Spring Harbor, the Brooklyn Hospital, Damnation Island, or any of the people involved.

At just past ten, the telephone rang, and he accepted the call from Dorothy Parker. This was a bit odd, for it seemed to be a tad on the early side of a weekend morning for her to be awake.

"Good morning, my large Hungarian bear," she said.

"Good morning to you, Dottie." 8 sat down at Millicent's desk and put his feet up. "And to what do I owe the pleasure of your voice this morning?"

"You see, the thing is, I've been invited to this dreadful luncheon out on the North Shore in Great Neck, and you see, the thing is, my husband was supposed to go with me, but he has completely jumped ship and has left this morning to go *golfing* with some of his pals. I just can't go alone."

"Great Neck? Scott and Zelda?"

Dottie snorted. "Do keep up with society, my dear 8. The Fitzgeralds are living across the pond in Paris. Rumor has it that Scott is finishing up a book set in Great Neck about some bootlegger millionaire, or some such thing, of love lost, found, and lost again or some rubbish such as that. Hopefully it'll be better than that *Vegetables* play he wrote about the postman who would be president."

"I'm in the middle of something right now," 8 said, not mentioning having shot and killed a man the night before, and his concern about leaving Asta alone. "Not sure I have time for a high society luncheon."

"I have been told that Max Lange, the host, is cousins with Lena Wall, and that she is visiting with them over the weekend."

"Lena Wall," 8 said slowly. "The wife of Herman Wall, director of the Department of Genetics."

"I don't believe that he will be present, but it might be a good opportunity for you to speak with the wife of the man you're researching, don't you think?"

"Do you think that it'd be okay if Asta came with us?"

There was a pause as Dottie digested this request. "You know what they say, my dear 8, not that I have anything against Asta, I think she's delightful, but two's a crowd and three's a drag."

8 chuckled. "No, I don't believe I've heard that said. The thing is, a man tried to shoot me last night, and I'm a little bit worried that Asta might be targeted as well."

"Whatever have you gotten yourself into now? Are you even safe to be around?"

Dottie agreed that it'd be fine for Asta to come along, but when 8 went up to wake her, she unequivocally said she was not interested, especially as she had nothing to wear to such a function. 8 tried to convince her as he made omelets, and continued to try to convince her as they ate, but to no avail. She had a book, *A Passage to India*, by E.M. Forster, that she was excited to begin reading. 8 knew better than to argue with her once her mind was made up.

At just past noon, therefore, he found himself sitting in the back of a motorcar that Dorothy had hired for the day along with a driver bouncing along the rough roads out to Great Neck. He trusted her to keep a secret and respected her ability to get right to the heart of the matter, so he brought her up to date on all that had happened in the last two weeks, some of which she already knew, but there were pieces he hadn't previously shared as well as new information.

When he was done talking, Dottie took a deep breath. "So, our darling Theda hires you to find who killed her husband and stole some priceless Aquila that is the symbol of a 2,000-year-old clandestine society in German called the Batavi. Her husband, Karl, was a doctor at the Brooklyn Hospital and on the board of directors for the Department of Genetics at Cold Spring Harbor. The hospital director, a gent by the name of Dank...worth, appeared to be hiding something and then later has a secret rendezvous with our dear Theda. The boxer, Jack Johnson, came to ask you to interfere on his behalf with the gangster, Charlie Luciano, who asked you to dig up dirt on a guy by the name of Wall who is bending the ear of Congress and is the director at the, do they happen to call the Department of Genetics DOG for short? That would be so much easier. This gent is married to Lena Wall who we're having lunch with today, and he also seems very suspicious. Is that it? Did I get it all?"

8 nodded. "Pretty much except for the fact that I had a run-in with two Germans over to the Bossert Hotel, and last night one of them tried to kill me and ended up putting a bullet in his own noggin. And the owner of the motorcar that ran Karl Vogel down went to a Klan meeting in Queens, and since has been visiting with Wall."

"Whew. I always thought my tombstone might say something to the effect that everything I did, I did against my better judgment. Well, being seen with you is certainly against my better judgment. My, you are in deep here, aren't you?"

"You got any advice?"

"Only, beware of those with money. If you want to know what God thinks about money, just look at the people who he gave it to."

Chapter 22

They pulled up a circular drive that went around a large fountain that appeared to have nymphs frolicking in the water. The mansion, or was it an estate, 8 wondered, was a massive structure built of stone and concrete, rising from the ground like the White Cliffs of Dover. It was newly built, he would guess, as the landscaping around the palace was freshly planted, not yet grown into the comfortable grounds of old money.

8 grinned wryly, thinking on how Dottie had just told him to beware of those with money, and then had brought him right here to the lion's den. He stepped out of the motorcar, jostled aside by a butler who helped Dottie from the automobile. They were led inside, two massive oak doors leading to a cavernous hallway that would've fit 8's entire apartment and then some.

The butler brought them to the library where fifteen or so people milled around with a mix of champagne flutes and glasses of liquor in their hands, clustered into small groups of two, three, and four. 8 wondered about what authors graced the extensive shelves as he followed Dottie to a man with a tray of champagne.

"No, I don't believe sweet water will do the trick this early, my dear," Dottie said to the man. "Be a darling and go find me a glass of gin and a whiskey for my friend." She turned and steered 8 to a man and a woman off in the corner. "Edna, you must meet my ambrosial escort, 8 Ballo. 8, this is Edna St. Vincent Millay and her husband Eugen Boissevain."

8 nodded, shook Eugen's hand, and wondered if he was supposed to kiss the woman's hand like some regal queen. Where Boissevain was in his forties, she was only about thirty, 8 judged. He was saved in his dilemma as she held out her hand.

"Call me Vincent," she said. As her hand disappeared into his she looked into his eyes. "My, you *are* a big six, aren't you. Are you big all over?"

Dottie laughed. "Don't mind her, my dear 8. Vincent grew up in the backwoods of Maine and has yet to learn the proper manners of a lady."

It was Vincent's turn to snicker. "Ah, they tried to instill that in me at Vassar, but it didn't take. Of course, Dottie is a paradigm of her particular stratum of society, be it high or low I can never tell."

The waiter came back with their drinks and was promptly sent off by Vincent for reinforcements of her own glass.

"Vincent and I both write for *Ainslee's*," Dottie said. "Short little snippets of drivel."

"Do I remember something about Vincent, here, receiving a Pulitzer Prize," 8 said. "For *The Ballad of the Harp Weaver*."

"That thing, it was just a string of words strung together," Vincent said.

"It seemed more familiar and intimate than that." 8 paused, remembering and putting the words together in his head. "*That was in the late fall. When the winter came, I'd not a pair of breeches, nor a shirt to my name, I couldn't go to school, or out of doors to play. And all the other little boys, passed our way.*"

"Good to know that somebody has read my work." Vincent plucked the fresh tumbler of gin from the waiter, her eyes pinned on 8, intense and mischievous. "Intimate?" she asked.

"I would say that you knew something of hardship," he said. "As a child. As well as a mother who loved you immensely."

"And what is it that you do, and why is it that you have a number for a name?"

8 chuckled. He told her about his mother being surprised that he was not a girl, and not having a boy's name ready, the mix-up of number with name that somehow never got corrected. "And to answer your first question, I am a private investigator," he said.

"A gumshoe?" Vincent asked, her eyebrows leaping up to wrinkle her forehead. "Oh, Dottie, magnificent. What a solace to the tedium of our normal luncheon crowd."

A bell rang. 8 followed as the others filtered from the library to the dining room with a table set for twenty-four. He was directed by Dottie to sit next to a curvaceous blonde woman with a bright smile and a narrow face.

"Hello," she said. "I'm Lena Wall."

Dottie had orchestrated well, 8 thought. "8 Ballo." This of course caused another explanation of his name and the comment that he was here as a guest of Dottie.

The kitchen help brought out turtle soup, which 8 tasted with trepidation though it proved to be delicious. "It is your husband who is doing all the wonderful work in Cold Spring Harbor," he said to Lena.

"He is doing God's work," she replied with a shine to her eyes. "Purifying the human race."

"We need more like him," 8 said, grimacing at the dirt he felt caking to his soul. "Out there as missionaries for God on earth, cleansing our society of the mongrel muck that has seeped into it."

"Max is a big supporter of his work," Lena said. "As, of course, is Mary Harriman, the Rockefellers, and of course, the Carnegies."

"Is he here?" 8 asked. "I'd love to meet him."

"Herman? No, he was unable to make it," Lena said. "He had too much to prepare for tonight."

"Tonight?" 8 asked.

Lena leaned closer, tickling 8's nostrils with a deliciously scented perfume of flowers and fruits. "He is a member of the Long Island branch of the Ku Klux Klan," she said. "They are having a meeting at the Howe Farm."

8 realized that her hand was on his thigh, and her lips were only an inch form his neck. She was most certainly flirting with him, as the actions were a bit more than just friendly. He turned his head so that he faced her. Her blue eyes shone brightly at him, black lashes fluttering, her red lips trembling ever so slightly.

"I am out this way for the evening and would love to attend a rally," he said. "I, of course, am a member of the Klan in Brooklyn, but do you think it'd be possible to be a guest this evening?"

"Herman is very welcoming to like-minded people." Lena licked her lips. "But the meet is back your way. In Queens."

8 put his hand on her knee, her skin warm to the touch, her breath hot on his neck. "What town is the Howe Farm in?"

*   *   *

"I lost him," Pearle said. "I sat down the road from his house, sitting out in the woods all morning because a Black man sitting in his car in that neighborhood has a death wish. Finally, he came out and went rocketing down the road. I was trying to keep up with him when I hit a hole in the road and got a flat tire."

8 had gotten himself dropped off at Pearle's place after the Great Neck luncheon, hoping that his buddy was there and not out following Herman Wall around. Of course, if he had been, that would've been fine as well, as they both planned on going to the same place this evening.

"That's okay," 8 said. "I know where he's gonna be this evening."

"That's great. I'll take the night off. Clarissa says that she's been missing her Pearle. I'll take a nap, clean up, put on some fine clothes, and take my lady out for food and music before bringing her back here for a nightcap."

"Speaking of, you got any of that good scotch whiskey around?"

Pearle walked to the bar and pulled a bottle from a shelf. He held it up. Bowmore. "Last bottle of this. They closed down about ten years ago. Appreciate this, because you might never get a chance at anything this smooth ever again." He took two glasses and poured two fingers in each. 8 followed him over and stood across from him, taking one tumbler, clinking it with Pearle's, and taking a sip.

"That is mighty fine," 8 said. "I thought you might want to go to a get-together this evening with me."

"Yeah? What you got that Clarissa don't?"

"Not me. It's the event we'd be going to. A costume party."

Pearle snickered. "I might do some sort of costume party with Clarissa, but I think I'll pass on attending one with you, Bo."

8 chuckled. "Both involve rolling around in sheets."

"What the hell you talking about?"

"I have the address of a Ku Klux Klan rally taking place over in Queens this evening at midnight that Herman Wall plans on attending. I thought we might go see what it's all about."

Pearle snorted. "You know I'm Black, don't you?"

"That's the beauty of the Klan. Once you put your white sheet and hoodie thing on it doesn't matter what your skin color, religion, or gender is. They are equal opportunity, those fellows in the Klan are."

"Last time I looked, my hands were black." Pearle held up his fist and inspected it.

"We'll get you a pair of gloves."

"What do you suppose they all do at those meetings?" Pearle asked. "Could be an interesting proposition."

"When you ever going to get a chance to go to a Klan rally again in your life?" 8 asked.

Chapter 23

Pearle had picked 8 up at ten, and then they'd gone and collected McGee down the street from his house. He'd not thought it a good idea to tell his wife that he was going to a Klan rally. Instead, he'd said he had to take care of some police business, which wasn't exactly a lie.

The road out to the Howe Farm was packed with cars, all of them turning down a long dirt driveway, all except Pearle, who drove on past. He found a small dirt road about a half-mile past in a wooded area and pulled the motorcar in there.

8 had picked up three authentic Klan outfits for them to wear as well as white gloves for Pearle. It turned out you couldn't just get a sheet and do a bit of sewing on that and add a pillowcase over your head but had to purchase it through the purser. The Klan uniforms and the bric-a-brac of various offices was a money-maker for the Klan leaders, often quite lucrative. This was not the only thing different about the Klan of today from its origins in the aftermath of the Civil War. While Black people were still targeted now in the '20s, the scope had broadened to include Catholics, especially the Irish and Italians, and the Jews.

8 had done some work for a fellow a few months back who'd told him this and had also mentioned in passing that he'd joined his local Klan thinking it was more of a club than a hate group. That particular chapter had sponsored a children's baseball team, held Sunday barbecues, the tri-Klub for teenage girls, and even a cradle

Klub for babies. It wasn't until the guy had bought his Klan gear and attended his first nighttime rally that he realized what they were really all about.

8 had given him a ring on the telephone, knowing the man had quit the invisible empire, hoping that he still had his Klan outfit. Not only did he, but he knew a couple of other gents who'd also quit, disillusioned by the mission of the Klan. Once 8 told him that he wanted to sneak in and reveal the true nature of the Klan, the man had readily agreed to gather the three outfits and drop them off with 8.

Pearle grumbled in disgust as he pulled the robe over his head. "Of all the stupid things I've done in my life, this here takes the cake."

"You can stay with the car, if you like," 8 said.

"Oh, c'mon, me lad." McGee pulled his robe on. "Let's go and see what these *shitehawks* are up to."

"Easy for you to say, you're not Black." Pearle pulled a white glove on. "Hey, these here are ladies' gloves."

8 chuckled. "Didn't have any white men's gloves down at the store. Figured you'd only be wearing them the once, anyway."

Pearle made more unintelligible disgusted noises.

McGee tied the belt on the robe. "Just so you know, these modern Klan lads hate us Roman Catholics more than they do you Black folks."

Pearle snorted. "Take that cross off your neck and nobody will know. But, any way you slice this pie, I'm still Black."

"Keep your hood and robe on, and let's give it the lash," McGee said.

"The lash is what I'm trying to avoid." Pearle pulled his hood over his head. "Can either of you see my face through these eye holes?"

"It's darker than a witch's tit out here," McGee said. "I can barely see *you* standing two feet from me."

"I think we're good." 8 pulled his own hood on. "Let's go see what's happening with our local Klan this evening."

The moon peeked out from behind the clouds as they left the trees and started across the farmer's field, illuminating a hillside to their right on which hundreds, perhaps as many as a thousand, figures in white sheet stood in formation, looking up. They held torches, a mixture of red, white, and blue flames licking the night air.

"Holy shit," Pearle said, staring at the mass gathering of sheeted men.

"Probably best if you both let me do the talking." 8 paused to take in the sight. "Especially you, McGee. You might be able to hide your cross, but you can't disguise that Irish brogue of yours."

They started walking again as fireworks began exploding into the sky at the top of the hill.

"Is that...?"

"I believe those fireworks just made the KKK symbol," 8 said. "Somebody knows what the hell they're doing."

"This is like being back in Kaiser Bill's war," Pearle said. "Only the explosions were bigger."

As the illuminated KKK slowly disintegrated on its way down to the ground, a cross, at least forty feet high, lit up. Over the back of the hill came a lone horseman at a slow walk while a thousand men held their breath.

Suddenly, a voice boomed over an electrified outdoor system, "Every Klansman will salute the Imperial Cyclops!"

A thousand right hands shot into the air. 8, Pearle, and McGee had by now reached the last line of the Klan and stood in formation, hands raised along with the others.

"Welcome." The voice of the Imperial Cyclops reverberated over this modern speaker system. "It is nice to stand in front of a crowd that is one-hundred percent American."

One thousand voices replied in full-throated mania. "America for Americans! America for Americans! America for Americans!"

The hands went back down as the Imperial Cyclops began speaking. "We of the Klan know that the pioneers who built America bequeathed to their own children a sole and sacred right to it, the control of it and of its future, and that no one on earth can claim any part of this inheritance except through our generosity. We believe, too, that the mission of America under Almighty God is to perpetuate and develop just the kind of nation and just the kind of civilization our forefathers envisioned when they created this grand country."

"America for Americans! America for Americans! America for Americans!"

"We understand that races of men are as distinct as breeds of animals; that any mixture between races of any great divergence is evil; that the American stock, which was bred under highly selective conditions, has proved its value and should not be mongrelized."

"America for Americans! America for Americans! America for Americans!"

"We hold firmly that America belongs to Americans and should be kept American. The whole purpose of the Klan is to bring this belief to fulfillment. We may make many mistakes, but we are doing this one thing, and no one else is even trying to do it. Within a few years the America of our fathers will either be saved or lost, and unless some other way is found, all who wish to see it saved must work with us."

"America for Americans! America for Americans! America for Americans!"

A man came up and gave 8 a torch, burning a bright blue. He looked around at the scene and wondered at the vagaries of the human condition. How was it possible that this hillside housed a thousand men who believed they were superior to other human beings simply because of the color of their skin, the church they decided to follow, or the genes handed down to them through generations, genes whose make-up they couldn't even be sure of?

"The Blacks walk among us with heads held high, eyeballing our women, their devious minds set to stealing, violence, and rape. The Pope controls the minds of the Catholics, sending them to our shores in droves, none so much as the Irish, but the Italians not far behind, bent upon acting as agents of the Pope to turn America into nothing more than another country to line the walls of the Vatican with gold and silver."

"America for Americans! America for Americans! America for Americans!"

8 had wondered where this new hatred of the Roman Catholics had come from, not having actually given it much thought until now. It seemed the fear was the control that the Pope had over his constituents. Men and women who put church before state, before their neighbors, before their country.

"These Papal warriors want to break up your clubs, invade your neighborhoods, take your jobs, and send the money back to the Vatican to be used to build their army of minions up even further and more powerfully."

"America for Americans! America for Americans! America for Americans!"

"The Jews are the spawn of Satan and spread their filth to our shores every single day. They make no attempt at becoming Americans but speak their strange language, dress in their ridiculous clothes, eat their odd fare, and wear outlandish hats over peculiar hairstyles. This alone makes them our enemies, but the Bible is more definitive in that they are the legions of Satan here to destroy our lives and cast us into a new Babylon to be lost forever."

"America for Americans! America for Americans! America for Americans!"

8 almost chuckled, biting back the disgust mixed with humor at this outlandish bombast. If they'd brought Marty along, he'd have the perfect trifecta of companions with him. A Black man, an Irish Catholic, and a Jew. These fellows probably wouldn't much like a bloke who consorted with all of these enemies of the white race of God-fearing Protestants.

He looked around, wondering which figure might be Herman

Wall. Or the Gold Bug fellow who had run down Kurt Vogel in the street. Maybe the rotund German named Funk. The tall fellow certainly wasn't here, as he was across the way in the Bushwick morgue. Would Kurt Vogel have been here if he was still alive? Perhaps. Was Theda Vogel a member of the Klan Klub for woman?

8 knew a few fellows who were involved with the Klan, other than the one who'd quit the organization and loaned him the outfit. He couldn't say that he cared for them much, but outwardly, they didn't appear to be monsters. They had families, worked hard, and were well-mannered. How was it that somebody like that came out on a Saturday night in a hood and robe, carried torches, and playacted like foolish children, but not just ordinary juveniles, but as the worst bullies on the playground?

"We are the last bastion of the old pioneer stock that made America great. The liberals are mongrelizing our fair country which will, in turn, bring its demise. The new Nordic blend which became the American race was the highest, most gifted breed the world has ever known. This present melting pot is a ghastly failure and has become our undoing. If we don't act now, with force and intensity, within a few years we will be supplanted by the mere force of breeding of the lowest possible standard of human being. With the current birthrate, the good and pure Nordic stock will become a hopeless minority in fifty years. The white race must be supreme, not only in Queens, not only in New York, not only in America, but in the entire world."

"America for Americans! America for Americans! America for Americans!"

"The time to act is now. The time to talk is past. Next week's meeting will have a special treat, and your Kleagles will begin assigning you missions to accomplish. War has been brought to our doorstep by the immigrants. The Jews, the Catholics, the people of color want to take what is ours by birthright. The time to act is now!"

"America for Americans! America for Americans! America for Americans!"

Pearle leaned closer to 8. "Let's get the fuck out of here before somebody realizes we don't have a fucking Kleagle."

8 nodded and touched McGee's arm and nodded over his shoulder. The three of them melted backward but were arrested by a voice out of the darkness behind them.

"Where are you going? Does the idea of taking action to protect our birthright make you piss your pants in fear?"

"Not at all," 8 said. "Just thought we'd beat the rush."

"You don't have the mettle to be Klansmen."

"No, I just told my old lady I'd be home by two, so I best be getting," Pearle said.

"You fucking Pope lovers. Probably blow him if given a chance, wouldn't you."

"Just get out of the way, me lad, and let us be going."

"An Irishman?" The man stepped out of the darkness and grabbed McGee.

Pearle shoved the man, who grabbed at his hood, and pulled it from his head.

"You're Black," he breathed in astonishment and then opened his mouth wide and yelled, "Hey, everybody, we got us here a N—"

That's when 8's fist broke his jaw, leaving it even wider, hanging down below his neck. A few men turned around at the ruckus as the three of them slid silently into the shadows, dropping their torches on the ground.

A high-piercing keening was coming from the man who somehow had remained on his feet and stood with mouth agape.

"Hey, what the hell happened to you?" a man asked.

Once safely in the shadows, the three of them broke into a jog. They were about halfway across the field and had a quarter of a mile to go when men carrying red, white, and blue torches came streaming after them. The fellow with the broken jaw must've somehow shared what'd happened and pointed them in the right direction, 8 figured, as he increased his pace, a delicate balance between speed and tripping and falling.

They reached the car, pausing for just a moment, looking backward. 8 thought it appeared as if they were being chased by the American flag, a thought that greatly disappointed him, as these bigots had appropriated the color and tarnished the flag and country that he loved.

As they pulled back onto the road, away from the farm entrance, hoping it wasn't a dead end, several automobiles came zooming down the road at a reckless speed. A few bright souls had thought to get their motorcars for the chase.

The lead one rammed into the back of the Nash, jolting the automobile into the ditch. Pearle twisted the wheel and veered back onto the road, flooring the accelerator as he did so. A second motorcar pulled up alongside of them, four men staring and shouting out the window at them, words that were lost in the rushing air and racing engines.

8 pulled out his .38 as the vehicle slanted toward them, bumping them and trying to force them from the road. He pointed the pistol and pulled the trigger just as they were jolted from behind and his shot went wide, blowing out the windshield. The automobile went off the road and slammed into a tree with a jarring impact that shook the road.

"Shite," McGee said. "I didn't think to bring my gun."

"See the case on the floor next to you?" Pearle said as calmly as if they were just out on a Sunday afternoon drive and was pointing out the picnic basket. "That there case has a Tommy Gun in it."

"*Feck* me, that's right jammy," McGee said.

Ten seconds later the Tommy Gun was chattering out the back window, and the chase was over. It seemed that the Klansmen liked to bully others when the odds were in their favor but didn't hold up when facing hot lead.

Chapter 24

"What time did you get in last night?" Asta asked from the foot of the bed.

8 took notice because she was naked from the waist up. "Pretty late. What time is it?"

"Just about ten. The day is wasting away on you."

"Nothing wasteful about lying around in bed."

Asta smiled wickedly. "It is if you're sleeping and not doing other things."

"I am fully awake now and open to suggestions."

Asta sashayed her way down the side of the bed to stand over him. "What kept you out so late?"

"I can assure you there were no women where I was," 8 said. "Not a one."

"Hard to go someplace in the city where there's no women. You play cards with the boys?"

8 put his hand around her bottom and pulled her tight to the bed. He rather liked looking up at her ample and quite bare breasts. "Actually, I took Pearle and McGee to a Klan meeting."

Asta giggled. "That'd sure be the bee's knees."

"No, really." 8 grabbed her hand and pulled her on top of him. "We wore robes and hoods and even carried torches."

Asta giggled again as she nuzzled her lips into his neck. "Are you lying to me, 8 Ballo?"

"It wasn't one of my grander plans." He turned her onto her side, his hand trailing from her lips down to her belly.

"Bringing an Irish Catholic and a Black man to a KKK rally? I hope that doesn't top your list of grand plans." She slid her hand into his pajama bottoms.

"It all went well until McGee spoke and made a fellow suspicious, who then pulled Pearle's hood off. Then things got a bit dicey."

Asta's hand paused, and her body went still. "Is everybody okay?""

"Oh, everybody's just nifty. Well, other than the fellow whose jaw I broke and maybe the men in the motorcars that we shot up."

"Oh, is that all?" Asta grasped him in her hand. "You wanna tell me about it?"

"Maybe later, over some food?"

"Where'd this all take place?"

"Some farm in the middle of nowhere Queens." 8 slid his hand down into her pajama bottoms.

"Some of the gals I work with say their husbands have joined the Klan. Dora, she's pretty angry about it. Doesn't understand why her husband would be a part of that."

8 bent his neck and kissed her, lightly at first, and then firmer with more intent. She moved her free hand to the side of his face, and then the back of his head, pressing him tighter to her.

8 moved his lips down to nibble on her ear. "Might be good if you could find out more about them. There was this fellow in charge of everything called the Grand Cyclops or something like that. It's easy enough to figure out who lots of these leaders really are, but we hadn't heard about this fellow before."

Asta moaned slightly. "I'll see what I can find out. Can we talk about it later?"

*   *   *

Luther Towers was a man of routine. He liked to read the newspaper in the morning with a cup of coffee. All of his suits were a dark blue, and he always wore a white shirt with a red tie. And he always ate lunch on Sunday at noontime in Brooklyn at a fancy French restaurant in Williamsburg. He wondered if that had to do with his ancestors originally being from that country. Of course, some 500 years ago they'd crossed over the narrow arm of the Atlantic to England, and then some 100 years ago, arrived on the shores of America.

Luther considered himself an American. A hundred years of heritage in this country should be long enough, he figured, to belong. And he was very proud of his United States of America. The pure America. Not the America of Blacks, Jews, and Asians. Not those Italians who formed gangs and ran liquor, breaking the prohibition laws. No, he was proud of the good white America.

That was the second reason, he figured, that he ate lunch every Sunday at *Le Pure Café* in Williamsburg. And while the neighborhood teemed with filthy Jews, they weren't allowed into this particular establishment. Luther didn't think particularly highly of the French, too many Roman Catholics, but the food was good, enough so for him to make the hour drive from Long Island every Sunday.

When Luther was seven years old, his mother had run off with a Black man. His father contended that she'd been abducted by the man, or perhaps hypnotized with some sort of Voodoo and witchcraft. That was when he first became aware of the poor moral character possessed by Black people. This notion swirled around in his head with no real basis until he was twenty-three.

That was when he saw that moving picture, *The Birth of a Nation*. That cemented in his mind the way in which Black men lusted after white women. His mother had not run out on him and his father, but rather, had been a victim, a heroine, stolen away, perhaps killed, maybe jumping to her death like Mae Marsh did as Flora when that deviant Gus chased after her. Luther had gone and watched that moving picture every day that week and then read the book by that fellow Dixon, only it was called *The Clansman*.

Luther sat at the same table every Sunday at noon and ordered the same dish. The Seafood Pot. It had fish, mussels, clams, prawns, peppers, tomatoes, and a few other things thrown in. The waiter knew well to bring him his glass of milk when the entrée came out and not before. As he set down the large bowl and glass of milk, the waiter asked, as he did every Sunday, if Luther needed anything else, and was told, like every Sunday, that he did not.

He liked his routine, but sometimes wished that he had somebody to share his Sunday meal with. Luther liked to fantasize that Lillian Gish would walk through the door and ask if she could join him, just like in the moving picture when she'd ended up marrying that Ben fellow who recreated the KKK down in South Carolina after the unruly Black people started causing problems. Much like Ben, Luther had become involved in several organizations including the KKK that meant to restore order. To make America great again, as the founding fathers intended.

The reality was that he'd never ever had a woman friend of any sort and had barely ever spoken to one. He wasn't sure if it was his appearance, tall and gangly with a narrow face and skin whiter than snow from which blue eyes burned forth. Or maybe he'd never learned how to speak with a lady, seeing as his own ma had left when he was so young, and there'd just been Luther and his pa left.

But, if he were able to shut out the world and concentrate hard enough, he could almost bring his fantasies to life and make them real. Almost.

"Excuse me, do you mind if I join you?"

Luther looked up at Lillian Gish. Light brown hair. Blue eyes. Five inches over five feet.

"Yes, please do," he said.

"I noticed you were alone, and as I am too, I thought we might share the table."

Her cheeks didn't have the dimples, and her mouth lacked the pouty tremble of Lillian Gish. The hair was darker than light brown.

"Pleased to have the company," he said.

"My name is Theda Lazur."

"Luther Towers."

"Do you recommend anything special?"

"I've only ever had the Seafood Pot, but it is perfectly fine."

She batted her lashes and smiled at him. "Would you mind terribly if I tried yours?" Without waiting for an answer, she plucked his spoon from the table, dipped it into the bowl, blew on it gently, and put it in her mouth.

This, he watched with rapt attention. This was certainly not part of the routine. But he thought that maybe, just maybe, he liked this intrusion into the ordered life of Luther Towers.

"It's wonderful." Theda clapped her hands in glee. "But I'm not that hungry. Do you mind if I just share some of yours?"

*   *   *

Smack had given Bettie an advance on her gig with his orchestra at the Roseland Ballroom. Her debut was slated for this coming Friday night. Everything was going so well, first singing with Peaches and his band and then at the Back Room with Smack, Hawk, and Louis. It was like a fantasy come to life. Except for the thing. The one thing.

Bettie had no idea if she ever wanted to have more children. She could barely take care of the ones she had, even if things in that department were looking up. But the fact was, it wasn't anybody's choice but her own. Hers and God's. It wasn't the choice of the baby's father, her aunt, and certainly not some white man in a hospital. She tried to tell herself to leave it alone, forget about it, walk away. Her future, for the first time ever, looked promising. Why ruin everything?

That 8 Ballo had seemed a fine enough man. Smack spoke highly of him, as did Hawk. Said he didn't back down from nothing. That was the kind of person she needed in her corner. Because she'd been violated, and violated in the worst way a woman could be violated. A doctor had made the decision to take away her ability to bear children. Most likely on the recommendation of another man, Ronald Dankworth.

She found who she was looking for in the park. He was a man who'd paid her to perform sexual acts on him several times before. That said, he was decent enough about it. She also knew that he dealt in stolen goods. He was a man who could get things, things that would be hard to obtain otherwise, particularly for a Black woman and at a reasonable price.

Bettie tried one last time to talk herself out of it. Friday she'd be singing at the Roseland in front of a huge crowd with an entire orchestra at her back. Everything she'd ever wanted. Soon, she and her son and daughter could move out and get their own place. Food on the table. Roof over their head. Why would she jeopardize that?

Let the private dick handle it. But what could he do, really? She was poor, Black, and overweight. Nobody cared about her. No policeman was going to arrest the doctor, investigate Dankworth's involvement, or otherwise care in the slightest. So what if a poor Black woman had been sterilized against her will?

Bettie took a deep breath and walked up to the man.

"Bettie, you are looking fine. Are you looking to make a couple of bucks?"

Bettie shook her head. "I'm looking to buy something."

"What?"

"A gun."

Chapter 25

It was almost six o'clock Monday evening when Dr. Bedford got off the elevator coming up from Damnation Island. 8 followed him onto the trolley. While his size was an attribute in many ways for a private detective, it was not optimal for subtly tailing somebody. Luckily, Bedford seemed preoccupied and not all that observant.

The good doctor got on the Brooklyn-bound trolley and backtracked the route that 8 had taken the other day, back to the downtown area. 8 studied him from his vantage point at the back of the trolley car. He was about a foot shorter than 8, had poofy hair that almost didn't look real, and a bit of plumpness to his belly. There was a smug look on his face that suggested he thought very highly of himself.

They changed trolley lines in Williamsburg, and, when Bedford got off in Brooklyn Heights, 8 followed at a discreet distance, which wasn't hard to do as the sidewalks were crowded at this hour. The man stopped and went into a café while 8 stood down on the corner. It was an hour before the man emerged. It turned out his house was just around the corner on Columbia.

As the man turned in to go through a gate, 8 closed the gap, and as Bedford stepped into an electric elevator on the side of the five-story building, he moved into the space next to him.

"What do you want?" Bedford demanded.

"Hello, Doctor." 8 smiled.

"You're that fellow who said he was from Mayor Hylan. Wheat, you said your name was."

"Let's go on up, and I'll tell you who I really am." 8 closed the gate and pushed the button, and the car started trundling its way up.

Bedford tried for angry, decided better, and went with indignant. "You have no right to be coming to my home. I will have you arrested."

"Are you married, Doctor? Children? Girlfriend? Boyfriend?"

"I don't see how that is any of your business. And I am not a homosexual."

8 gathered the front of his suit jacket in one large hand and gently shoved him into the back of the elevator as it came to a stop. He had his .38 in a holster under his own jacket but didn't think he'd be needing it.

"I'd hate to have to punch your lights out and then shoot somebody you care about because you couldn't answer one simple question."

"I live alone."

"Excellent," 8 said.

They stepped off the elevator onto the rooftop. Somewhat incongruously, an abode style house was on the far side, and in between several potted trees and a rock garden. 8 prodded Bedford in front of him to the front door of the sun-dried brick building that looked as if it'd been plucked from the New Mexican countryside and dropped on top of this building. As they approached the front, 8 turned and was met with a wonderful view of the Manhattan skyline.

"You'll not get away with this," Bedford said loudly. He stopped and tried to wrest his way from the grip on his arm.

8 merely tightened his hold. He'd once broken a man's elbow just by squeezing. "Be a good fellow. I just want to talk."

As they reached the door, it opened, and a man stood there with a gun in his hand pointed at 8.

"My butler and cook." Bedford smirked. "Now kindly unhand me."

8 eyed the butler. There was a tic in his left eye, and his breathing was ragged like he'd been running. Or was nervous. 8 placed his other hand in the small of Bedford's back and flung him forward into the butler. The man was knocked backward, the pistol flying upward, and before he could bring it back to bear, 8 hit him in the chin with a punch that had his legs and shoulder into it. He was knocked back against the inner door to the hall, his eyes glassy, and then he slid to a sitting position. 8 stepped forward and plucked the weapon from his hand.

"Anybody else I should know about?" 8 asked.

Bedford's smugness was now completely gone. His eyes flickered this way and that, and it appeared he might've pissed himself.

8 slapped him lightly on the cheek. "Answer the question?"

Bedford shook his head. "No."

8 opened the inner door, and the butler toppled to a prone position, not quite unconscious, but not quite capable of movement either. 8 shoved the short, plump Bedford through the doorway, tripping over the butler as he went.

"Sit." 8 pointed to a chair with the pistol. He grasped the butler by the collar and dragged him into the room, shutting the door behind them.

8 looked around the large central room, The interior was comprised of woodwork with a heavy-beamed ceiling, stained and oiled, from which were suspended two old iron candelabras.

"You certainly seem to have good taste," he said. "I quite like your home, Dr. Bedford."

Bedford was now crying, tears running down his cheeks, and a blubbering noise coming from his mouth in heaving gasps. "What do you want?"

"Just to talk, Doctor. As long as you're honest with me, nothing more."

"About what?"

"It seems that your facility on Welfare Island is engaged in unauthorized sterilizations, which is against New York State law."

"That's, that's not true."

8 picked up a chair and sat in front of Bedford. "Do you know Ronald Dankworth?" Bedford said no but his eyes said yes. 8 slapped him. Hard. And then again. Harder.

"Okay, okay, don't hit me. I know who he is. He's the second-in-charge at the Brooklyn Hospital. We both have the same job and have reason for interacting with each other."

"That's better. Now tell me about the sterilization program."

"There is no sterilization program. I don't know what you're talking about."

8 stood and looked out the window behind Bedford. It was a floor to ceiling arched window with wooden doors that opened outward and overlooked a small yard and several trees. He pushed the window open, grasped Bedford by his poofy hair, and tilted him over the edge, just grasping his ankles before he went plummeting down to earth five stories below.

Bedford tried to scream but only whimpered. 8 pulled him back up and in, back to the chair he'd been sitting in. "Trust that I'm very serious, Dr. Bedford, and do not like to be lied to. Last Monday, Ronald Dankworth sent you a patient to have her appendix removed. She was a young, poor, Black woman, and your doctor decided to tie her tubes at the same time so that she wouldn't be able to have any more children. Was this Dankworth's idea, the doctor who operated, you, or somebody else who is playing at being God?"

"I can't tell you, please, you have to believe me."

"Do you want to go back out the window?"

Bedford looked over his shoulder at the window, open, swaying slightly in the breeze. "It wasn't my idea. I wanted nothing to do with it. But they made me. You have to believe that I was against this horrific thing."

"How is it that they made you?"

"They threatened to reveal my secret."

"What is your secret?"

Bedford shook his head. "No."

The butler groaned and sat up, his eyes trying to focus.

8 looked from him back to Bedford. "Who threatened to reveal your secret?"

"If they know I told you, they'll expose me, and then they'll kill me."

"I will get it out of you one way, or another," 8 said.

"You have to tell people that I wanted nothing to do with this, that it wasn't my idea."

"Tell me what they had on you."

"It was only once. But he was such a beautiful young man. How could I know they'd paid him? I thought he loved me." Bedford sighed. Leaned his chair back so that he toppled backward and then flipped himself over the small ledge of the window and disappeared from view.

8 just missed grabbing his leg as he fell, and watched the man hit the ground with a resounding thump. It didn't look to be a soft landing and even from here, 8 could see that the man's neck was crooked at an impossible angle. It seemed a prudent time to leave.

That potential lead just fell through the cracks, 8 thought wryly, wincing at the unintended pun. He'd had a heart-to-heart with the butler who seemed to think it was a good time to leave town. Even if he didn't, he had no idea who 8 was, and Bedford had jumped to his own death, witnessed by the butler.

If 8 had been more worried, he would've gotten out of the area immediately, but as it was, he just went a few blocks to where Theda Vogel lived. It being Monday evening, 8 was hoping that she'd be home, and alone. He was right on both counts.

Theda poured him a drink and settled down next to him on a sofa. It was really a mixture of a sitting room and a library as shelves lined the walls filled with books. "You didn't bring your escort with you this time?" she asked.

8 was taken momentarily off guard, but then remembered he'd previously visited with Dottie, who'd perhaps saved him from the seductive wiles of the woman now sitting next to him. This made him even more uncomfortable.

"I wanted to ask you about Ronald Dankworth," he said in a rush.

"What about Ronald?"

"Your husband worked for him. What kind of boss was he?"

"Why do you ask me?"

8 shrugged. "I feel like something is off about him. That he might be involved in… unsavory business. That you might have felt that, too."

"Ronald? Applesauce! I wouldn't think so. He's too much of a bluenose to be involved in anything criminal."

"Bluenose?"

"You know, a prude. A stick in the mud."

8 nodded. "If that's the case, why'd he have you over to his room at the Bossert the other night?"

Theda laughed. "I thought that bumping into you outside was a bit suspicious. Why didn't you just come right out and ask me right then? And, no, he did not *have* me in his hotel room."

"Well, I'm asking now. What were you doing there?"

"Did I hire you to investigate me, Mr. Ballo?"

"I suspect that Dankworth may be involved in illegally sterilizing young women, so I was following him. You just happened to show up on the horizon."

"Ronald wanted to go over some things with me. There are some death benefits due to me from the hospital and whatnot. Nothing nefarious, I can assure you."

"What is it that you want from me, truly, Mrs. Vogel?"

"Lazur. I am returning to my maiden name. But why so formal, all of a sudden? Let's remain friends. 8 and Theda." She smiled warmly at him, a touch of mischief at the corners of her mouth, her lips twitching, her eyes bright.

"I am beginning to get the impression that your concern is not to bring the murderer of your husband to justice. Maybe more on finding this missing Aquila?"

Theda looked around like somebody might be listening, even though they were the only ones there. She slid closer and whispered, "That eagle is priceless. If I were to find it, I'd never have to worry about money again."

8 looked around. "You seem to be doing okay for yourself."

"The building manager has given me three months to pay my rent or vacate the premises. I've had to let all the staff go. Without Karl's income, I have nothing. There were some savings, but they are going quickly. Without the Aquila, I'll have no choice but to marry some wealthy man to live, well, as a girl wants to live. More than likely, it'll be some old and wrinkled fellow who will disgust me, but I will do what I have to in this man's world to live the life I deserve."

8 thought those two concepts contradictory, but he'd never had to walk in a woman's shoes. He did understand that societal constraints prevented most women from having successful and profitable careers, though. While 8 had never seen reason to get hitched, he was able to pay his bills, even if the income was sometimes erratic.

But, 8 thought, of course she could go back to work if she wanted. Working for the Department of Genetics gathering information on people, or perhaps as a secretary somewhere. Either way, it would not allow for the extravagant lifestyle she'd adopted.

Of course, he now felt bad, as he was going to let Theda know that he was going to need some more money to continue the investigation and search. That would have to wait, and from the sounds of it, was only going to happen if he did find the gold eagle and return it to Theda. But hadn't Karl Vogel only been holding onto it for safekeeping? In reality, it belonged to an organization called the *Rein Adler of the Batavia*, or the Pure Eagle of the Batavia. A clandestine clan that had existed for 2,000 years and would most likely not hesitate to kill a woman, or a gumshoe for that matter, to get the eagle back.

"Karl is dead," Theda said. "But the Aquila is still out there."

Asta had called in sick to the telephone company today and spent the day in the office and had promised 8 a nice Dutch meal for dinner. He looked at his pocket watch as he walked, having extricated himself from thoughts of Theda's husky voice, dark eyelashes, womanly curves, and flirtatious manner. He had an inkling that he was one of many men on whom she inflicted her feminine wiles to whatever end necessary. If he walked fast, he'd not be late, and wouldn't have to jump on a trolley.

He thought about what Theda had said about having to marry wealthy to live the lifestyle she chose. If she didn't recover the Aquila, that is, and if the RAB didn't kill her. His own apartment could fit in Theda's sitting room/library, so he certainly wasn't marriage material for the dame. He had his uses, she knew, and one was to find the eagle.

This line of thought caused him to wonder, not for the first time, what Asta's aspirations were. Even though she was six or seven years younger than he, she was no spring chicken, not when most women her age had already married. Did she hope to become Mrs. Asta Ballo? It wasn't like he had much to offer. An apartment that was small and had seen better days and a business that barely paid the bills.

They'd never discussed children; heck, they were only living together because some fellow had threatened her. But, 8 figured, she most likely wanted to have a few of them. He saw how her eyes lit up whenever she saw babies, how she giggled at the antics of toddlers, and her eyes shone at a little girl in a pretty dress. But did he want a passel of little Ballos running around underfoot? He grinned, thinking it'd be kind of nice, but then grew somber as he thought about how his profession could quite easily put them in danger.

It was a tough enough world out there for an adult, what with all the twisted people out there. It was bad enough having gangsters out there running drugs, hootch, girls, and killing anybody who got in their way. Fellows like Luciano, Siegel, and Lansky, all of who he was associated with. Now, there were groups grown out of a shared hatred of others—the eugenics people, the Klan, and the Nazis. Was this really a world in which to have and raise children?

He'd turned the corner onto Bushwick Avenue when an automobile pulled over, and Comb-over, Lucky Luciano's beef, leaned out the window. "Get in."

8 figured that Baldy must be driving. He also supposed if he was going to have regular interaction with the two men, he should probably learn their names.

8 opened the back door and slid into the expansive space next to Luciano. "Nice motorcar."

"She's a beaut." Luciano said. "Made a limited number of this model, the Rolls Royce Silver Ghost, a few years back up to Springfield, Massachusetts. When the opportunity arose to get my hands on one…" He shrugged. "I got a message that you called me earlier today."

"I'm running a bit late for a dinner date," 8 said.

"With the lovely Asta Holm?" Luciano took out a cigar and lit it as the motorcar drove off down the street. "Are you eating out, or is she cooking for you now?"

There was a veiled threat in Luciano's words, however lightly said. "Had a little run in with a German fellow on Friday night. Thought it might be best if she stayed with me for the time being."

"What is she making, if you don't mind me asking?"

8 did mind and wished that he hadn't agreed to intercede with the gangster on the behalf of Jack Johnson. But, sometimes, you just had to play the cards dealt to you. "Steampot. A traditional Dutch

dish."

"Yeah? What's in it?"

"Potatoes, vegetables, cabbage, and sausage. Very tasty." 8 sighed. "Look, Mr. Luciano, it's been a long day, and I'd like to get home."

"Heard about that thing with German *compagno* the other night. That have anything to do with Wall?"

"Not sure. But I did have another interesting day on Saturday. I attended a luncheon out to Great Neck, think the fellow was a bootlegger..." 8 trailed off, realizing that he was perhaps talking to the king of bootleggers in New York. "Anyhow, Mrs. Herman Wall was also in attendance. A sultry woman by the name of Lena. She let it slip out that her husband was preparing for a Klan rally out in Queens that very night."

"Lots of fellows in the Klan," Luciano said. "That's just about as normal around here as death and taxes."

8 doubted that Luciano paid much in the way of taxes, but also knew that he was not lacking experience when it came to death. "This particular Klonverse seemed more like a militia prepared to wage war than sponsor a baseball team."

"Klonverse?"

8 chuckled. "Yeah. I was doin' some research earlier today. Seems the Klan has fancy little words for normal things. The Invisible Empire has a Supreme Grand Wizard and at every level there is a board of officers with titles like Klaiff taken from bailiff, the Klokard from teacher, and the Kludd, just to name a few. The Klonverse is the local county organization, one step above the individual town group. In this case, I believe it is a combination of Queens County and Kings County. This is run by a Grand Titan and a board of the Seven Furies."

Luciano stared at 8 for a long minute before bursting into laughter. "You're fucking shitting me?"

8 shook his head. "The more you read up, the stranger it gets. There was an Imperial Cyclops presiding over the meeting I snuck

into, but I can't find any information on who he is, exactly. There are Wizards, Dragons, Giants, and Terrors. There is an Exalted Cyclops, the head of the local Klan chapter, but this person yielded a bigger stick than that, and being called the Imperial Cyclops suggested that he has a leadership role in the entire world organization."

"And you think that Wall may have been this Imperial Cyclops?"

8 shook his head. "I don't know. His wife told me he was preparing for the rally, but it's pretty hard to recognize anybody at one of those things."

"'Cause of the hoods they wear?" Luciano swore. "What are they hiding from? At least us gangsters don't walk around with a bag over our heads. We are who we are."

"It protects their identity, but I had a fellow tell me today that it's also about the mystique they project. The Klan parades down the street, and people stare and wonder what that's all about, and next thing you know they're carrying a torch, making secret handshakes, and lynching Black people."

"What is it they hope to achieve?"

"That is a hard one to figure out. Some of it is just money. Turns out you got to buy the uniform from their purser for big bucks, and then they also solicit donations. And then there's the political angle in that they seem to be caught up in politics, and not just local things like who sits on the school board. Maybe your immigration bill? I mean, Wall plus the KKK is sure an interesting equation."

Luciano stared out the window as the automobile came to a stop in front of 8's apartment. "If it could be proven that Wall is using his anti-immigration policy just to enrich himself or the KKK, that'd probably sour Congress on him. They'd distance themselves from him pretty damn fast."

8 nodded. He was thinking that he might be able to connect Wall to far worse atrocities than a for-profit business that preyed on the fears of working-class white men. That was just standard fare for the rich. But he had more investigating to do to acquire that proof.

Luciano handed 8 a stack of cash. "Buy something nice for Miss Holm. Keep up the good work, Mr. 8 Ballo. Have a good dinner. And let me know what you find out about our friend."

Chapter 26

The next day was spent researching the Klan, the Department of Genetics, and any connection that might exist between the two. There was the obvious shared contempt of those who were different. It was some sort of fear, 8 figured, that immigrants of color, Jews, and Roman Catholics were going to steal their way of life.

As far as 8 could tell, both the very wealthy and the very poor white people of western European stock were equally fearful. Where did this anxiety stem from other than a deep-seated apprehension that they were lacking in some fashion? Such were his muddled thoughts as he walked to pick up Asta from work.

The Department of Genetics, or DOG, as 8 had begun calling it, credit to Dottie for that bon mot, was the arm of the monster that operated right out in plain view for the world to see. They worked to pass laws that would prevent "more inferior" races from coming here and to stop those that were here from reproducing. They were rich and educated and motivated in their aims of homogenizing America, creating one dominant color and culture.

The Ku Klux Klan was the silent army that created fear through threats and intimidation, and quite possibly, from the sounds of it, might have one division that had begun taking steps for an eradication of those inferior races by sterilizing the unwanted. They were the Invisible Empire, as they called themselves, doing everything that the DOG was unable to do itself officially.

And it was in this way that they were connected, 8 had realized, halfway through the afternoon. They were two parts of an umbrella organization that was looking to erase certain segments of the human race from existence. They were not separate entities at all, but were one and the same, a Janus, two faces, one for public consumption and one for their more shadowy endeavors.

And the connection between the two of them appeared to be Herman Wall. Assistant to the Superintendent of the DOG, a man who had his hands in hospitals, insane asylums, prisons, and yet who also had the ear of Congress. As far as 8 could tell from the journals, essays, and books he'd pored over, many scientists, thinkers, and intellectuals thought that the science behind Wall's theories on breeding, genetics, and ethnic purity was based on false evidence, and he was well down the road to thinking that, too.

But nobody cared. Because some very powerful people wanted to believe.

Where did the death of Karl Vogel, the theft of the Aquila, and the Germans fit into the equation, if at all? There were still too many questions and not enough answers.

At that point in his ruminations, Asta spilled out of the telephone offices with a large smile as she waved to him. She was quite the woman, 8 thought. Hard working, intelligent, positive, and always with a smile. She wasn't the trending beauty of the time with short, black, bobbed hair and a rail-thin body and dark eyes. Instead, she was short, blonde, and had womanly curves, features that he loved about her.

"Hi ya, handsome." Asta stood on her tiptoes and kissed him. "I suppose we can do this now that we live together in sin."

8 winced slightly, quickly hiding his discomfort behind a grin. It wasn't the kiss, which was quite nice, or the sin that he minded, but rather the living together part that gave him pause. "How were the connections today?"

"Oh, the usual. I had one cake eater who asked me to go out with him, a dope fiend who made no sense whatsoever, a couple of dumb

Doras and a few saps, but for the most part, everybody was pretty nice and friendly."

"Fellow asked you to go out with him?" 8 tried his best at a growl. "What'd you say?"

"Told him he'd have to check in with my big six. And that he happened to be a big 8, actually."

"Well, if you didn't make plans with this hombre, maybe we can go get some dinner."

"Actually, my *schat,* you have plans."

"First, I hope that you calling me *schat* is not what it sounds like, but is some type of Dutch endearment, and second, what plans, pray tell, do I have?"

Asta giggled. "*Schat* is sweetheart. And second, your Joseph Grady has agreed to let you into Ronald Dankworth's office."

Sweetheart? 8 supposed he was okay with that. Better than what it sounded like. "How'd you work that?"

"I passed the message through his wife Jill that it was worth a double sawbuck if he did, and another visit from an unhappy big 8 if he didn't."

"No more bruises, scrapes, or complaints from her since I last paid him a visit, I trust."

"Jill said that Joe has been on his best behavior, even laid off the hooch some. Not sure that'll last, but so far, so good."

8 nodded. "And the plan is for tonight?"

"Jill said he takes a smoke break at ten outside the employee entrance. If you're there, he'll get you inside the hospital and let you into Dankworth's office."

8 looked at his pocket watch, wondering if it was time to modernize and get a wristwatch. A couple of weeks back he'd been looking at a Cartier Tank Cintrée model, figuring that if it was good enough for General John Pershing it was good enough for him. He chuckled under his breath, knowing full well that he'd never earn enough to buy that particular watch, but maybe a less expensive

one would do the trick. Perhaps, now that Luciano had given him a hundred bucks to keep digging into Wall, it was time to splurge. Okay, he was also supposed to buy Asta something nice.

"I'll walk you home and then skedaddle on over there," he said. "We probably have time for a quick bite on the way if we keep moving."

8 waited in the shadows past the overflowing garbage bins, hopefully soon to be picked up for transport to Governor's Island and the incinerator. At ten o'clock on the dot, the door opened, and Joseph Grady stepped outside with a nervous look to the left and the right before lighting a Lucky Strike.

8 moved closer but stayed to the shadows. "Hello, Joe."

The man started as if he'd been punched. His body was still skeletal, but it appeared that perhaps a trace of color had entered the pallor of his cheeks since last time 8 had seen him a few weeks back.

"That you?" Joe asked.

"8 Ballo."

"You got the twenty?"

"Yep. Give it to you once you get me in Dankworth's office."

"Let me finish my cigarette. Put this on."

8 stepped from the darkness to be illuminated faintly by the grimy light. Joe tossed him a white doctor's jacket that buttoned down the front.

"Remembered you was a big hombre," Joe said. "Got the largest one I could find."

8 pulled the jacket on, his arms and shoulders stretching the fabric to the limit. He had a hard time finding clothing that fit, and he just didn't want to draw attention to himself as they walked through the hallways.

"Perfect fit," 8 said drily.

"Let's go. Follow me, and keep your trap shut."

8 thought that was pretty bold from the small, sickly man but

bit his lip and followed through the doorway and into the hospital. They entered the administrative wing, the halls almost empty at this hour, a few cleaning staff mixed in with a few men in suits filtered past them into the hallway. Outside Dankworth's door was a bucket with a mop and a cart with other cleaning supplies including a straw broom.

"I already cleaned in there," Joe said. "You go look around while I mop the hall out here and the office across the way, and then I walk you back out of here." He held out his hand.

8 grasped and turned the knob to the door. It was unlocked. "You let me know if anybody comes." He handed Joe the twenty and slipped into the office.

He put the light on and surveyed the office. There was a desk, four filing cabinets, and a closet. 8 began with the desk, scanning the calendar on top that had appointments penciled in and scribbled notes in a shaky scrawl. On the 13th, BY was scrawled. And then again on the 22nd. BY. Bettie Young had checked in here on October 13th, been taken back into this office by Ronald Dankworth, and then transported to Damnation Island. The 22nd of October was tomorrow. Something to ponder.

8 opened the top drawer of the desk. Ink pens, pencils, paperclips, note pads—organized meticulously. The bottom right drawer was locked. None of the other drawers had the key. And nothing of interest. He went to the filing cabinets and browsed the contents. One was for employees. Another was for sponsors, charities, and donors. Nothing on Herman Wall or Karl Vogel. No Dr. Bedford.

The closet held several doctor's white coats, a pair of shoes, and not much else. 8 sat back down at the desk, shrugged, leaned down, and popped open the locked drawer. The wood splintered and the mechanism busted, so it'd be obvious somebody had been here.

He pulled out a file that said confidential. There was a newspaper article about a druggist in Freeport on Long Island named Ernest Louis. 8 remembered reading the story from August about how a young girl said the Jewish owner had grabbed her arm when she was looking at perfume, the police found nothing to substantiate this accusation, and the Klan had taken matters into their own hands, driving him and his family from town. Then, in September, emboldened by their actions, the Klan had held a parade with over 2,000 participants.

His musing and search were suddenly interrupted.

"Hello, Dr. Dankworth, what brings you back in this evening?"

8 could hear the fear tinging Joseph Grady's voice from the hallway. He looked around the room.

The door handle turned, the door starting to open, and then Dankworth's voice asked, "Why is this door unlocked?"

8 shut the drawer and stood, sliding the folder marked confidential into the back of his pants.

"What's that, Dr. Dankworth?" Joe's voice trembled.

The door was thrust open, and 8 decided he might as well sit back down.

"You! What are you doing in my office?"

"Stopped by to ask you a few questions, Dankworth." 8 leaned back in the chair and put one foot on the desk. "Have a seat."

"You are in my seat." The man's voice cracked slightly as the words left his mouth. "I am calling the police. There were two of them at the front desk when I came by."

"I know what you've been doing here, Dankworth. Go ahead and call the police. I'm sure they'll be fascinated by what I have to tell them."

Dankworth stepped forward and grasped the telephone on his desk. "Hello, hello."

8 ripped the cord from the wall, his bluff called. He didn't have a shred of proof that Dankworth had done anything wrong.

Dankworth turned for the door.

"How many patients have you sent to Damnation Island to be sterilized?" 8 asked.

Dankworth paused at the door. "I don't know what you're talking about." He went on out the door.

Time to go, 8 thought. He followed Dankworth out the door and went the other way. Joseph Grady was nowhere to be seen.

*   *   *

Luther stood just down from the corner table where Herman Wall, in his cowboy hat, and Heinrich Funk, the rotund German, sat. They were at a speakeasy just before midnight, a nice enough joint, quiet at this time. It wasn't one of those rowdy speakeasies that featured music, dancing, and entertainment, or a blind pig where the drunks fell about over cheap liquor. A muted silence enveloped the bar, men nursing drinks, talking in low tones or reflecting over their own.

Only once in a while had Luther had to step in front of a man who had a thought to sit down in that corner. The last bloke had looked up at him, craning his neck. Luther had shaken his head. That was all. The man had turned and went back the other way.

Luther listened as his boss, Herman Wall, conversed with the German, Heinrich Funk. Funk's tall, thin associate was not with them. Luther knew that this was because that gumshoe with the funny name had shot and killed him. That's what happened when you sent an amateur to do the job.

"When will Herr Hitler be released from Landsberg Prison?" Wall asked.

"He will be out on the street before Christmas," Funk replied.

"And what of this book that he has dictated that will change the world? The one called *Four and a Half Years of Struggle against Lies, Stupidity, and Cowardice*? A struggle, by the way, that I know well, but we are changing, here in America."

Funk blew his nose into a handkerchief and almost immediately took a swallow of brandy. Then he leaned forward and spoke in a hoarse whisper. "The rumor is that it has a new title. Simpler. More direct. To the point. Very German."

Wall looked down his nose at the man. "Be very German and tell me what this new title is."

"*Mein Kampf.* Meaning *My Struggle.* The battle that led Herr Hitler to the realization that the Jews are nothing more than germs of the human race and must be exterminated."

"Exterminated seems a tad bit extreme, don't you think?"

Luther glanced sideways at the table, wondering what Wall was playing at.

Funk again blew his nose. "There are many different means of reaching the same end, *mein freundin.* It is quite clear that the Jews mean to rule the world and must be stopped."

"That is why I wish to make a gift of the Aquila to Herr Hitler. To merge our similar ideologies and work together to create a superior race, one not tainted by the Jews and Blacks, nor controlled by the Pope."

"Your offer of returning the Aquila to its rightful place is well appreciated. Herr Hitler said that you would succeed in retrieving this age-old symbol of the purity of our movement, this pure eagle of our organization. I had my doubts, but he assured me you were the man for the job. But what of the men who took it?"

"They have been dealt with."

Funk looked like he wanted to ask more but shut his mouth as he looked at the man's grim countenance. "Thank you, Herr Wall. When can I expect to have the Aquila once again in my hands? I must make preparations to return to Germany. It would be an incredible honor if I could present it to Herr Hitler upon his release from Landsberg."

"And Herr Hitler is the... legitimate owner of this Aquila?"

"Not the owner, as the Aquila is owned by the pure blood of Germany, but more the protector. Herr Hitler is the *Führer* of the *Rein Adler of the Batavi,* and as such, the Aquila is his to, what do you say? Look after? Or, I suppose, safeguard would be better, *ja?*"

"I will be able to have my man, Luther, deliver it to you on Friday. Noon in Fort Greene Park. The day of the gathering."

Funk looked up at Luther. "*Ja.* I will be there."

Chapter 27

The two flatfoots, police patrolmen Davies and Evans, had been called into the Lieutenant's office on Tuesday night just past ten o'clock. They were working the eight-to-eight shift, but only two hours in, they'd been beckoned back to the Butler Street Station they worked out of. The two men not only worked together, but also were best of friends outside of work, having grown up together and joined all the same clubs and organizations.

Lawton Evans had been destined to join the police department ever since he'd been born and given his name, or so he always told everybody. He was a third generation Englishman from the county of Suffolk, proud of his heritage, but even more gratified to consider himself an American of pure blood.

When approached three years back by the local Kleagle, his answer had been an emphatic, hell yes! Evans was tired of the Italians who had crept into his neighborhood, and outraged by his Jewish neighbors who dressed, spoke, and acted so strangely, and all the while walking around like they were superior to good Americans. And, when, four years back, the Butler Street Station hired a Black patrolman, Evans had had enough.

He'd been a foot soldier for the local Klan, helping to define the jurisdiction of their Klanton, discouraging filthy foreigners from moving in, encouraging the Jews, Blacks, and Italians to move out. He didn't know much about Asians, figuring they were best contained in Chinatown up to Manhattan, and didn't really have anything against the Roman Catholics, but the powers that be expressed a distaste for the powers of the Pope, and he was on board with what his brothers desired.

When told to report to Lieutenant Schulz, therefore, Evans had an idea that this wasn't just police business, not that there should be a separation between the two. Both the Klan and the police enforced the laws of justice and moral purity.

"Shut the door," Lieutenant Schulz said as Evans followed Davies into his office. "And have a seat."

"Yes, Lieutenant Klarogo Schulz," Evans said, doing as he was told. He was quite pleased with himself for acknowledging aloud that this was to be police *and* Klan business.

Schulz was one of the Twelve Terrors of the local Klan, an honor to show that he was an official of the organization, and in this case, the Klarogo, or the inner guard of the council. He had cunning eyes over florid cheeks and a large belly below.

"Evans. Davies. We have a situation that needs to be rectified," Schulz said by way of greeting once they were seated. "There is a man with the unique moniker of 8 Ballo who needs to be dealt with."

"Ballo? Is he Italian?" Davies asked.

"Hungarian, actually, I am told, but he consorts with all sorts of ill-bred vermin. His closest pals are a Black man, a Jew, and an Irish Catholic."

"If you find yourself in the toilet bowl, Klarogo," Evans said, "then chances are you are shit as well."

Schulz looked at him with those beady eyes and then rewarded him with a laugh that shook his jowls. "Quite right you are, Evans."

"What is it you want, Klarogo?" Davies asked.

"Earlier this evening, this vermin, 8 Ballo, broke into the office of one of the Seven Furies of the Grand Titan and stole some documents that are very sensitive. I need you to arrest him and retrieve those papers."

"Do you want him brought here, Lieutenant Klarogo?" Evans asked, again mixing police and Klan business together."

Next to the Schulz's office was a supply room. In it stood Captain Archipoili, who was not looking for supplies at all. He'd learned several years ago that in here you could clearly hear everything in the office next door. When he'd seen Davies and Evans walk through the department only partway into their shift and go into the Lieutenant's office, he'd known something was up.

Archipoili well knew that the Klan had grown in numbers in the Butler Street Station over the past few years, and that Schulz was a bigwig in the organization and that the two patrolmen were flunkies as well. For the past two years, he'd learned much by standing in the corner where the pipes led next door, the passageway acting as megaphone.

Thus, he clearly heard the last directions given by Schulz. "No. Once you have the papers in your possession, take him down to Gravesend and bury him with the other vermin."

* * *

Bettie Young was outside of the Brooklyn Hospital. She'd followed Dankworth when he'd initially left at five o'clock to go to a restaurant. Bettie had stood across the street by an apple vendor's wagon. Every once in a while, she reached into her handbag, fondling the butt of the pistol within.

It was still too light, too many people, too many excuses. Plus, Bettie told herself, she wanted to ask Dankworth a few questions before she killed him, the biggest one being simply, why? He spent three hours in the restaurant. Bettie had just about decided that he must've left via a back way and was about to call it a night and return to her children when the door opened and out he came. He was with three other men, and they all shook hands, and went off in separate directions.

Bettie followed him back to the hospital, trying to bolster her courage. All she had to do was walk up behind him, place the barrel of the pistol to the back of his head, and pull the trigger. Bang. How hard was that? Drop the gun and then turn around and walk away. She'd prefer to walk away and not be caught. She didn't want to end up in prison and executed. But she couldn't let the man get away with what he did to her. It just wasn't right.

So, there she was, outside the employee entrance to the Brooklyn Hospital when that gumshoe, 8 Ballo, came out, moving fast. She thought about calling out to him, but why was he here? Was he investigating what had happened to her or was he like all other men, working in league together to make her life a living hell? More than likely that was why Dankworth had come back here, to meet with the man, and be told that some poor fat Black woman was out to get him.

Perhaps that was why Ronald Dankworth looked so agitated when he came out the door about twenty minutes later. His face was twisted in fury and fear, a look she well knew from so many men, especially those who paid her for sexual favors. It was commonplace. They were angry at their doubts, dismay, and dread of everyday existence and channeled that into an anger to be unleashed on those weaker than themselves. On many occasions, Bettie Young had been the victim of such fury fueled by fear.

She had to walk fast to keep up with Dr. Dankworth. He hurtled down the sidewalks bumping people and cursing as he went. When he went into the Butler Police Station, Bettie's anxiety skyrocketed, certain that the gumshoe had given her away, and she was now being reported to the police as a threat to Dankworth, probably some elaborate lie that painted her as some lunatic.

He wasn't there long, not long enough for Bettie to decide to call the whole thing off, as she stood on the corner caught between her own fear and fury. She continued to follow him as he rounded a corner, and suddenly they entered a quieter street with fewer lights.

There were no people in sight. It was the right time and place. Bettie picked a space in the middle of two streetlamps. She shortened the distance between them, her hand grasping the butt of the pistol.

"Just point and pull the trigger," the man who sold it to her said. "Several times if you want to make sure. It is loaded. If you need more bullets than that... well, chances are you already screwed it up, and you are up shit's creek."

As they passed the streetlamp, Bettie was ten steps behind him. About fifty feet to the darkest part between the two lights. She quickened her steps, closing the gap. Five feet. Trying to be quiet. Now was the time. Dankworth stopped and turned, and Bettie froze.

"What do you want?" he demanded.

Did he recognize her, Bettie wondered?

All of a sudden, his face changed, a transformation that Bettie knew well. It was as if a switch were flipped. Rage to lust. Two emotions connected in many ways.

"How much?" he demanded to know.

"What?" Bettie held the pistol, struggling to understand the question, but she knew what it was.

Dankworth waved his hand impatiently. "My wife is away to the country for the week. I'll give you five dollars, and you let me do anything I want to do with you."

"Where?" Bettie muttered, thinking it might provide the opportunity to ask the burning question of why before she killed the man who'd stolen her fertility.

"I live right here." Dankworth pointed to the steps of a two-story home wedged between other similar ones on either side. His face contorted with a salacious hunger mixed with self-loathing. "Two hours."

Bettie nodded yes.

*   *   *

8 was just considering asking Asta if she was ready to move to the bedroom when there was a pounding on the door. With all that was going on, he went and got his .38, holding it behind his back, as he opened the door. If it was a friend, all fine and good, and if it was an enemy, best to get it over with.

It was Stephen McGee. "We got to get you out of here."

"What's that?"

"I'll explain as we go. Asta, too. Don't be a *scut*. We got to leg it."

8 grabbed his holster and slung it around his shoulder, sliding the pistol back in. He grabbed his hat and jacket as Asta put her shoes on.

Footsteps on the stairs.

McGee closed and locked the door.

"This way," 8 said.

The fire escape was out the bedroom window. He opened the window. McGee went first, and then 8 helped Asta through, as somebody started banging on the door.

"Police. Open up."

8 stepped through. His neighbor was sitting there in his pajamas smoking a cigarette. They stepped around him. As they started to descend the stairs, 8 heard his door splinter. He kept meaning to replace it with something more substantial, of thick oak perhaps, as he did have a tendency to make enemies. It seemed that the time was ripe for a new one.

They were on the last flight of stairs when a voice rang out above them. "Stop. Police. You are under arrest."

Asta paused in front of him, and 8 nudged her along. "Keep going, sweetheart. They're not the kind of police we want to speak with."

Pistol shots rang out, and 8 heard the clank of bullets on metal as they dropped into the alleyway. 8 took the lead, knowing the way, and they ran down behind the buildings, across an empty lot, and to the next street.

"Don't suppose you brought a police motorcar, did you?" 8 asked.

"They don't sign out paddy wagons to flatfoots like me," McGee said.

"Don't suppose the police are going to be able to help us, are they?" 8 asked.

"Who were those men?" Asta asked. She looked more excited by the drastic turn of events of the night than fearful. "What did they want?"

"In here," McGee said. They went down some steps and into a hallway. Behind the stairs that led up, was a closet. On the other side of the closet was a door. They went through and into an Irish speakeasy. "We should be safe here."

They got a table in a dark corner by the back door and ordered two Irish whiskeys and a gin.

"I suppose we owe you a thanks, Officer McGee." 8 raised his glass. "For what, I don't yet know."

"Captain Archipoili over to the Butler Street Station gave me a ring at the precinct," McGee said, pausing to take a slug of the brown liquor. "Said the Klan was after you for some papers you took. And they planned on burying you down to Gravesend once they had them."

"So, those fellows back there weren't really police?" Asta asked.

"Oh, those lads were police all right. The Klan has their talons in deep in the department, they do."

"And here in Bushwick at the 83rd as well?" 8 said.

McGee nodded, finished his Jameson. "'Fraid so. Lots of Germans at the precinct. Don't like us Irish, not so much. We even got us a Protestant who they don't like, just on general principles, or maybe they think he's Catholic, I don't know."

"What are we going to do about it?" Asta asked, her eyes shining.

8 looked at her. It was tough to tell if she'd be safer with him or without him. She had been followed, possibly randomly, or possibly a message from either the Germans or the Klan.

McGee cleared his throat. "Archipoili said the Lieutenant over there, a real piece of *shite*, mentioned that you acquainted yourself with a Black lad, a Jew, and a Catholic. That rules us out as a hideout until this all blows over. Maybe the two of you should get on the train and get out of town. Go to New Jersey for a vacation."

"Don't think this thing is going to blow over." 8 turned the empty glass over and over in his hand. "But we got to get off the street. Find a hideout. Somewhere the Klan won't find us."

"The Klan is everywhere," McGee said. "There isn't any place they can't find you."

8 stood up. "Wait here. I gotta make a telephone call. Saw a pay phone booth up on the corner. I'll just be two minutes."

Even though it was dark, 8 felt like a glowing target in the wooden phone booth as he made the connection.

"Yes?"

"Is Mr. Luciano in?"

"Who is this?"

"8 Ballo. Tell him it's urgent."

The line went quiet. Not the sound of being hung up, which gave 8 pause for relief.

"The gumshoe." It was Lucky Luciano's voice.

"Mr. Luciano. I've gone and stirred up the KKK. I need a place to lay low for a bit while I get a handle on things. Me and my gal."

Luciano laughed. "You want me to put you up in a love nest somewhere."

"I was thinking in your neighborhood of lower Manhattan. Not where you live, but the tenements where the poor Italians and Jews all live."

"No Klan member would dare show their face there," Luciano agreed. "I might got a place. What you got for me?"

"I *got* a confidential file of the vice president of the Brooklyn Hospital. Haven't even got a chance to look at it yet, but it sure riled up the hornet's nest fast. Police from Butler Street just tried to kill me."

"I'll send you a car for you and *la ragazza*. He'll take you to a safe place. You leave the file with him. Where you at now?"

8 gave him the name of the speakeasy and the address and went back inside.

Chapter 28

Pearle had been watching Wall for almost two weeks and had been about to give it a rest. For all his shadowing, the only interesting tidbit had been his meeting with the owner of the motorcar that had run down Karl Vogel. It wasn't even Pearle who'd connected Wall to the Klan, as that had been 8's finding, talking with the man's wife while at a luncheon, while Pearle was left sitting in his automobile eating cold chicken.

As of late, once he realized that Wall was in his office at Cold Spring Harbor from nine to five, Pearle had been taking care of his businesses during the day. He'd decided it was more important to watch the man outside of his workspace, for chances were that the man wouldn't risk tarnishing his image at the office. And there were only so many hours in the day for Pearle.

Although, as far as Pearle was concerned, politicking for forced sterilization of prisoners and those with mental deficiencies, as well as restricting immigration from a select few nations, was damning enough. If it was up to Pearle, he'd take the man to some quiet spot and give him a beating and then maybe another until Wall decided that he should pursue a new career, perhaps as a social worker.

8 had suggested that society frowned upon such behavior, and they had to find something more substantial to destroy the man's credibility instead of his face. A connection between Wall and Dankworth and Bedford would be a start. They'd still have to prove his involvement in the forced sterilization of a woman. Even that

might not be enough, Pearle thought with disgust, because she was poor and Black, a bad combination in any scenario.

Pearle had thought that connecting Wall to the Klan would do the trick, but apparently many people thought that it was just a club, no different than the Elks Club—the Best People on Earth they called themselves—in their racist exclusion of Black people from their ranks. No, Wall would have to be seen to be directly linked to some of the more nefarious Klan activities such as threatening, destroying property, or lynching somebody before anybody would care. And even then, all those white members of Congress would probably turn a blind eye.

The ties between Wall and the German who'd tried to kill 8 and that stolen Aquila, Pearle thought, were certainly worth pursuing as well. Pearle had an inkling that this German presence here in America was representing that nationalist party gaining traction in that country, the Nazis, they called them. They had a similar ideology, Pearle knew, and to belong to their group, one had to be of pure Aryan blood, some bullshit dreamed up by that fellow Hitler who claimed they were part of some superior race that didn't even exist.

Herman Wall, the Klan, and the Nazis all thought that Jews and Blacks were vermin and Catholics couldn't be trusted. That, Pearle thought, was too much of a coincidence. During the long hours of surveillance, Pearle had spent a great deal of time reading up on these groups in books from the library, and he was starting to put the pieces of the puzzle together. Racist pigfuckers, Pearle thought, all drawn together like nails to a magnet.

Last night, that tall fellow had come and picked up Wall in his automobile at ten o'clock, just as Pearle had been planning on calling it a night. Pearle followed them to a speakeasy in the Park Slope neighborhood of Brooklyn. He hadn't been able to go inside as it didn't allow Blacks, but an hour later the two men had come out with another fellow. A heavyset man who instead of saying goodbye, had said *Auf Wiedersehen*.

When Pearle had been in the Great War, fighting in France against the Germans, hunkered down in trenches, sometimes no more than fifty feet from the enemy, there'd been an opportunity to pick up snippets of the language. Enough to know that *Auf Wiedersehen* was German for goodbye.

This left Pearle with a dilemma. Continue following Wall and see if he had any more stops on his agenda or follow the chunky German. He chose the latter, tailing the man just a few blocks to a mansion. That was it, the connection between Wall and a German had been established.

Pearle figured that 8 would be interested in hearing about this, but maybe not after midnight, so he'd waited until this morning before calling the office. There was no answer until nine, when Millie picked up, saying she didn't know where 8 was, but that wasn't unusual.

He had to check in on a garment factory he owned in Bushwick, so after he did that, he swung by the office. Before he entered the building, though, an automobile pulled up next to him, and a man in the front passenger seat leaned out.

"Pearle Hill. It's been a long time."

Pearle turned his head to look. "Bugsy Siegel. Don't believe I've seen you since you put a bag over my head."

Bugsy Siegel gave a broad smile that could've turned him into a moving picture star if he hadn't gone the route of bootlegging, numbers rackets, prostitution, and murder. "That was for your own protection. To prevent you from seeing things you shouldn't be seeing."

"You come to see 8? I was just going in to see if he was around."

"Actually, I'm here looking for you. Millie said you were going to stop back by. I got a message for you from 8."

"Yeah? You and him tight these days?"

Bugsy scowled. "Here I am doing you a favor, and you got to give me attitude."

Pearle grinned. "Just fun to push your buttons, my man." He refrained from adding that it was always fascinating to watch Siegel get angry and watch his eyes begin to protrude from their sockets, a quirk that had given him his nickname, short for bug-eyed.

Bugsy shook his head. "Don't push too far. I got a better handle on my temper these days, but you don't want to tempt it."

"What's the message?"

"Seems the Klan is after his head for some papers he took. Lucky put him up in a hideout, along with Asta. He suggests you might want to do the same thing, lay low."

Pearle snorted. "The Klan been after me my whole life and aren't going to be stopping anytime soon. Not going to stick my head in the sand and hope they don't find me. If you run into that privileged white man 8 Ballo, you tell him that bullies don't like public places."

Bugsy laughed. There might've been a hint of respect in his eyes. "That there is the truth. Want another truth? Bullies don't much care for their knees being smashed by a baseball bat either." He laughed again, louder, an infectious guffaw that made Pearle smile in return.

"Well, if you see 8, you tell that piker that I'm going to kick some German Eugenics Klan ass, and he should pull his head out of his own ass and come give a hand."

*   *   *

Bettie woke in stages. She wasn't quite sure when as it was all in a fog. Words, faces, emotions had flitted through her being, and she had no idea what had been real and what had been a figment of her bewildered mind.

It was hard to breathe. She was wedged into something. Her hands were tied across her stomach. Bettie started to panic, gulping deep breaths of air that didn't exist. With deliberate breaths, she calmed herself, breathing through her nose. She was a survivor. No matter what this world had thrown at her in her twenty-three years of life, she had moved forward, never giving in, never giving up.

Once Bettie had relaxed her breathing, she took stock of her situation. Something was stuffed into her mouth. She was squeezed into a tight space that felt like it was made of wood. Her hands were tied with coarse rope. It was dark, oh so dark, but tiny slivers of fainter blackness suggested cracks in the top of whatever prison she was in. That gave her a bit of relief. At least she wasn't in a coffin, buried in the ground, alive or dead, it didn't matter. That was the worst, a fear she'd carried her entire life.

How did she get here? Her mind trudged backward. She was going to kill Ronald Dankworth. The man who'd sent her to Damnation Island to be sterilized against her will. She'd followed him from work. To a restaurant. Back to the hospital. She'd seen that gumshoe who she'd spoken to on the recommendation of Smack.

She'd been about to pull the pistol out of her bag and place the barrel at the back of Dankworth's head and pull the trigger and kill the son-of-a-bitch. Then, he'd stopped, turned, and propositioned her for sex, mistaking her for a whore instead of an assassin. Bettie had agreed, following him up the steps into his home, thinking the privacy would allow her to force him to answer the question that consumed her like an inferno, hellfire licking at her soul. Why?

If not an answer, a confession that he'd indeed decided to play God with Bettie Young, taking away her ability to have any more children. They'd gone inside, a hallway leading into the living space. Dankworth had taken his jacket off and that is when Bettie pulled the pistol out. His face was almost reward enough. Surprise, confusion, and finally fear raced across his face with alacrity.

"What do you want?" Dankworth asked.

"Go sit over there." Bettie gestured to an armchair just off the hallway.

"Take what you want and leave."

Bettie pointed the pistol at his dick. "Move."

He went to say something, thought better of it, and went and sat down. Bettie sank gratefully into a chair opposite of him.

"You don't remember me?" she asked.

Dankworth shook his head. "How would I know you?" His tone suggested that him knowing a Black woman was an impossibility.

"You brought me into your office and had me taken to Welfare Island to have my appendix removed. Only, they didn't just do that. They spayed me like some scrawny stray bitch dog. Do I look like a goddamn bitch to you?"

"What? No. I didn't do that!" But that was not what his tone or eyes said.

"I have just one question for you." Bettie raised the pistol slightly. "Why?"

Dankworth opened his mouth. Shut it. Repeated. "Look at you," he said finally. "You are a disgrace to humanity. Your spawn will destroy the entire human race. Day by day we grow weaker because of—"

"Thank you. That's all I needed to hear." Bettie pulled the trigger. Only there was no explosion. No bang. Just a click. She tried again.

And then Dankworth punched her in the face, and she toppled from the chair where he started kicking her. And then it went dark. And it was still dark.

Bettie winced, the punch and kicks explaining the aches and pain suffusing her body. Then she heard voices.

"Tell me about this PI. 8 Ballo. What did he take?" A cold and chilling voice dragged across broken glass.

"A folder that had record of the women who I've sent to Welfare Island to be sterilized. Names and dates." Bettie recognized this as Dankworth's voice. "Not to worry. Just names and dates."

"Unless somebody tracks down these women and realizes they've been sterilized without their knowledge or consent."

"Relax. None of them even know."

"Unless they're subjected to a medical exam."

Dankworth scoffed. "Poor. Black. Feeble-minded, most of them. Who's gonna bother?"

"Regardless. This PI must be stopped. He's learned too much already."

"I'm on it. He'll be gone within forty-eight hours."

"He better be. Gone for good." There was a pause. "Why did you bring her here?"

"I didn't know what else to do with her."

"Kill her. Dump her body. Get rid of her."

"You talked of a special treat for the Klonvokation tomorrow night."

There was a pause, long seconds, as Bettie breathed slowly through her nose.

Then the chilling voice replied, "That might be just the ticket. Good thinking."

Chapter 29

8 had woken up after only four hours sleep, his mind abuzz. The file he'd taken from Dankworth's office included a list of seventy-three names, all women. Each woman had a date next to their name and the name of a New York hospital. At City hospital on Welfare Island, forty-three of these women had lost their ability to bear children; the others all around the city. Bettie Young was one of those names listed, along with the date of her operation.

He'd convinced Luciano to let him keep the list so that he could continue investigating what it all meant. He didn't share with the gangster that he was almost certain that it was a list of women who'd been forcibly sterilized with or without their knowledge. There was as yet no proof behind his suspicions, but 8 happened to know a journalist who was very good at turning over stones and finding creepy crawly things underneath.

The tenement didn't have a telephone, and the thin walls made privacy difficult, sleep impossible. There was food in the cupboard and coffee and tea. His plan was to hide out for the day, let the Klan cops cool their heels, and get back into the fray. By ten in the morning, he was ready to bounce off the walls and knew that the patient route wasn't going to happen.

He was sitting in the cramped kitchen at the table in a chair far too small for his bulk when Asta came in, stretching her arms languorously over her head. She was not much of a morning person but looked marvelous all the same, 8 thought. He was about to suggest a distraction when there was a banging on the door.

8 motioned Asta back into the bedroom. The unit was all one straight line, from living area to kitchen to bedroom, all three rooms about ten-by-ten feet. Another hour in this zoo cage, and 8 was going to start breaking down walls, so the interruption was welcomed, even if it was corrupt cops come to kill him.

He stepped to the door, .38 held at the ready. "Who's there?" He quickly stepped to the side as he spoke.

"A Jew and a Black man here to talk to an over-privileged white Christian who's gone soft, according to the Black fellow, anyway."

8 thought it sounded an awful lot like Bugsy Siegel, but he didn't lower the pistol as he unlocked and opened the door. It was Bugsy, and behind him, Pearle. What an unlikely duo to show up at his hideout in a tenement home on the Lower East Side of Manhattan.

"I heard the Girl Scouts were starting to sell cookies door to door," 8 said. "And I didn't believe it, but here you are, living proof."

"Ah, we have found the hiding bear. Have you decided to hibernate for the winter?" Bugsy pushed past 8 into the room with Pearle behind him.

"Bugsy says you're hiding out from the Klan," Pearle said. "What'd you do to tick them off?"

"I liberated a file from a German fellow named Dankworth," 8 said. "But no, I'm done hiding out. It didn't really take."

"I got a proposition for you along those lines," Bugsy said. "Me and Meyer were talking after Lucky gave us a call about your predicament. We came to the conclusion that we don't much care for the Klan. As a matter of fact, as of today, we're declaring war on those bastards. And we plan on starting by giving our good friend, 8 Ballo, some protection."

8 wondered what sort of strings would be attached to such an offer. There was no such thing as a gesture of good will when dealing with Bugsy Siegel and Meyer Lansky. "Thank you, but no thank you," he said. "I have my own resources."

"You got the Klan gunning for you, you're going to need more than Pearle Hill, no offense." Bugsy looked at Pearle and shrugged. "They're going to find you when you least expect it, and they got no honor. It'll be a knife in the back on the street or a gunshot to the face when you're sleeping. Cowardly bunch, if you ask me. Bullies that dress in disguise and hunt in groups and at night."

"Me and Pearle been fighting boys and men like them since we were ten," 8 said.

Bugsy nodded. "Meyer said you wouldn't accept any help. He usually knows these things."

Asta stepped out of the bedroom, now fully dressed, still tousle-haired in a very sexy way. "Good morning, Pearle. And Mr. Siegel, I've heard so much about you."

Bugsy's eyes widened, a smile coming that covered half his face. "Well, good morning to you. You must be Asta Holm."

"If you think it'd be okay with Mr. Luciano," 8 said, "Asta will be staying here for a few days while I get this sorted out."

"The hell I am, 8 Ballo," Asta said.

8 briefly thought about arguing but knew it was pointless. "Looks like we won't be needing the place after all."

Bugsy dropped 8 and Pearle off at the *Brooklyn Eagle* and was then going to drop Asta off back in Bushwick at the office. Again, 8 suffered pangs of conscience allowing her to be driven anywhere by the likes of Bugsy Siegel, much less back into the hornets' nest of riled up Klansmen, but it wasn't his decision to make.

They found Marty at his desk, head down and fingers ferociously clattering away at the keys of an Underwood typewriter. His small, slender frame was matched by a childlike face making him appear far younger than his true age, mid-thirties Ballo guessed. 8 took a moment to marvel at the man's long pianist fingers leaping between the cockeyed round buttons with letters on them. Typing was not a skill that 8 had ever attempted, much less mastered, and he was always amazed by Marty's speed.

"What do you want?" Marty didn't stop or look up. "I got a deadline."

8 laid the two pages of names on his desk. "I need to hold onto this, but you should take a few minutes to copy it down for yourself."

"Told you, I'm on a deadline. No time."

"This is a list of seventy-three women and the dates on which they were sterilized either against their will or without their knowledge at hospitals all over the city."

Marty's fingers froze in place, and he slowly looked at first the pages, and then at 8 and Pearle. "You're shitting me."

8 shook his head. "I wish I was. I'm not a hundred percent certain, but I was approached by a young lady named Bettie Young who went out to Welfare Island to have her appendix removed, and they went ahead and clipped her reproductive tubes while they were at it."

"And she knows this how?"

"Seems the doctor didn't realize she didn't know about it. He was just doing what he was told, not realizing that she wasn't aware that this was part of the plan."

"On whose orders was it done?"

"A fellow by the name of Dr. Bedford. Don't believe I ever got his first name."

"I should be able to find him easily enough," Marty said. "He practice out on Welfare Island?"

"Think you'll need a shovel to find him," Pearle said.

Marty flicked his eyes over at Pearle. "Why's that?"

"On account of him jumping off a very tall building just around the corner from here," Pearle said. "Might've been something 8 said to him."

"The big fellow does have that effect on people sometimes," Marty agreed.

"It seemed the good doctor was afraid of some secret of his being revealed," 8 said. "Said something about they'd humiliate him and then kill him."

"And you got this list from him before he jumped?"

8 shook his head no. "Got this from a locked desk drawer of Ronald Dankworth at the Brooklyn Hospital. He seemed upset by it enough to get the Klan after me, luckily McGee warned me before a couple of corrupt cops came by to make me disappear."

"You been busy," Marty said. "What do you want from me?"

"Do what you do," 8 said. "Dig out the story, flesh out the details, write it, print it."

"You say the Klan is involved?"

"I don't know. You know all the rest. Seems like it originates from the Department of Genetics out to Cold Spring Harbor. Could be that the Klan is involved. Maybe something to do with some German fellows as well."

"Why do you say that?" Marty asked.

"Well, the head of that whole eugenics' thing, Wall, is German, as is Dankworth. Oh, and yeah, some German fellow tried to kill me the other day."

"I take it he failed, as you're here. You get a chance to ask him any questions, or should I be looking him up myself?"

Pearle chortled. "Better bring a shovel."

Marty eyed him again. Shook his head. "I read about that, but your name wasn't mentioned in the story. Any leads as to why?"

"Actually, I haven't had a chance to update 8 on this yet, but I did follow Wall over to a speakeasy in Park Slope, upscale kind of joint, where he met with a German guy. I followed that hombre to a mansion in the nicest section of Park Slope."

"How'd you know he was German?" Marty's family had come from the Rhine River area of western Germany. This was one of just several languages he spoke.

"On account of him speaking German," Pearle said. "And he fit the description of the man 8 tussled with at the Bossert Hotel. Not the one he shot in the face, but the other one."

"You don't need a shovel to follow up with him, too, do you?" Marty asked.

"Nope. He's still walking and talking."

"It would seem that there is a definite connection between the Germans, maybe that Hitler guy, and the Department of Eugenics, and that fellow Wall." Marty drummed his fingers on the desk. "May seem a bit strange, but have you noticed any swastikas in any papers you've come across from the eugenics crowd?"

"Swastikas?" 8 said.

Marty grabbed a piece of paper and sketched out a swastika. "The Nazi party under Hitler has adopted this as the symbol of their movement. Funny enough, the Hindus have used it for thousands of years to signify new beginnings and the vastness of infinity. Buddhists also thought highly of it, as have many others." He searched around the clutter of his desk and pulled out a book. "Take a look at this. It details the symbol's significance throughout history before this guy Hitler came along and appropriated it for his own particular brand of evil. See if Wall, or the Klan, also uses it."

8 took the book. "I'll keep an eye out."

"Where do we start?" Marty asked.

"First, copy down these names and dates," 8 said. "And do your investigating thing, and I'll do mine and we'll compare notes."

Chapter 30

Bettie Young was in a barn. Gagged. A grain sack over her head. She'd been hung by her arms so that her feet barely touched the floor. The strain of standing straight on the balls of her feet had been too much, and she dangled from the rope like a deer carcass left to bleed out.

Only, she wasn't dead. She hadn't been shot. She wasn't gutted and waiting to be cut into venison. Bettie Young was alive. And she was a survivor. Just when things were looking up in her life, the rug had been yanked out from underneath her feet. And Bettie wasn't going to allow that to happen.

She hadn't seen the man who'd brought her here. She'd still been in that box, which had been loaded into a truck, she thought. She had seen lights flash overhead as the vehicle bumped and bounced its way down the road and then away from the city, lights that were replaced by flashes of stars.

After what seemed to be days of being jostled, banged, and bruised, the truck had finally come to a halt. After a few minutes, Bettie had felt the box being lifted and carried, had heard the creak of wooden doors, before she was dropped to the ground, startling her. Before she knew what was happening, the top of the box was ripped open, and she was grabbed and pulled upright, her face slammed down in the straw. That was how she knew it was a barn. That and the smell.

For the past hour, the sounds of arriving automobiles had filtered into her addled brain. Her head was thick, her thoughts like pea soup. Even through the grain sack, she perceived flashes of lights, the rumble of motors, the crunch of tires over rough road.

Then came the creak of those doors, a high, raspy, rumble. Movement, a whoosh of fresh air, the sounds of many feet. Light filtered through the seams of the sack over her head. Dancing light. She sensed the presence of somebody in front of her. The sack was pulled from her head.

Standing in front of Bettie was a white-cloaked apparition wearing a pointed hood that made the figure look to be ten feet tall. One of the chimera's hands held a torch. There was a red circle embroidered on its breast with a white cross inside and a drop of red in the middle that looked to be blood. Behind it was a group of perhaps twenty others in similar costume. The apparition in front of Bettie reached out and removed the gag from her mouth.

"Tonight, your ability to taint the pure blood of the human race will be erased." The voice was chilling, more so as she recognized it as that of the man who'd been with Dankworth when she'd first woken in the box. "Science shows that you are an infection upon the body of humanity. A blight sent by God to test us. Tonight, we will take a step toward the purification of the blood that flows within our veins. Tonight, you will be removed. Tonight, you will die. It is our duty to erase you so that you do not erase us."

* * *

Thursday afternoon found 8's office abuzz with activity. Asta had set up shop out in the main room with Millicent, and Pearle sat across the desk from 8 in the interior office. Marty had given them another pile of newspapers to pore through. They were looking for a few things all at once: suggestions of impropriety at the Department of Genetics, any mention of forced or unknown sterilizations, Klan activity in the area, and news of Germans in Brooklyn, whether it be visiting nationals or suspicious immigrants. And, of course, any ties linking these four things together in any way.

8 had just picked up the afternoon edition of the day's *Brooklyn Eagle* down on the street from a newsboy and was perusing his way through the latest news, skimming for anything related to the chaotic mess he'd become immersed in. The Democratic candidate for president, John W. Davis, had made a harsh denouncement of the Klan during a stop in Cleveland the previous day, but still trailed Coolidge hopelessly in the polls.

In what was turning into a heated presidential race, Mayor Hylan of New York City had called out President Coolidge as being a tool of Wall Street and the Klan. 8 noted this with interest, wondering about the connection between that venerable financial institution and the clandestine club of hatred.

The Klan came up again in the murder trial of that former police officer, a fellow by the name of Patrick Ryan, for the killing of Ferdinand Downs. The men who'd been with Downs said they were chasing a bootlegger, but Ryan claimed that Downs and the others were after him because he was a Roman Catholic, and they were members of the Klan. Many thought that Ryan was to be finally exonerated for shooting and killing Downs in self-defense, but yesterday's trial had ended in a hung jury and back to jail Ryan went, a place he'd been since May. 8 remembered reading about the funeral, out in Suffolk County, where 10,000 Klansmen had shown up to pay their respects.

Special Deputy Assistant Police Commissioner and head of the Narcotics Division, Carleton Simon, had attacked the graft and corruption inherent in the Chinese tongs while speaking to a men's club in Bedford. 8 wondered about the seeming indifference the Klan had to the Asian population of the city, figuring that it was because they mostly kept to themselves, hiding away in Chinatown.

As 8 moved onto the *Brooklyn Daily Times* and the *Standard Union*, he was amazed at how often the Klan was popping up, in everything from politics to murder trials. He'd never quite realized before how integrated they were into every political, financial, governmental, and social organization in the city, and by extension the country as a whole. Congressmen, governors, mayors, bankers, policemen, firemen, judges—many were Klansmen, and, yes, possibly even the President of the United States.

"Got something here about the Rockefeller Foundation working with the Kaiser Wilhelm Society to create an institute in Germany to further the Eugenics Movement," Pearle said. "Not sure what it means, but it sounds like all them high-binders like the Rockefellers, Harrimans, and Carnegies are in on this together. And this is a link to Germany."

"Especially that grifter fellow," 8 said. "Adolph Hitler."

"He seems to be the one leading the racist hatred in Germany," Pearle said. "Especially of the Jews, but also gypsies, homosexuals, and those feeble of mind or body. I'm sure us Black hombres aren't far behind."

Asta stepped into the doorway, newspaper in hand. "Apparently DOG has amassed 750,000 index cards on people, each rating their worth as a human being based on things such as hair and skin color, hair texture, disease history, incontinence, jeez. But also if someone is easily offended, depressed by alcohol, suffering from wanderlust, having philosophical tendencies, loving sentimental drama, being open or secretive, trustful or suspicious, whiny, using good penmanship ability, and even how well they play chess!"

"Incontinence?" Pearle asked, his face twisted in puzzlement.

"What is wanderlust?" 8 asked.

Asta shrugged. "Incontinence, that's bed-wetting and such, I think. Wanderlust, couldn't tell you."

"How'd the Department of Genetics amass all these rating cards?" Pearle asked.

"They had a whole team of field workers who were trained to interview and judge people on these criteria."

"Yeah," 8 said. "Theda Vogel was one of those field workers."

"Seems like your mystery lady is dirty up to the elbows in all this," Asta said.

8 looked at her. She'd slipped seamlessly into the group, into the work, and had proven quite astute in her research. And she was witty and beautiful. Things to ponder. "*Our* client is far from a woman of the cloth. But the fact remains that her husband was killed on purpose, not accidentally as the police reported, and he had a very valuable heirloom taken from him that quite possibly belongs to her."

Asta wrinkled her nose. "Whatever. That high pillow at DOG has bragged that their work is acclaimed the world over, especially in Germany."

"You mean Herman Wall?"

"That's the one. I read an article here how he has been working closely with a German scientist by the name of," Asta looked down at the paper in her hand, "Eugene Fischer."

Millie stepped past Asta into the room. "Couple of Germans recently published an essay in favor of killing off the incurably feeble-minded, their main argument being based on the work of Wall. And this other German has been in contact with Wall about the Black shame, whatever that is."

Pearle cursed, breathed loudly, composed his face. "There's this lie circulating through Germany about how the Black regiments in France ran amok, raping women and children. I guess that was in our free time between shooting Germans and dying in the trenches."

"Where'd you read that?" 8 asked. "I wouldn't mind taking a look."

Millie snickered. "Wouldn't do you much good as it's in German."

That Millie spoke and read German had made her a valuable member of the team, as they didn't have to constantly bombard Marty with questions and translations.

"How about the Italians and the Asians?" 8 asked. He wanted

confirmation of what he was pretty sure he already knew. "Do the Germans hate them as much as the DOG and the Klan seem to?"

"Didn't the governor of Georgia just say something about building a wall of steel, a wall as high as Heaven, against the admission of a single one of those Southern Europeans, meaning, I guess, the Italians?" Asta sat down in a chair to the side.

"But the Germans don't seem as concerned about them, not like the Klan and DOG," Pearle said.

"Let's focus on anything that connects all the groups together," 8 said. "DOG, the Klan, and the Germans."

"That hombre, Hitler, he has nothing but praise for the United States, from immigration laws to sterilization, to classification of citizens," Pearle said. "I even read an article where he talked about how we exterminated almost an entire race, the Native Americans, to create a better world here, and that Germany could learn from that."

*   *   *

Luther Towers lay in bed, his mind a bowl of mush, his typically ordered, calculated, black and white world now a puddle of gray. It was not a bad feeling, just not a natural one.

His tall and slender body was completely naked. Luther imagined he looked like a skeleton lying there. Next to him was the woman he'd met the other day at the restaurant. Theda Lazur. It was she who had thrown him into disarray. Today, he'd been coming out of the Brooklyn Hospital after meeting with Ronald Dankworth and had literally bumped into this wildly exotic woman.

Theda had convinced him to have a drink with her, one that turned into two, and then three. Luther was not a drinking man. But there was something intoxicating about this woman. Maybe it was the fact that no woman had ever paid him any mind whatsoever. He'd never been with a woman, had barely spoken to one, that is, in anything but a businesslike manner. But Theda?

As they sat in the juice joint, she'd touched his arm. His leg. Her scent made his knees week. He was treated to glimpses of her cleavage, the two round orbs of flesh sending blood racing to his head, making him lightheaded, or was it the drinks? Finally, she'd taken his hand, said that she lived just around the corner, and that she wanted to show him something. He no more could've said no than he could've been friends with a Jew.

Luther thought of her body, writhing on top of him, under him, in front of him. How her lips curled ferociously before they attacked his mouth, nipped at his neck, bit harder at his chest. She now lay with those delicious orbs of flesh totally exposed, a sheet covering down there, smoking a cigarette. He felt himself stirring again.

"Quite a coincidence running into you coming from visiting with Ronald," Theda said. "I was just talking to him the other day and your name came up."

"What's that?" Luther tensed. Why would Dankworth mention him to this woman?

Theda put her cigarette out and turned on her side to face him, her breast pushed against his arm, her hand lazily grazing his chest in small circular motions. "I'd brought up to him that the *Rein Adler of the Batavi* had gone missing, and asked whether he knew anything about that or not. He said that he didn't, but that you might."

"I don't know what that is," Luther said.

Theda ran her hand down over his long abdomen, her fingers tickling, teasing, exploring ever lower. "It's a golden eagle. But you don't trust me. Ronald said you knew of it."

"Trust you? In what way?"

"My ancestors were some of the original Batavi who rebelled against the Romans, wiped out the Legion, and took the Aquila. My family has been in the order for many generations, but as you most likely know, women are not allowed. I've never gotten a chance to see this symbol of German pride and superiority."

"What is it that you want from me?"

Theda leaned her lips to his ear, her tongue flicking his lobe, as her other hand grasped his member firmly in her hand. "I'd just like to see it, just the once."

* * *

There was a knock at the outer door, currently shut and locked, with the Klan targeting them.

Pearle retrieved the Tommy Gun from the corner and went out and sat at Millicent's desk while 8 took out his .38 and went to the door.

Asta and Millie peered through the inner office doorway.

"Who is it?" 8 asked.

"Fletcher Henderson, looking for Mr. 8 Ballo."

8 opened the door. Smack Henderson was a short and compact man with a receding hairline that made his face seem particularly oval. "What brings you down our way, Smack?"

The man looked over 8's shoulder where Asta was emerging from the office. "Well, normally speaking, the opportunity to see Miss Holm would be plenty enough, but I got some other things to discuss with you."

The man made no pretense of admiring Asta's beauty ever since first meeting her the previous year. 8 was not sure if he should be annoyed by this or take it as a compliment. "Come on in. We've been keeping this door locked on account of the Klan being on the warpath. You didn't see anybody out there wearing a pillowcase on their head, did you?"

Smack looked nervously over his shoulder and hurriedly stepped inside. He reached out and shook 8's hand, his long fingers disappearing in 8's paw. He caught sight of Pearle at the desk with a Tommy Gun, and he gave a small start. "You expecting somebody, Mr. Hill?" he asked.

"Never can be too sure," Pearle said, leaning the weapon in the corner and standing up as 8 locked the front door. He shook hands with the pianist and bandleader. "How ya been?"

Smack shook his head, a worried look on his face. "Did a young woman by the name of Bettie Young come in here last week?"

"Sure," 8 said. "As a matter of fact, she said you recommended she come to me."

"So you know about what they done to her."

8 nodded.

"Well, now she's gone missing."

"What do you mean missing?" 8 asked. "Maybe she's just taking some time for herself."

Smack shook his head. "She was supposed to sing with my orchestra last night at the Roseland Ballroom. She wouldn't of missed that unless she was dead or in a real bad way."

Chapter 31

"Point and shoot," 8 said. "All you do is pull the trigger. Point like you would point your finger at somebody. Don't jerk it."

Pearle had gone to get his motorcar and returned with pistols for Millicent and Asta.

"I've shot a gun before," Asta said.

"So you have," 8 agreed.

They were upstairs on the third floor in his apartment. The women were going to spend the evening and night, while he and Pearle went to check on a few things out in the world. When they got back, they were going to bed down in the office on the second floor.

A knock came at the door. A lot of weapons turned that way as 8 stepped over, but it was only McGee.

"Don't think you need any of my boys outside," McGee said, stepping into the room. "Seeing as you got a passel of *manky* goons out there already."

"What's that?" 8 asked.

"The street is crawling with Jewish gangsters," McGee replied. "Looks to be Meyer and Bugsy's lads. I'm thinking they're protecting you."

8 scowled. Then grinned. Bugsy couldn't very well strong-arm him for a favor when 8 had flat out refused his offer. And there was something heartwarming in the gesture, even if it came from a pack of heroin dealers, gamblers, pimps, and murderers.

"I expect they have a vested interest in this business," 8 said. "On account of the Klan hating the Jews. Maybe we just keep our head down and let the gangsters and racists kill each other off."

"Bad as Meyer and Bugsy are, I'd take them over the Klan any day," Pearle said.

"Where you lads off to?" McGee asked.

"Thought we'd pay Ronald Dankworth a visit," 8 said. "See what he might know."

"I'll stay here until you get back." McGee walked into the kitchen. "You got any of the good stuff so I can have a wee dram while you're gone?"

Ronald Dankworth had taken the rest of the week off, the receptionist at the Brooklyn Hospital told 8 and Pearle. No amount of cajoling could get her to share the man's address.

"Seems to me that Theda Vogel most likely knows where the man lives," 8 said, once they were back on the street. "Seeing as her husband worked for Dankworth, and she just lied to me about the reason for spending an hour in a hotel room with the man. How about we swing up to her place?"

"Sounds like a plan," Pearle said as they clambered back into the Nash automobile. "You think Dankworth has something to do with this Bettie Young going missing?"

8 shrugged. "He personally checks her in and arranges for her to be transported to Damnation Island to have her appendix removed where they also sterilize her, and then I find a list in his desk drawer that seems to suggest that he's been involved in at least seventy-three other instances of the same crime? Seems to be as good a place to start as any."

Pearle nodded. "You think he found out that she'd come to you about investigating the whole pile of shit?"

"Could be." 8 hoped that his involvement wasn't the reason she'd gone missing.

Pearle pulled the automobile to the side of the street into a space just down from the Vogel residence. The doorman was adamant about not letting Pearle into the building, and upon calling up to Theda's apartment with no answer, would not let either of them inside.

8 looked at his timepiece, wondering where she could be, but it was obvious that the grieving Widow had a full social calendar. Back at the motorcar, he looked up at her windows, and thought he might've seen a curtain move, but couldn't be certain.

"You think she's actually here?" Pearle asked as they got back into the Nash.

"Could be. Not sure why she'd pretend not to be."

"Be easy enough to get past that buster at the door and go up and find out."

8 contemplated this, looking up at the window. "What are we going to do, bust down her door?"

"Only if we have to."

"No. Either she's there or she's not. If she is, she's going to be pissed off because she didn't want to see us. I'll give her a ring on the telephone in the morning. How about we take a ride out to that mansion in Park Slope where you saw the German fellow go?"

"You're the boss," Pearle said, pulling out onto the street. "Something off about that woman, though. I can sense it in my bones."

"She's willing to do anything to be wealthy, and I don't mean just well off, but stinking rich," 8 said.

"Don't suppose that's all that different than most people," Pearle said. "What do you mean by anything? Sex? Theft? Murder?"

"I wouldn't put anything past her."

"You think there's any chance she killed her husband?"

8 went to reply, stopped, and turned to look at his friend. "I hadn't thought of that. Why?"

"To get her hands on this Aquila thing."

"But they had it, already, didn't they?"

"Ah, but what if Karl Vogel was protecting it on principle, as an emissary of the Rein Adler of the Batavi group."

8 nodded. "He was going to give it back. But Theda wanted it for the wealth it would bring. They fought about it. She paid somebody to run him down and steal it."

"Just a thought."

"It has merit."

Pearle stopped the motorcar. "That's the place he went into."

8 looked in wonder at the mansion. It was a two-story affair of brick and stone, the roof of the second floor like some storm-tossed ocean of swells and ebbs bursting into the sky, a mishmash of gables, arches, and domes. "That joint has to be a hundred feet long." It was separated from the sidewalk by a wrought iron fence, its top a collection of jagged spears and miniature gargoyles.

"It's owned by a hombre named Hans Krüger. Couldn't find out much about him other than he owns a good chunk of everything."

"German fellow, huh?"

"What's the play?"

8 looked to the west. "Sun's down. Another fifteen minutes, it'll be pitch black. How about we see if we can get around back, climb the fence, and peek in some windows. See if our boy Heinrich Funk is in there."

"And if he is?"

"Let's take it one step at a time."

Off the side street, they were able to clamber over the fence with little difficulty. Even though both large men, they were quite agile for their size. Pearle left the Tommy gun behind and carried a huge Colt revolver stuck into the back of his pants, and 8 had his .38 in a shoulder holster.

They crept through the scant bushes surrounding the mansion, finding most of the bottom floor windows lit up. It was at the back third window that they hit pay dirt.

The window was a massive affair with curtains pulled open. The inhabitants must have felt comfortable with their privacy in the rear of the palace-like structure. 8 looked down, almost expecting to see a moat.

Light illuminated a large room filled with men in suits, smoking cigars, with tumblers in hand. Several men had large bushy mustaches, a few played billiards, and in the middle of the room was Heinrich Funk. He was in conversation with Herman Wall.

"I'd give a pretty penny to hear what they're saying," Pearle said.

"I have a feeling it'd only anger you," 8 said with a quiet chuckle. "If I was a guessing man, I'd say that's a room full of rich Germans."

Through an open doorway from the center of the mansion came a tall, thin, balding man. Ronald Dankworth. He went over to Wall and Funk. Whatever he said agitated them. Wall began to wave his arms angrily, and Funk's face grew red, and you could almost feel the perspiration popping out on his forehead.

After a minute, the three men left the room. 8 and Pearle scurried around the side of the mansion and watched as the three men exited the front door.

"Quick, over the side fence," 8 said as the men turned and walked in the opposite direction. He boosted Pearle up and then followed him over as they rushed to the corner.

"Automobile or foot?" Pearle asked. The sidewalk was empty in front of them.

"You get the motorcar, and I'll go on foot," 8 said.

He went at a fast walk down the sidewalk past the Krüger mansion on his right. At the end of the block, he saw the three men down the side street and turned to follow them as an automobile pulled up next to him.

Awful quick for Pearle, 8 thought, looking over at it as a man got out with a pistol pointed at his head.

"8 Ballo? I'm Lieutenant Schulz. Can you come with us, please?"

"What for?"

8 cast a look down the street where the three Germans had now disappeared. Then back the other way, the direction from which Pearle should be soon coming.

"I am not going to quibble with you, Mr. Ballo. I don't believe you have the document any longer, anyway. So, I'm going count to three and then I'm going to shoot you. Or you can get in the car."

A second man in uniform stepped around the back of the automobile. He also had a pistol leveled at 8.

"Document?" 8 asked.

"One."

"How do I know you are really police?"

"Two."

"Okay, okay, I'm coming." 8 stepped forward, hoping to maybe grab this Schulz fellow and use him for a shield, but the man sidestepped.

"We just have a couple of questions for you, Mr. Ballo." Schulz gestured to the open door to the backseat of the automobile. "No more stalling. Your friend, the Black bloke, has found that he has a flat tire. We just need to speak with you."

8 didn't believe that for the slightest part of a second, but he didn't see any play. Better to wait for an opportunity in the car. He climbed into the backseat. The second man went back around and climbed in beside him holding a gun to his ribs, while Schulz got in the front with the driver.

"Where we going?" 8 asked as they pulled out on the street.

"You are going to a grave in Gravesend." Schulz guffawed, caught his breath, and then howled even louder. "But first you'll—"

An automobile slammed into them from behind, throwing their heads forward, the driver's into the steering wheel and Schulz's into the dashboard, and the two behind them against the front seat. The pistol at his ribs went off, luckily no longer pointing into his side, but the bullet still burning across the top of 8's stomach.

The man looked up blurrily.

8 reached sideways and cupped his hand behind the man's neck and slammed his face into the seat again as he pulled the trigger, the bullet again going wide.

Schulz was turning with a pistol in hand when 8 socked him in the nose. He wasn't able to get much behind it, but it still snapped the Lieutenant's head back.

The driver turned, gun in hand. 8 grabbed his wrist and hauled the man over the seat. The driver grasped 8's neck with his other hand as he slammed into him.

The man next to 8 was scrambling on the floor for the pistol he'd dropped. Blood poured from his nose as he searched for the weapon.

Schultz steadied his pistol, and the window behind 8 exploded. Then he jerked sideways, clapping his hand to his cheek as a gunshot exploded outside.

8 slammed the driver through the window as Pearle opened the front door.

Schultz brought the pistol up, his hand clasping his face, blood bubbling around it. Pearle drove a fist into the man's neck, and a gurgle burst from his lips, spraying blood as the gun dropped from his hand.

The man next to 8 found the pistol and started to bring it up as 8 hit him with a right-handed punch, turning and putting his weight behind it. He could feel the man's jaw shatter under the impact, perhaps already fractured from being slammed into the seat.

8 opened the door and shoved the man through it, following along behind. The driver, who he'd thrown through the window, stumbled into Pearle, who turned and threw the man to the ground, and then leaned down and slugged him in the face, and the man sagged into the street.

Schultz tumbled from the automobile, again with pistol in hand, as 8 raced around the front. He knocked the Lieutenant's arm upward, the bullet whistling into the heavens, and then grabbed it and wrested it from his hand.

"Glad you could make it," 8 said to Pearle. "Don't much like it down in Gravesend."

Pearle looked up from the unmoving man on the ground. "Sorry. Had a flat tire. Slowed me down."

8 grasped Schulz by the neck and slammed him back against the hood of the automobile. "Who sent you?"

Schulz tried to laugh, spit blood, and looked back up, eyes shining hard. "You're a dead man. I'm a policeman. Any minute now, more coppers are going to show up. And then you're dead. Do you get it? Dead."

Pearle looked at 8. "He's right. We need to skedaddle. This don't look good at all."

"We'll bring him with us," 8 snarled angrily.

"And what? Torture him? That ain't what we do. If you want, I'm not opposed to putting a bullet in his head, so he can't be coming at us no more, but I'm not down for peeling fingernails, Bo."

8 took a breath. "No. You're right. That's not who we are. Let's get out of here."

"They're just going to come at us again. I say we put a mercy bullet in their noggins first."

"You said it. That's not us."

"But they're going to try again."

"If it's not them," 8 said, "it'll be somebody else. At least we'll be able to recognize their maimed ugly mugs coming at us."

Pearle sighed.

Across the car, the man with the broken jaw stood up with a Tommy Gun that he must've retrieved from the boot of the automobile. He was a macabre figure, moving as if in slow motion, but too quick for either of them to react.

Then his body jerked, once, twice, too many times to count, the rattle of a machine gun coming from the shadows.

Bugsy Siegel stepped into the streetlamp, smoking Tommy Gun in his left hand, three men behind him. He pointed at 8 with his right hand, and then mimicked cocking the fingers. "Looks like you owe me one, Ballo," he said. "And yeah, that is who *we* are."

Bugsy motioned with the barrel of the weapon. One man grabbed Schulz by the neck and the other two picked up the unconscious man as an automobile pulled up in the street. They threw the two men in the back, two of them crowding in as Bugsy stepped to the passenger side front seat door.

Bugsy turned and laughed. "Good thing I'm not above killing trash and torturing vermin." He climbed in the automobile, and it roared away.

Chapter 32

They'd driven the battered Nash around the block and parked it. The front bumper clanged on the ground, matching the damaged rear bumper from the other night at the Klan rally. The right front tire had been slashed, and Pearle driving it had mashed the rim.

"What now, Bo?" Pearle asked.

"Now we go back and visit Theda," 8 said. "And if she won't see us, we'll sneak in and break down the door. If she's not there, we'll wait for her to return."

"It does seem that she is the linchpin to this whole mess," Pearle agreed. "She hires you to find who killed her husband and stole the Aquila. She knows Wall and Dankworth. Her husband, if not her, was a member of the Batavi group that I'm betting your hombre Heinrich Funk is involved with. The eugenics people, the Klan, and the Batavi. All in her web."

They found a trolley stop that'd take them back up to Brooklyn Heights, luckily with a car just about to leave, and they managed to jump on just as it began to trundle its way uptown.

"I wouldn't want to be those coppers right now," 8 said. "Rumor has it being interrogated by Bugsy Siegel can be a painful process."

"Feels right, somehow, a Jewish hombre turning the tables on some Klansmen."

"Not sure anybody deserves that fate, but yeah, I know what you mean."

"I guess Bugsy was good to his word, keeping an eye on us, for protection and the like," Pearle said.

"The fellow saved our lives," 8 said. "But not sure I like being in his debt."

"Beats being six feet under."

"That it does. That it does."

The trolley rumbled to a screeching stop, sparks flying, and they disembarked just around the corner from Theda Vogel's apartment. As they approached the front door, a tall man was walking away from them, and 8 briefly thought it might be Dankworth, tall and thin, but realized this man was even taller. He shook his head to clear it from seeing killers on every sidewalk.

They didn't have to sneak in and break down the door, as this time Theda answered the doorman's telephone call, inviting them up. The elevator operator kept eyeballing Pearle, but didn't say a word, perhaps he'd noticed both men were splattered with blood and thought it best to keep his mouth shut.

Theda opened the door to them wearing a robe, black with yellow sunflowers bursting forth and red sleeves, that reached just to her knees. Her hair was tousled, as if she'd been sleeping, but she had a cigarette in a long holder, and a tumbler in hand that 8 was guessing was gin.

"Hello, 8," she said with a sexy smile. Then she caught sight of Pearle. "You brought a friend. And he's…Black."

8 brushed past her into the apartment. "Hello, Theda. Yes, you are right on both counts."

Pearle was left facing Theda. "Hello, Mrs. Vogel. I am Pearle Hill."

"So you are." Theda turned and followed 8 into the apartment. "There are drinks on the trolley in the library."

She led the way, 8 and Pearle both pouring themselves large glasses of brown liquor from a decanter, and then they all sat down. It tasted mighty fine, 8 thought, letting the liquid burn its way down his throat.

"Is that blood in your hair and on your jacket?" Theda asked. She didn't seem particularly perturbed.

8 nodded. "Not mine. Been a tough night."

"Have you found my Aquila yet?" Theda asked.

"No. Do you know a man by the name of Heinrich Funk?"

Theda flinched slightly. Took a deep breath. "That is the man who my husband was going to turn the Aquila over to. He is a high-ranking member of the Rein Adler of the Batavi. What of him?"

"Do you know where we can find him?"

Theda shook her head. "Does he have the Aquila? Was he the one who... killed my husband?" Her breath caught in her throat and a small sob slipped out from her glistening lips.

"I just saw him in the company of your friend," 8 said.

"My friend?"

"Ronald Dankworth."

Theda's face paled. "Ronald was with this man, Funk?"

8 nodded. "Why do you suppose that is, Theda?"

She shook her head. "I don't know. They are both acquaintances of my husband. I suppose they might know each other."

"Who has the Aquila, Theda?"

"That is what I hired you to find out." A bit of fire had crept back into her voice.

"I thought you hired me to find out who killed your husband."

"Yes. Yes. Of course. But it is one and the same person, is it not?"

8 was starting to doubt the veracity of anything that she said. "What were you doing at the Bossert Hotel with Dankworth the other night?"

"I... I told you. I was, uh, going over some benefits owed to me from the hospital."

8 chuckled. It sounded harsh to his own ears. "That sort of thing is conducted in offices, Theda. Not in hotel rooms."

"What are you saying? That I am some sort of quiff? A wanton woman, a bereft widow, finding solace in the arms of men such as Ronald Dankworth?"

"I just want to know what you were really doing there," 8 said.

Pearle got up, refreshed the gin in Theda's tumbler, and then the whiskey in their glasses. "I thought that he might know where the Aquila was," Theda said tightly. "My Aquila. He denied any knowledge of any such thing. And now you tell me he was meeting with Heinrich Funk—the man sent here to retrieve it for the Batavi."

8 nodded. That had more of the ring of truth—if not all the truth—to it. "Do you know where Ronald Dankworth lives?"

"Do you think he knows where the Aquila is?"

8 thought about that. He wanted to find Dankworth primarily because he suspected the man knew what had happened to Bettie Young, knew if the young woman was alive or dead. But it seemed quite possible that he might also know of the whereabouts of the Aquila.

"Yes," he said.

*   *   *

8 and Pearle were parked outside of a two-story row house with concrete steps up to the front door. There were lights on inside, and a shadowy figure could be seen moving behind the curtained windows.

"Looks like he's home," Pearle said.

"With any luck, Dankworth brought Wall and Funk home with him," 8 said.

"One way to find out."

"How 'bout I stand to the side, and you knock on the door," 8 suggested. "He doesn't know you, and there's not much chance he'll open the door for me."

Pearle snickered. "Yeah, the Klan hombre is much more likely to open the door to a Black man at ten o'clock at night."

"If he asks what you want without having opened the door, tell him you have a message from Theda Vogel."

"Ila," Pearle said. "That'll do the trick. He'll be so tickled he might even kiss me."

"I'm guessing that Theda and Dankworth did more than talk for that hour they spent in the hotel room. What I don't know is why? Theda strikes me as a cagey woman who gets what she wants by any means necessary. Do you think that Dankworth actually knows something about the Aquila?"

"One way to find out," Pearle said again and went up the steps.

8 followed him and stood off to the side between the door and the window.

Pearle knocked twice.

The door opened immediately, as if Dankworth had been expecting somebody. His bushy eyebrows raised in surprise, and he dropped the satchel in his hand as Pearle shoved him backward into the house. 8 followed, pulling the door shut, and picking up the bag.

"What do you want?" Dankworth demanded of Pearle as 8 entered the room.

"Just a few questions, Ronnie," Pearle said.

Dankworth looked at 8. "You."

8 nodded. "Me."

"I thought you'd be in jail by now for breaking into my office," Dankworth said.

8's eyes swept the room. Very spartan. One wall had a painting with a red background, a white disc in the middle, with a black hooked cross inside. On the floor, next to the armchair, in the corner, was a woman's shoe. 8 had seen that shoe before.

"Get out of my home."

Dankworth's tone was belligerent, the voice of someone accustomed to people listening to him. Pearle failed in that endeavor, striking him across the face with an open-handed blow, and then back the other way. His round spectacles were knocked from his face, two red marks spring to life on either cheek.

"I'll see you lynched for that, you disease-infected animal."

This earned Dankworth several more slaps and backhands.

8 laid a hand gently on Pearle's back, who gave one last slap, and stepped aside, saying, "I loosened him up for you."

Dankworth sagged backward into the sofa. His lip and nose were bloody, coating his mustache.

8 sat down next to him. He nodded at the wall, where a flag emblazoned with a swastika hung in a proud frame. "I take it you're not Hindu?"

"What? Hindu?" Dankworth stuttered, eyes wild in his battered visage.

"The swastika. Very important symbol in the Hindu religion. Long before your friend, Hitler, appropriated it for your particular brand of hatred."

"It is a symbol of our movement, the National Socialists," Dankworth said, sitting forward and picking his glasses off the floor. "The red is the social ideal, the white is the nationalist ideal, and the hooked cross is the mission of our struggle for the victory of the Aryan man."

"Mm. The Hindus saw it as the revolving sun, infinity, and continual creation."

"What do you want? I'll have you..." Dankworth started to bluster, looked at Pearle, and shut his mouth.

"Do you know where the Aquila is?"

"The Aquila is not my concern."

8 thought it interesting that the man hadn't professed ignorance. "Whose concern is it?

"What do you want with the Aquila?"

"I was hired to find it."

Dankworth nodded. "That is the item that was stolen from Karl when he was killed."

8 nodded.

"Perhaps you should ask your client where it is. She knows."

"Theda?"

"She may not know where it is now, but she will know where it will be."

"How do you know that?"

Dankworth had settled his cracked spectacles back on his face. "They will kill you, you know. You're a dead man." He looked up at Pearle. "And you they will mutilate and stuff your own cock into your mouth and let you bleed out like the animal that you are."

8 raised his hand to stop Pearle from striking Dankworth. It didn't work. This time it was a punch to the jaw, snapping the man's mouth shut with a clack. A tiny piece of red flesh fell to the floor as Dankworth was slammed back into the sofa. 8 realized it was the tip of the man's tongue.

"We need him to be able to speak," 8 said.

Dankworth was crumpled into the sofa, a dazed look on his face, but conscious.

"Depends on what he's saying," Pearle said.

"Ronald, could you please try and be more civil," 8 said. "My friend here has a temper. It seems that he doesn't much like the idea of having his own cock stuffed into his mouth."

"Or being referred to as an animal," Pearle said.

"How about you give a little nod if you understand," 8 said.

Dankworth tilted his head down and up. And then groaned. His hand went to his mouth. Touched his jaw. Felt his tongue. Groaned again.

"How does Theda know where the Aquila is?" 8 asked.

"I told her that on Friday, it will be at Fort Green Park. That Herman Wall hath agreed to return it to Heinrich Funk. Friday at noon." Dankworth fumbled to speak without the tip of his tongue.

"Why did you tell her that?" 8 asked.

"It wath a moment of weakneth. Afterward. We were in bed. I shouldn't have told her. If anybody findth out, he will kill me."

"Who will kill you?"

Dankworth groaned. His eyes fluttered. 8 was worried that the man was going to pass out. He grabbed him by the shirt collar and pulled him forward. He twisted the man's ear to garner his attention.

"There is a shoe in the corner behind that chair that belongs to Bettie Young. Do you know where she is?"

"Bettie who?" Dankworth muttered.

8 twisted his ear again. "Bettie is a young lady who you sent off to Damnation Island to be sterilized without her knowledge. She is currently missing. And her shoe is in the corner of this room. I believe you know who she is. Furthermore, I believe that you know where she is."

"I don't know what you're talking about."

"Well, look what we got here," Pearle said. He'd just peered into the satchel that Dankworth had been carrying when he opened the door. "Were you on your way to a party?" He pulled out a white robe and triangular hood.

"Is Bettie Young still alive?" 8 asked.

"That damn..." Dankworth paused, looked at Pearle. "Not for very much longer. She is going to be burned at the stake tonight at midnight. To teach her to never forget her place. To thend a methage that Blackth, Jewth, and Catholicth should know their fucking plathe."

8 looked at his pocket watch. It was just past ten. "Where?"

Dankworth shook his head. 8 tweaked him in the eyeball.

"The Brown farm in Gravesend." Dankworth had started to blubber. "He will kill me. You didn't hear it from me. You understand."

"Who will kill you?"

8 wasn't sure if he heard the crack of the pistol, the smashing of the window, or the thunk of a hunk of lead impacting Dankworth's forehead first. With brain and pieces of skull fragments coating his face, 8 dropped to the floor and rolled over.

A bullet hissed in the space he'd just occupied, striking the wall behind with a crack. Pearle had worked his way over to the window, pistol drawn, as he peered out. 8 crawled into the hallway and to the door.

"Cover me," he said. "I'm going out."

He jerked open the door and slid outside, bounding down the steps. Nothing. Nobody.

An automobile came down the street. 8 stepped behind a lamppost with pistol aimed. It was a man with spectacles who looked completely innocent and harmless.

It was as if the gunshots had come from a ghost.

Chapter 33

8 and Pearle weren't sure if anybody had even heard the gunshots but thought it best to get out of there anyway, just in case.

"Don't think we got much time to get to Gravesend and find this Brown farm," Pearle said. "Little less than two hours to midnight. My automobile is out of commission. Trolleys don't run that way this time of night and would probably leave us off miles from Farmer Brown's anyway."

"Maybe McGee can get us a police motorcar," 8 said. He nodded to a telephone booth down and across the street. "Hope somebody is in the office."

The line rang and rang. 8 begged the operator to let it go a bit longer.

"Yes, lad," McGee said.

"It's 8. We got us a bit of a situation, McGee. Can you get a motorcar and pick us up?"

"What sort of situation?"

"We don't have time. I'll tell you on the way."

There was a pause. 8 could imagine McGee fighting back the urge to ask more questions like what had happened to Pearle's automobile and where they were going.

McGee cleared his throat. "That wisecracker friend of yours is here. You know, Dorothy Parker. The aces and eights lady. Came by looking for you. I believe she said she was in her automobile. Struck me as strange, you know, a lass—"

"Tell her that you need to borrow it and come get us. There's a life on the line, here, McGee." 8 looked around. "We're at a telephone booth on the corner of Henry and Pierpont in Brooklyn Heights. Hurry."

Twenty minutes later, a 1923 black Ford Model T came screeching up to the corner. 8 had spent the time making a few more telephone calls to find out the whereabouts of the Brown Farm in Gravesend.

"No. No way," 8 said."

Dorothy Parker was in the driver's seat. Asta sat next to her. McGee and Millie were in the backseat. Dorothy had on goggles like aviators wore. The automobile had the top off with just a windshield to protect against the cold night air.

"I thought you were in a hurry," Dottie said. "Get in."

8 opened the driver's door. "We are going to a farm in the middle of nowhere to try and save the life of a young Black woman. A passel of Klan members are intent on lynching her at midnight. This is no place for women."

Dottie slammed the door shut. "If you want my automobile, you got me right alongside of it."

"Sorry, me lad," McGee said. "They ganged up on me."

8 looked at Asta. "Asta?" She glared back at him. He looked at his secretary/receptionist, Millicent Winter.

"You need me," Millie said. "In case somebody is speaking German. You're not leaving me behind. Not all Germans are bad."

Meanwhile, the hour of death was creeping closer and closer for Bettie. He walked around to the passenger side. Pearle squeezed into the back. Asta was forced to sit on 8's lap, half in the car, half out.

"Where to, my big 8?" Dottie asked.

8 pointed forward, and she pressed her foot firmly down on the accelerator, and away they went. He turned his head. "When you

get a chance, you might let your buddy, Captain Archipoili, know that Ronald Dankworth is lying dead in his home back down Henry Street with a bullet in his skull."

"Was it ye who shot him?" McGee asked, having to yell so the words weren't lost as they zipped down the road in the open-air automobile.

8 shook his head. "It was a ghost," he said.

"Where do they have Bettie at?" Asta asked. Her eyes were shining brightly with the excitement of it all. So much more thrilling than the humdrum of being a telephone operator.

"A farm in Gravesend," 8 said. "Take a right on the next street," he said to Dottie.

"I brought the pistol that Pearle gave me," Asta said. "Right there in my bag."

8 turned his head to the backseat. "Millie, we can let you out. You shouldn't be putting yourself in danger."

"Are you saying you don't trust me because I'm German?"

"No, I…" 8 realized she had a wicked grin on her face.

"I'm in this now, right up to my chin," Millie said. "And I aim to see it through."

"Okay, then."

8 mused on the widening circle of his gang. Not too long ago it'd been Pearle, McGee, and Marty. It seemed that it now included his friend, Dorothy Parker, his employee, Millicent Winter, and his lover, Asta Holm. He supposed that these three tough women were every bit as capable as the three men. He grinned in the dark of the front of the motorcar, thinking that the three of them were probably tougher than Marty in a fight.

As the jalopy bounced at breakneck speed on the road to Gravesend, 8 mused that he'd been mistaken all along. He'd always assumed that he wanted a woman like Camila Morales, the young lady who'd broken his heart back before the Great War, marrying another while he was off fighting.

A woman to keep home for him. To cook him meals and greet him at the door when he came home from work. Somebody to raise their children and make sure they did their homework. 8 had always thought that what he wanted was somebody grounded, stable, and supportive of him.

Now, as 8 looked at Asta's shining blue eyes, hair blowing freely in the wind, and mouth bared in a ferocious grin of excitement, he realized that maybe he'd been wrong all this time. The perfect match was somebody who walked beside you, not behind you.

What he truly wanted was a woman who shared his sense of adventure, for these exhilarating exploits were truly why he was a PI. Sure, it paid the bills, and sure, plenty of it was as dull as watching paint dry, but here, now in the moment, was what it was all about. The pure electrifying thrill of experiencing life and making a difference.

"We got time to swing by my car and get the Tommy Gun?" Pearle asked from the back seat. "It'd sure come in handy."

8 weighed that in his mind. They were cutting it awful tight. But the weapon would certainly be of use. "Take a left," he said.

"Who is this Bettie?" Dottie asked.

"A client," 8 said. "Who could use a helping hand."

"A Black lady they are gonna lynch because of the color of her skin," Pearle said.

"This is the Klan threatening this young lady?" Dottie asked. Her eyes, behind the goggles, were pinned to the road as they bounced over bumps and took corners on 8's directions.

"Stop here," 8 said and Dottie slammed on the brakes.

Pearle jumped out of the back, went to his Nash, and retrieved the Tommy Gun from the boot.

"Yes on the Klan," 8 said. "Go left at the next turn."

"What do you think their stance is on mongrels?" Dottie asked, whipping around the corner. "My father was a Jew, I went to Catholic school, and my stepmother, the housekeeper, was a Protestant."

"Who really cares what religion you are?" Asta asked. "Other than a bunch of fellows in sheets who know their wives mock them and their bosses believe them to be shit on their shoes?"

The Brown Farm was in a corner of Gravesend that didn't see much motorcar traffic. 8 directed Dottie to drive past the farm, and then down a side road to another crossroad. A plan began to form in his mind as they returned to the front side of the farm. The six of them got out of the car and crept up behind the barn, and then moved to a vantage point by a machine shed. The night was clear, but the moon was just a waning crescent, the sickle-shaped sliver providing just the faintest of lights.

This light was enough for them to see a cross in the middle of what looked to be a cow pasture with a fence separating them from it. A person was strapped to the crucifix, their feet raised about five feet off the ground, hovering in the air over about twenty figures in Klan uniform.

"Thank you esteemed members of the White gentile race of good Christians who don't believe in a false Pope. Tonight, we have a special treat for you, one that you will bring back to the Klan in your neighborhood and replicate going forward."

At least, 8 thought, this was not a gathering of over a thousand members like the one they'd last witnessed. This must be some sort of inner circle, the upper echelon of the most trusted, the most important men all of whom embraced the violent aspects of the organization.

"The time of passive opposition is past. No longer will we simply parade in protest against the influx of vermin into our midst. No longer will we turn a blind eye as Blacks dilute our offspring into some inferior race. No longer will we allow the Jews to steal our money and try to change who we are as Americans. No longer will we allow the Pope in Rome to determine our future. Today, tonight, right now, we are going to make a statement of our intention to preserve the master race of good American and German stock, men who will preserve the sanctity of public schools, free speech, free press, the pursuit of happiness, and our homes."

A pyre of sticks and wood was piled at the base of the crucifix. In the gloomy light, it was difficult to tell if the person to be burnt alive was Bettie Young.

"And now, gentlemen, I'd like to introduce you to the master of ceremonies for this evening, the Imperial Cyclops of the United States of America."

Twenty sets of hands and twenty mouths clapped and roared their approval. A hooded horseman appeared walking slowly forward. The horse came to a stop between the crucifix and the gathering of sheeted figures. Torches, set into the ground, flickered. The air grew thick as death, and the Klan Konvention fell silent.

"The basic principle of blood states the blood of every single person on this planet contains the soul of a person and likewise, the soul of his race. The Volk. God himself has created the most perfect union of purity ever known. It is the new Aryan-American race. The race of the future. The salvation of mankind."

Behind the shed, out of earshot of the gathered men, 8 shared the plan hurriedly with the others, pointing and speaking quickly, for it looked like there was little time to dilly dally.

It took them five minutes to get into place. 8 could clearly see that the writhing figure on the crucifix was Bettie Young. All the while, the ceremony droned on.

"We are in the throes of creating a New World Order. The Aryan Race which has created all the artistic, scientific, and engineering marvels that we see before us today will now be mixed with the American Race which is the future. But we are challenged with a threat from the Blacks, the Jews, and the Roman Catholics who wish to return us to the darkness of being barbarians and living in caves."

C'mon, McGee, 8 thought. It's time.

"Today, tonight, we take a stance in defense of the Aryan-American Race of the future. The race of pure blood undiluted by inferior stock. This will be the spark that will ignite the grand solution." The Imperial Cyclops stepped his horse over to a torch and pulled it free from the ground.

C'mon, McGee. 8 took careful aim at the Imperial Cyclops. It was possible that the plan was going to have to be altered.

The Imperial Cyclops walked his horse to the pyre under the feet of Bettie Young. "Let this be a lesson for all of you on how to deal with impure blood in your neighborhoods. This will be a spark that will sweep the city, the state, the country, and the world." He leaned down with the torch.

"Stop. Police." McGee's voice came from the darkness over by the fence separating the shed from the pasture. "By order of the New York City Police Department, you are ordered to cease and desist."

The Imperial Cyclops paused, turned his horse toward the voice. "This is of no concern of yours. Leave."

"Everybody come toward me and away from the lass," McGee said.

"And why would we do that for one man," the Imperial Cyclops said. "An Irish Catholic at that? Leave now or we'll add you to the fire."

"I have an entire unit here. Surrender or we open fire."

The Imperial Cyclops walked his horse toward McGee. "I think he's bluffing, boys."

Dottie sent a burst from the Tommy Gun over their heads, and the Konvention scattered, some dropping to the ground, others running and crawling into the darkness. The horse of the Imperial Cyclops spooked and reared, whinnying in fear.

8 and Pearle rose to their feet from behind the water trough and scrambled over to the crucifix.

McGee, Asta, and Millie scattered a couple of pistol shots into the ground and air to add to the idea that there was a complete police unit lurking in the shadows.

The Grand Cyclops pulled a rifle from the scabbard on the saddle and began to return fire as his horse whirled and pranced and reared.

Pearle climbed onto 8's shoulders and then stood up on them, pulling a knife and cutting the bindings on Bettie's ankles, waist, and wrists. He grasped her around the midsection as he made the final cut, and then let her slide down to 8's waiting arms before jumping to the ground himself.

Gunfire was now flashing in the gloomy night from all over, all aimed at where McGee and the others had been. 8 hoped that they were well gone by now, hoofing it back to the car and the road. He and Pearle each grabbed one of Bettie's arms and slung it over their shoulders, hotfooting it in the opposite direction. She was conscious but didn't seem to have control of her limbs. The plan was for the others to get to the motorcar, circle the farm, and pick them up on the far side.

They'd gone about two hundred yards when the voice of the Imperial Cyclops cut through the din of the chaos. "Stop firing. Hold your fire. Somebody has freed the Black woman. Find them. Find her."

8 risked a glance over his shoulder where men were retrieving torches and fanning out in search of them. Bettie's legs started to work slightly, increasing their speed. 8 realized she was still gagged and yanked the cloth from her mouth. She coughed, hacked, spit— all the while they kept moving.

The Imperial Cyclops came charging in their direction, his rifle searching the darkness, and Pearle was forced to take a snapshot with his pistol to slow him down, giving them away to the other Klansmen searching.

"Take her," 8 said, releasing his hold on Bettie. "Get to the road. I'll catch up."

They'd known each other too long for Pearle to argue. They worked together like two hands of the same being, of the same mind, of the same body. 8 went to one knee, steadied, and took a shot at the approaching Imperial Cyclops. He couldn't tell if he'd hit his mark, but the horse veered away to the side.

Bullets splattered the ground where 8 had been but he'd already rolled and scuttled away. He took another shot at a flash in the darkness and moved again. When the pistol emptied, he reloaded, shooting and moving, all the time toward the road, following Pearle and Bettie, diverting fire from them. Step by step, the circle of Klansmen following him got closer.

And then he was at the road. The motorcar was waiting for him. Bettie was in the front with Dottie and Asta. McGee and Pearle were providing covering fire.

The Imperial Cyclops came galloping their way, the rifle in one hand, reins in the other, bullets from all angles raining down upon them.

"Let's go," 8 said, leaping on the side running board as McGee and Pearle did likewise on the other side.

Dottie gunned the motor, the tires kicked up dirt, and the car went rocketing off into the darkness as the Imperial Cyclops jumped the fence to the road and opened fire with his rifle.

Dottie didn't slow for several miles, but there seemed to be no pursuit. She pulled over so they could climb in, and, as she slowed the automobile, Asta sagged forward, her head crashing into the dashboard.

8 grasped her shoulder to pull her back, and realized it was sticky with blood. With horror he eased her back into the seat, her head lolling to the side, her lifeless eyes staring at him.

Chapter 34

The next hour was a blur for 8. A bullet, most likely from the Imperial Cyclops' rifle, had blown apart the back of Asta's head, most likely killing her immediately. There was little time to react to the death as they had to continue on before the Klan came after them in their own cars.

The motorcar stopped. 8 looked up from his feverish thoughts. They were at Pearle's house. He realized the others were getting out of the car.

Pearle opened his door. "Come inside, Bo."

"What about Asta?" Her lifeless body was propped onto his lap, her blood on his face, on his jacket, seeped into his shirt.

"She'll be here when you get back. Come inside. Just for a moment."

8 set Asta gently in the middle of the seat and gently let her body sag against the door. Pearle gave him a hand, and he got out, as Dottie found a blanket in the boot and laid it over the inert and empty body of his friend and lover.

"She's gone." 8 found himself going through the open door of Pearle's house.

Pearle poured six glasses of brown liquor and handed them around the circle. Bettie took the tumbler tentatively, her eyes flitting around the group, strangers who'd saved her from burning to death, people she hardly knew. Dorothy, her face grave, took the first one and slugged down a healthy shot. McGee swirled his glass, anger like storm clouds crossing his face. Millie was crying, tears coursing down her white cheeks. 8 realized that he, too, was crying, silently, his eyes pooled, blurring his sight.

"She was an amazing woman." Pearle raised his glass. "A lady of the highest caliber."

8 felt the liquid burn down his throat. Pearle went to pour him more. He shook his head and put his hand over the top. "I've got things to do, yet."

"Why'd you all… what… what just happened?" Bettie asked.

"We been looking for you," Pearle said. "Ever since Smack came to the office and said you didn't show up for your gig."

"And you risked your lives to save me?"

"Seemed to be the thing to do."

"Thank you. Thank you so much. I'm so sorry for…"

"Asta. Asta Holm." Dottie took another belt of liquor. "She was a gorgeous human being. One of the finest."

"The lass was a princess, she was," McGee said.

"Somebody's going to pay for what they did," 8 said.

"They'll pay everything," Pearle said. "And still owe some."

"What's the plan?" McGee asked.

"The plan is I'm going to find this Imperial Cyclops fellow, beat him to within an inch of his life, and then I'm going to torch his remains and watch him burn."

8 took a step to the door but was halted by Pearle's hand. "Let's lick our wounds for a couple of hours, Bo, and we'll get started at first light."

8 looked at him. Pearle's eyes burned fiercely, and 8 realized his old friend was right. "Okay, then. Can you put Bettie up here until we get things straightened out?"

Bettie looked as if she were about to fall asleep standing up.

"Not a problem," Pearle said. "You should shack up here, too, for a couple of hours."

8 shook his head. "I'm going to bring Asta home."

Dottie dropped 8, Millie, and Asta off at his apartment, and then was going to take McGee to the precinct station before going home herself.

8 carried Asta up the three flights of stairs with Millie trailing behind. She'd offered to stay behind, and he took her up on it, having plans of his own. Plans that were far too wild and dangerous to include Pearle. 8 knew that his friend would try to talk him out of what he was going to do, and upon failing, would silently go along and back his play. But it was pretty much a suicide mission that 8 was bent upon, and he couldn't ask Pearle to follow.

8 didn't want Asta to be alone, and asked Millie to stay with her, and then exited the apartment without an explanation. He didn't believe that it was just the local Klan. He was convinced that it was a gathering of the leadership of all the city. And he had an inkling that the Imperial Cyclops was Herman Wall.

His neighbor owned a bicycle that he rode to work every day and parked in the hallway at night, and this 8 took with him as he left. It was thirty-five miles to Herman Wall's house in Cold Spring Harbor. It took him four hours, his ire mounting, ratcheting higher and higher, his sadness cycling into anger, so fiercely that he thought he might burst.

When he found the house empty—no Herman Wall, no wife, no living being present at all—8 burnt the place to the ground.

There'd been many fights, much heartache, and one Great War, but the simmering anger he was experiencing tinged everything in red hues and dark shadows that he didn't recognize. Asta was dead. Killed because 8 had agreed to allow her to come, rather than forcing her to stay behind. It'd been no place for her. Not for Dottie nor Millie for that matter. He, Pearle, and McGee had cut their teeth on the streets and then the Great War, but Asta was a woman from the peaceful country of the Netherlands who worked as a telephone operator.

8 had tossed the house before creating a pile of linens and clothes

in the dining room and dousing them with gasoline. He had then rolled up a copy of the *Brooklyn Eagle*, lit it, and used this as his fire starter before walking out the front door. There'd been some paperwork in the house about the Klan, but nothing incriminating, nothing worth keeping as evidence. 8 had already convicted the man in his own personal court of law. Tried. Found guilty. Condemned.

The next stop was the Department of Genetics located in Cold Spring Harbor. People walked here and there as 8 approached the building. It was then, and only then, that he realized the sun had risen, and the day was already several hours old. The receptionist told him that Wall was not in, and as a matter of fact, had called to say that he wouldn't be coming in that day at all, quite unlike him.

8 had the thought that she might be lying to the man before her who smelled like smoke and had red anger rimming his eyes, so he pushed on past her and into Wall's office, but the man was indeed not there. A security guard had come into the room at that point, and 8 knocked him to the floor and walked out without a backward glance. 8 wasn't collecting evidence—he was on the hunt.

8 rode the bicycle to a trolley stop and took the cars back to Fort Greene Park. There was to be an exchange at noon today, according to Theda, with the Aquilla being given to the German, Funk, to be returned to Germany. This was some gesture of good will, an offering that would unite the *Rein Adler of Batavi*, the ancient organization of Germans now apparently an integral part of the Nazi movement with which it shared so many ideals, and the Americans.

8 had his bowler pulled low over his eyes as he strolled through Fort Green Parke, his eyes searching for any of the players who he knew. Funk. Wall. Wall's assistant, Luther Towers.

Was the American version of the Nazi party represented by the KKK, 8 wondered, as one would think after last night? Or was there some nefarious collaboration between the Department of Genetics and the Germans? Both the DOG and the KKK were formidable institutions that could certainly aid in the transformation of

America to a white Aryan America paradise where Blacks, Jews, and Asians were all excluded from business and society. The poisonous combination of DOG, the KKK, and the Nazis was a terrifying notion, and one that had to be stopped.

Both the DOG and the KKK had powerful and wealthy members and benefactors who could bankroll the agenda of marginalizing, degrading, sterilizing, and exporting minorities from the shores of the United States of America. Both organizations had networked their way into the political machine that drove the country. Judging from what he'd seen and experienced in New York City and Brooklyn, 8 could only assume both organizations were currently holding office at local, state, even national levels.

Marty had schooled him on that fellow Hitler, with Millie helping fill in many details, and 8 could envision an alliance between the fascist politician and DOG and the Klan. Apparently, Hitler was coming out of prison—after the failed uprising he'd led called the Beer Hall Putsch—even stronger and more powerful than when he had entered it. His following had grown, especially with the release of *Mein Kampf,* his vitriolic missive justifying his worldview of racist hatred that had sent tremors into every corner of the world.

All 8 could be certain of was that he, 8 Ballo, was responsible for the death of the woman he'd been coming to love, a bright spark in the shadows cast by these various hate groups. He knew that he'd spend the rest of his life punishing himself for this egregious offense, but more immediately, he meant to punish those responsible for Asta's death. Even if that meant bringing the DOG and the KKK to the ground, destroying any ties to the German Nazi party in the process.

He knew that Wall belonged to both organizations. But where was the man? 8 looked at his pocket watch. One o'clock. A full hour after the Aquila was supposed to have been handed off, according to Theda, if she were to be trusted.

"If she were to be trusted," 8 said the thought aloud.

He sat down on a bench. The day was overcast and cool, people mostly hurrying through the park on business or some mission, not many lollygagging about. On a warm day, the park would be packed at this time with people eating their lunch, mothers with their children, men handing a flask back and forth, and boys playing dice games.

Pearle sat down next to him. "Millie said you left right after Dottie dropped you off."

8 nodded. "Had some things to do."

"You smell like smoke."

"Burnt a house down."

"Anybody in it?"

"Unfortunately, no."

"We got some work left to do, then."

"What are you doing here?" 8 asked.

"Watching your back, Bo."

"How'd you know where to find me?"

"I was with you when Dankworth told us about the exchange of goods was supposed to take place here at noon, remember? I figured I'd find you here. Been following you in circles for the past hour."

"Not really an exchange of goods. Wall was going to give Funk the Aquila."

"Everything is an exchange of goods," Pearle said. "Wall ain't giving the man something without expecting something back."

8 nodded. "I was just thinking that the first thing I was going to do was to smash that accord between them. Let the Germans know that America is off limits."

"Ha," Pearle said. "Now you sound like them, cutting back immigration status based on nationality."

8 gave him a tight grin. A very tight grin. "Just the racist shitheads."

"What's the plan now?"

8 shrugged. "Find Wall. Make sure he doesn't make the… exchange of the Aquila to Funk. Then beat Wall into a confession before putting a bullet in his noggin."

"You thinking that Theda Vogel fed you the wrong information about this exchange going down at noon here today?"

"Thought had crossed my mind." 8 sighed. "Or she tipped them off that we'd be here."

"How about we get you a bite to eat, bring you home to get cleaned up so you don't stick out like a hobo in the Waldorf Astoria, and then we go see about tracking down the beasts who killed Asta, and maybe along the way put a hurting on a bunch of racist motherfuckers?"

Chapter 35

Millie had laid Asta out in 8's bed, cleaning and washing her body and wrapping her gently in a blanket. She reposed, looking cold and beautiful, almost as if peacefully sleeping. Almost. 8 wanted to lie down next to her and pretend that none of this had happened. He wanted to erase the moment Theda Lazur Vogel had first walked into his office and everything that had followed.

But that wouldn't do the trick, he knew, for even without Theda pulling him in, Herman Wall still existed. The Imperial Cyclops had said, "Today, tonight, we take a stance in defense of the Aryan-American Race of the future. The race of the pure blood, undiluted by inferior stock. This will be the spark that will ignite the grand solution."

What he couldn't be sure of—though he had horrifying notions aplenty—was what the grand solution was.

"You ready, Bo?"

8 looked up, remembering where he was, standing over the body of Asta, in his apartment, preparing for something that was more than revenge. That was the burning spark that drove him, to be sure, but there was more to it. There was an evil here, today, in Brooklyn, that had to be stopped before it bound itself up with other evils of the world to become an unstoppable force of heinous proportions.

"What do you suppose that Cyclops fellow meant about the grand solution?" 8 asked his friend, his eyes still staring at Asta, so calm, so peaceful, so dead.

A banging came from down the stairs. *Bam. Bam. Bam.* 8 took his .38 out, walked out the door and down the stairs. A man was pounding on his office door. A very large man. Jack Johnson.

"Okay, okay," 8 said, putting the pistol away. "I'm kind of busy right now, Jack. Maybe we can chat some other time."

"Heard something interesting last night up to the Cotton Club."

"Yeah? What's that?"

"Fellow was talking about that Herman Wall you told me about, the one out to Cold Spring Harbor that wants to get rid of us Black folk because we muddy the water. He said that Wall was going to be meeting with him and some other, *Cher-Mans*, he said, but I think he meant Germans. That it was going to be a pact between eugenics, the Klan, and the Germans to make the world a better place to live."

"Yeah? When they supposed to have this meet-up?"

"Tonight. Didn't get a time. Just tonight."

8 nodded. "You get a location?"

Jack shook his head. "Didn't say an address, but I did hear them talk about a place in Park Slope."

8 looked over his shoulder at Pearle. "Thanks, Jack. That's a big help."

Pearle was driving them around in a Ford truck he'd picked up from one of his warehouses. 8 guessed that it'd been modified to enclose the bed in wood paneling. It'd make a fine vehicle for transporting illegal liquor, but, as far as 8 knew, his buddy's business enterprises were all aboveboard and legal.

It was eight o'clock by the time they pulled up across the street from the mansion that stretched half the block behind the wrought iron fence. The bottom of the dwelling was fully illuminated, light blasting out from the windows, while only a few of the upstairs rooms were lit.

8 had noticed several Black men, walking with hurried steps,

down the street and around the corner to the rear entrance of the mansion. They wore white tuxedos, well-shined shoes, and had very dark skin. An automobile pulled up on the corner, and a bevy of Black women piled out, also going down the side street.

An awful lot of Black people going to the house of what he presumed was inhabited by white supremacists, 8 thought, pondering the implications of that.

It was here that Pearle answered the question 8 had posed before they'd left the apartment. "So the problem for the KKK here in America is the Blacks, the Jews, the Asians, and the Roman Catholics. In Germany, it seems the Jews are the focus."

"So?" 8 asked.

"Well, then," Pearle continued, "if that's the problem, then the grand solution would be the elimination of all of them."

They sat in the front cab of the truck chewing that one over for a bit until 8 cleared his throat. "By expulsion and sterilization."

Pearle shook his head no. "That's a step on the way, sure, one that's being practiced already. But the grand solution is bigger. More extreme. Grandiose violence like you can barely imagine. Or maybe you can, having been in the trenches like me."

8 nodded. "I was thinking the same thing. Extermination. The massacre of anybody not born of pure Aryan American stock."

"If we allow that Imperial Cyclops hombre to achieve his aims, we're talking the eventual annihilation of half the population of Brooklyn including myself, Bettie, Dottie, Marty, and McGee. The good news is that you and Millie will most likely be spared."

"Impossible," 8 said. "Some hideous pipe dream conceived in the minds of a few demented and deranged individuals. If they actually moved in that direction, they'd be stopped immediately."

"Who would stop them?" Pearle asked. "The Department of Eugenics *is* the government. Both they and the Klan are run by the richest men in the country and boast representation in every facet of our society. You were at the rally the other night where thousands turned out in fucking sheets and hoods to listen to hateful rhetoric. They cheered fanatically and hung on every motherfucking racist idea."

"This stuff doesn't just happen. There are too many good people."

Pearle laughed coarsely. "No, it doesn't just happen. It happens one small step at a time, until you realize that you're already there. That boats are transporting Africans to foreign shores to be enslaved, beaten, raped. That the Roman Empire is conquering and killing entire cultures just to expand their political boundaries. That the Roman Catholic Church is burning people and torturing them in the name of their God. That Columbus is exterminating entire Native American populations in the search for gold. Goddammit, 8, this motherfucking shit happens all the time, and we are on the cusp of the worst fucking atrocity of all. The extermination of entire races of people based on the color of their skin, their religion, their culture—right here in motherfucking Brooklyn, New York, the United fucking States of America."

"Guess we should do something about it, then," 8 said.

"What? How are you and me going to take down the entire Klan?"

"It's not just the Klan." 8 took two cigars out of his pocket, snipped them, lit one and handed it to Pearle, and then lit the other for himself. He took a puff and blew the smoke out the window. "You got the eugenics people to think of. And then don't forget the Germans and that fanatic, Adolph Hitler. What we are, is in the middle of some sort of devil's triangle. Three perfect storms coming together, and one of two things is going to happen."

Pearle puffed on his cigar, blew smoke out. Looked at the tip, rolling the cigar in his fingers. "Yeah, what's that?"

"They're going to combine into one motherfucking huge storm, or they're going to bounce off each other and go in three separate directions."

"Not sure which is better, one colossal motherfucker, or three pretty bad storms going three different directions."

"Well, Julius Caesar said it and Napoleon practiced it, so I imagine, good enough for them, good enough for me."

Pearle gave him the look. "Said what? Practiced what?"

"Divide and conquer, my good man. Divide and conquer. We might not be able to take down the Klan, or DOG, or Hitler, but what we can do is to make certain that they leave Brooklyn in three different directions."

Chapter 36

8 Ballo sipped on an Old Fashioned as he viewed the scene. He was in a great room filled with men and women wearing masks. He, too, had a mask on. It was, after all, a masquerade ball. What is it, 8 wondered, about these people and masks and costumes, be it the Germans or the Klan?

They'd settled on the plan when the first guests had arrived, a man and a woman, both who pulled masks on over their faces, he in black tuxedo, she in a glamorous gown, before going through the gate to the front door of the mansion in Park Slope.

When a Black man in a white tuxedo had come rushing past their parked car, intent on crossing the street, obviously late, Pearle had jumped out and grabbed the man by the arm, asked a couple of questions, and offered him fifty bucks. The man gave up his waiter's uniform in exchange for the money and Pearle's very expensive clothes. He also gave Pearle a bag he'd been carrying, his mask.

The mask, a Black man's face marked by a very wide and toothy-white smile, covered the entire face. It was like the caricature of the Black-face performers who stumbled around on stage mocking Black people as idiots and imbeciles. Once he was done cursing, Pearle put it on, told 8 he'd see him on the other side, and crossed the street and down the side road to the back entrance where the servants were entering.

That had left 8 to find his way in, which turned out to be cheaper, and extremely satisfying as well. He'd gone a few blocks up to a darker patch of the road and waited for the right opportunity. He allowed a few couples to go by, growing anxious that he was being too picky.

After a bit, a single man in a black tuxedo came striding along. 8 had asked him if he too was going to the masquerade, and when he said yes, 8 had knocked him out. The first punch knocked him to the ground, and it was probably the third strike that caused unconsciousness, but 8 walloped him several more times for good measure. He was done playing nice.

The tuxedo was tight on him, but so were most clothes. There was an invitation to the Aquila Klonvocation of the Grand Solution in one pocket of the man's overcoat. In the other was a mask that covered the eyes and had a huge beaked nose, the width of a hot dog, but longer.

Now, 8 stood in a milling mass of people, trying to drink from the tumbler without getting his nose into the glass, watching and waiting for those he sought.

All the waiters wore white tuxedos and the hideous mask caricatures of grinning Black men, but 8 had picked out Pearle immediately, knowing the gait and stature of his friend better than he knew his own. Pearle was sifting through the crowd with a tray of champagne glasses, mostly for the ladies, the men opting for sterner liquor.

A woman was chattering to 8 about this or that, he wasn't quite sure exactly what, as he merely nodded and agreed every once in a while. She was quite pretty, and if his lover hadn't just been killed, and if this hadn't been a gathering of the most vile and racist people in the entire world, he might've been interested. As was, it took great self-control to not reach out and snap her neck.

A woman across the room caught his attention. She had dark hair, her face partially obscured by a black mask with purple feathers sprouting from it, but he recognized her mouth, her lips, her figure, and her legs. It was Theda Lazur Vogel. She was talking to two men, but her attention also seemed diverted, her eyes flickering this way and that way around the room.

"Champagne, Mistress?"

It was Pearle at their side, offering a flute to the prattling woman, but his eyes flashing at 8 behind the mask. She took the proffered glass with a white-gloved hand and a disdainful look.

"There are stronger drinks over at the bar, Master," Pearle said, nodding his head. "Over by the wall."

Even in his enraged state, 8 smirked slightly at Pearle having had to call him Master, obviously a requirement of the waiters. He looked at his almost-full drink and then in the indicated direction. By the bar was a rotund figure that must be Heinrich Funk, a huge, hooked nose sprouting from his mask, speaking to a second man, who Pearle was hinting was Herman Wall.

"It's not time for another drink quite yet," 8 said. "I'll let you know when I need one. I believe that lady over there could use a champagne, though." He nodded his head at Theda.

Pearle nodded and walked off, even if skirting a careful edge around Theda.

8 made his excuses to the woman and walked off in mid-sentence. He wasn't sure if she was aware he'd even left. This was pretty much as far as their plan had developed. Get disguises, enter the mansion, find Funk and Wall. The question was, what now? He slowly moved closer to the two men, avoiding drawing attention to himself, but wanting to get close enough to eavesdrop.

The two emotions driving 8 Ballo were a bottomless rage and a thirst for revenge. The overwhelming need to avenge Asta's death surged through his veins, the hot blood burning the nerves of his body with an angry agony that demanded satisfaction. The other fiery need, mixed with the few wisps of rationality left in his fevered being, was to vanquish these forces of hatred, or as he'd suggested to Pearle, doing anything to prevent them from uniting. If it was not already too late.

8 sidled up to a group, his back to Wall, only a few feet separating them.

"Hello, Emil Petrus." The man next to 8 held out his hand.

"Gustav Brandt." 8 shook the man's hand.

Behind him, Funk was saying, "The *führer* has agreed to the alliance. America's government-backed eugenics movement meshes neatly with his agenda. The Aquila will cement the friendship between the Department of Genetics and the scientists within our movement to bring about the new world order that we all are working towards."

"Are you an American?" the man, Petrus, asked 8.

"Uh, yes, but I am very much a supporter," 8 replied.

"The Aquila is upstairs," Wall said. "Let us retire to the study and enact our pact of friendship so that we may move forward towards the grand solution."

The two men eased off, touching arms and shoulders as they moved through the masked crowd.

"It is time for the rising of the pure bloods," the man Petrus said. "Time for us to take back what is ours. For too long, good Aryan Americans have been bypassed, forgotten, and—"

"Excuse me," 8 said. "I need to find the men's room." He walked away from Petrus in mid-sentence.

Pearle was staring at him from across the room. 8 nodded at Funk and Wall, and then toward the stairs. He saw Theda also watching the two men move across the floor, her blue eyes luminous behind her dark mask.

8 joined a trickle of men moving toward the stairs. He slowed his pace, watching Funk and Wall ascend, followed by a spate of masked men flowing up behind them in a resolute torrent, maybe fourteen or fifteen in all.

He waited until they were all at the top before approaching the stairwell. There were two men, maskless, but with faces like stone, standing at the bottom with arms crossed. As 8 started to pass, they squeezed together, blocking his egress.

8 gave them the haughtiest stare he could pull off in a mask with nose shaped like a long hotdog. "Stand aside, my good men. Mr. Wall has requested my presence upstairs."

The two men looked at each other, gave almost imperceptible shrugs, and stepped aside.

8 was halfway up the stairs when he heard Pearle's voice behind him. "Mr. Funk has asked that I bring up a tray of cocktails."

He didn't bother turning, knowing that Pearle would have his back. It was pretty much a suicide mission, walking into a roomful of bigots, but 8 was banking on the fact that most, if not all, of the men were unarmed.

8 counted sixteen men in the study as he entered. He worked his way into a corner hoping to avoid notice.

Funk cleared his throat from behind the desk where he stood next to Wall, and the assemblage grew quiet. "Welcome, everybody, on this historic day that will join the two master countries of Germany and America together to form the most powerful nation the earth has ever known. The German-American Empire. The bonding of the Aryans and the Americans. You all are here on the first step of this historic journey in creating the master race, *die Übermenschen.* For those of you who don't know, this is Herman Wall of the Department of Genetics who has been doing outstanding work towards scientifically determining the qualities of men such as us— as well as those defining lesser beings, the inferior races, enough so that when we reach the final solution, ridding our lands of the latter, not an eye will blink, not a single protest will be made."

The room broke into enthusiastic applause.

Wall allowed the clapping to die away before speaking. "Thank you, Heinrich, for inviting me. There is much work to be done yet, but I can assure you that the pieces have been put in place to elect men here in the United States who are sympathetic to our cause. With the proper support in Congress, the President is ready to announce his allegiance to this new alliance that will change the course of history. To mark this momentous occasion, this joining together of the pure of blood, I would like to offer a token of our unification. The *Rein Adler of the Batavi.*"

He held up a gold eagle statue, no more than a foot in height, the very object that had brought 8 onto the case in the first place. Such a simple thing really, for such a big fuss, but, 8 reckoned, people died every day for flags, so why not for a golden eagle?

The men in the room were madly pounding their hands together, stamping their feet, and yelling cheers, hurray, *hurra, prost,* some whistling, others yelling nonsensically.

8 saw Pearle slide into the back of the room, setting his tray on a small table. 8 nodded to him. No time like the present. He pulled the .38 from his waistband at his back, and holding it down to his side, began to move toward Wall and Funk.

The cheering subsided. Wall turned to Funk, holding out the Aquila, as 8 stepped up to them.

"You killed my love and now you're going to pay the price," he said. "You racist bigoted bastards."

Chapter 37

Wall froze, his eyes turning from Funk to 8. "You're that private dick," he said.

"That's me. You shoot any women lately, or try to burn any alive, for that matter?"

"What are you talking about?"

A man pulled a tiny pistol, what 8 thought might be a Remington, from his pocket and aimed it at 8.

"Why don't you slink your ass out of here," the man said.

8 looked at him. "Why don't you drop that pea shooter before your brains get splattered all over the room?"

"What are—"

The man reacted to the cold metal of the pistol pressed to the back of his head, his mouth pantomiming a fish out of water.

"How about you hand it over nice and slow," Pearle said, holding his free hand out to the man's side. The man complied.

Wall took the diversion as an opportunity to act, stepping forward and crashing the Aquila into the side of 8's head. 8 took the blow without blinking, his hand going to his ear in wonder. He struck Wall across the face with his pistol, looked at the weapon, and dropped it in his jacket pocket. Then he picked up Wall, one hand around his neck, one in his crotch, and threw him into a wall, the shock sending shudders through the entire building.

Funk slunk backward as 8 turned on him, closing the distance in two quick steps. He grabbed the man by the throat and pinned him to the wall. "How about you, Kaiser Bill, were you at the Klonvocation last night as well?"

The click of Pearle's pistol cocking could be clearly heard in the hush of the room. "I wouldn't think it a good idea to take another step in that direction, if I was you, I'd stand right where I was."

8 looked over his shoulder at a man slowly settling back, his face ashen. 8 turned and drove his fist into Funk's belly, an explosion of air whooshing from his mouth. "Answer me. Were you there?"

"Was I where?" Funk managed to gasp.

"In Gravesend for the burning of a Black woman," 8 said, slapping the man across the face.

"No, no, please, I don't know what you're talking about."

Wall staggered to his feet—the Aquila still clutched in his hand. He stepped forward awkwardly, his leg not quite working correctly. 8 turned and drove a fist into his nose, blood and cartilage showering forth as Wall fell over backward.

A man stepped forward, a look of outrage on his face, an expression which went ashen as the barrel of Pearle's pistol struck him in the back of the head. He slumped to his knees and toppled over.

"Next person steps forward gets a motherfucking bullet in the noggin," Pearle said.

8 stepped over to Wall as Funk slumped to his knees. He picked Wall up by the jacket lapels and slammed him into the wall. "Did you pull the trigger? Tell me. Did you pull the trigger that killed her?"

"I don't know what you're talking about." Wall was blubbering, blood running down his face, the spectacles gone from his face, leg crooked at a strange angle. "Please. Don't hurt me."

The door to the study slammed open, and Luther Tower stepped into the opening and shot Pearle in the back. Pearle crumpled to the ground, his own Colt pistol falling from his hand.

Luther stepped over to him, his pistol pointed at 8, and kicked the

Colt out of reach of his hand.

"Everybody out," he said. "Leave Herman, Heinrich, and myself to clean up the trash."

The other men in the room didn't have to be told twice, rushing toward the open door and fighting to get out of the room.

8 looked at Pearle who was softly moaning and writhing on the floor. At least he was still alive. He punched Wall in the face with all the force he could muster, getting his legs, back, and shoulder into the blow. The man's jaw cracked and splintered under the impact, and his mouth gaped strangely open as he toppled forward onto the floor.

Luther smirked. "I believe that your anger is misplaced, Mr. Ballo."

"Oh, yeah," 8 said. "How so?"

"Herman Wall and Heinrich Funk were not even at the Klonvocation last evening. Herman is merely the Klabee, or treasurer, of his Klan and doesn't rank highly enough to have been invited to the intended roast. And Heinrich? He's not even in the Klan. But they are both very important people to my plan."

"I take it you were there," 8 said. His eyes widened as he thought of the man on horseback, and how tall he appeared from his mount, realizing that he was, indeed, tall, and not just on horseback. "You're the one who killed Asta."

"I don't know of what you speak." Luther stepped closer, the gun steady in his hand. "But I do know that you've become a thorn in my side."

"You are the Imperial Cyclops."

Luther laughed harshly. "I am. Understand that I rule the Klan. The Imperial Grand Wizard is merely my puppet. I am the voice of the Klan. The voice of a pure-blooded America."

"That was you on horseback last night in Gravesend. You were the one who was going to start the bonfire to burn a woman alive."

"Ah, now I understand. I wondered if that was you and your

friends who interfered with my plans. But no, we were not planning on burning a woman. We were going to roast a breeder intent on diluting the blood of America and corroding its greatness from within, one brown mixed blood at a time."

"You killed the woman I love." 8 clenched and unclenched his fists, wondering if he could take a bullet, wrap his hands around Luther's neck and kill him, before succumbing to death. "And for that, I will kill you."

Luther cackled. "Ah, one of my bullets did indeed find their mark. I'd rather of killed the Black vermin but will settle for eliminating a person who interferes with the valuable work that I am doing. And now you will be next."

"If you're such an important muckety-muck, why is it that you play second fiddle to him?" 8 nodded at Wall, who lay on the floor groaning, one hand clutched to his broken jaw.

"I have found that the position of second fiddle, as you call it, lets me escape attention, being out of the spotlight. I can accomplish more from that position. But don't be mistaken as to who has been calling the shots at the Department of Eugenics. Herman is my mouthpiece to the scientific community, to the public, and to Congress. But I am the one dictating that policy."

8 eased forward a step. The longer he kept the man talking, the better his chances. At the same time, if Pearle was still alive, his time was leaking away. "You are creating an alliance between Adolph Hitler's Nazi party, the Department of Eugenics, and the Ku Klux Klan to create an Aryan American race, a power like the world has never seen. In the process, you will exterminate those who you believe to be less human. The Blacks. The Jews." He said it as if in awe, knowing that true believers like Luther could not resist the echo of their own rhetoric from the mouth of another.

"And those weaker, of course. The feeble-minded. The promiscuous. The criminals. And of course, the Asians." Luther raised the pistol and aimed it between 8's eyes. "You have proven to be a capable enemy, Mr. 8 Ballo. It is too bad that you have thrown your lot in with the mongrels of the world."

"If you're such a wonderful specimen of humanity, why don't you lay down that pistol and fight me man to man." 8 eased forward another step.

Luther cackled again, the sound like nails being dragged through broken glass. "I fear that I do not have time to entertain that possibility. But rest assured, that if the time were available, I'd gladly tear you apart limb by limb."

"That's something I'd like to see." The voice came from the doorway.

8's eyes flickered over that way. Bugsy Siegel had moved inside the room, a Tommy Gun in his arms, pointed at Luther. Fanning out behind him was a chopper squad of six other men, tight-faced Jews in overcoats, collars turned up, fedoras pulled low.

Luther turned sideways, keeping the pistol leveled at 8, his eyes taking in the new presence in the room. "And you are?"

"Bugsy Siegel at your service. One of them Jewish mongrels of inferior blood you been talking about. Now drop the gat. I'd like to see the gumshoe take you apart, real slow like, before I put a bullet in your head."

"As tempting as that all is, it doesn't make much sense to me," Luther said. "If you're going to kill me anyway, I might as well take him with me." His finger tightened on the trigger.

"Don't really matter one way or the other to me," Bugsy said. "But I'll tell you what. You win the fight, and you can walk out of here alive. On my mother's honor."

Luther looked at him, his eyes searching for the truth behind the words.

"Ben, can you have one of your men check on Pearle?" 8 asked, using the man's given name to remind him of who was the friend, who the enemy. "This bigot shot him in the back."

"I'm okay, Bo," Pearle said, propping himself up, back against an armchair. "Just a flesh wound. Knocked the wind out of me though. Nothing that's going to kill me. And nothing that's going to prevent me from watching you beat this bastard to death."

"Very well, then," Luther said. "I accept your offer." He dropped the pistol and with the same motion spun on his heel and kicked 8 in the side of the head, sending him crashing to the floor. "You see, my father, he had a bunch of Chinamen working for him when I was a child. One of them took me under his wing and taught me Shaolin Kung Fu. He also soiled me in the name of God and gave me insight into the creation of the Master Race."

8 sat up, rubbing the side of his head. He'd not even seen the blow coming. One moment he'd been standing there looking at Pearle, assessing his health, and the next he was flat on his face. He stood up and faced Luther, who'd dropped into a crouch, his long legs split apart, his arms up in front of him, hands turned sideways, wiggling ever so slightly.

This was the man who'd killed Asta. 8 rushed at him, Luther pivoting, swiveling, and chopping the flat of his hand into 8's neck, setting him to gagging as he staggered past.

This was the man who intended to exile, sterilize, and exterminate all those who he thought inferior to his pure Aryan American blood. 8 turned, moving in more slowly, more controlled. Luther thrust a flat-edged hand at his throat, and he deflected it with his left, but the tips of the man's other hand, feeling more like a splitting maul, slammed into his cheek, bringing tears to his eyes.

Luther swept 8's feet out from underneath him, and he toppled to the floor. In an instant, the Imperial Cyclops, Luther Tower, was crouched over 8, raining blows into his face. 8 rolled and threw the man off him, both of them coming to their feet at the same time. 8 could feel the stickiness of blood on his face, his breathing was ragged, and a blackness of rage was starting to overcome him.

Everything slowed down in the room, and the lights appeared to dim. Luther was a shadowy figure, a ghoul of sorts, across from him. 8 concentrated all his will upon this apparition of death, this grim reaper of souls. He could hear a roaring sound and realized faintly that it was him, a guttural howl of fury rising up through his body, his throat, hurtling its way out of his mouth with a mighty roar of rage of all that was wrong with the world.

Luther slid forward, his leg sweeping around, but now, 8 watched all of this as if in slow motion. He caught the leg as it neared his head and swung the man, using his own weight against him, crashing into the wall. Not giving him a chance to recover, he followed it up, slamming the man in the face, once, twice, three times, before he crumpled to the floor.

8 picked him up and threw him over the desk. Luther rolled over, his eyes wild in his head, the faintest glimmer of fear leaking into the pupils, as 8 followed, kicking the man in the chin, the crack sounding throughout the study like a gunshot.

Luther kicked 8 in the groin as he came at him again, staggering him backward, but only for a moment. As Luther rose to his feet, 8 drove a fist into his solar plexus, doubling him over just as his other fist crashed into Luther's cheek, the skin splitting to reveal the splintered bone below.

And then again. And again. Until Luther's face was pulp, a bloody mess of nothing—with each blow 8 trying desperately to erase the man from existence.

8 stood up, the roaring subsiding, the room slowly coming back into focus. Bugsy Siegel, standing as if in awe, a look of admiration mixed with a sick pleasure adorning his face. Then, one by one, the chopper squad came into focus, all with varying degrees of horror stamped upon them as if imprinted for life.

Pearle. 8 looked over where his friend sat propped up. He stumbled over to him, fear washing away the tide of anger. Pearle's eyes belied his statement that he was fine. There was a bullet wound just above his right breast. 8 leaned him forward to find a matching hole. He ripped his own tattered shirt from his body and wrapped it in a makeshift bandage around the wounds.

"Why don't you two get out of here," Bugsy said. "Take the man to a hospital. We'll clean up the leftovers."

8 pulled Pearle to his feet, pulling the man's good left arm around his own shoulders as he grasped him around the waist and began hobbling to the door, where he stopped, turned back, and surveyed the scene.

Heinrich Funk stood in shock, not having moved since the fight had begun. Herman Wall lay on his back, gasping for breath, groaning and moaning in pain. Luther Tower lay without moving. It was impossible to tell if he were alive or dead.

"Just a moment," 8 whispered in Pearle's ear.

He propped his friend against the door and went back into the room. 8 picked up the Aquila from the corner, and went back to Pearle, carrying the golden eagle in his left hand, supporting Pearle with the other. They hobbled out the door to the stairs.

Halfway down, they heard a series of double taps. Pop-pop. A couple of seconds in between. Pop-pop. And then again. Pop-pop. The alliance between the Klan, the DOG, and the Nazis had been effectively ended. The murderer of Asta Holm had been sent to Hell.

When they reached the bottom of the stairs, Theda Vogel was standing there. 8 handed her the Aquila. "I believe this is yours," he said. Then, he and Pearle continued out the front door of the mansion in Park Slope, down the steps, across the street, and into the truck.

Epilogue: Eight Days Later

8 sat in the lobby of the Brooklyn Hospital waiting for Pearle to be brought out. He had the *Brooklyn Eagle* in front of him, wondering if he really needed to read the latest story by Martin Hoffman, the third in the past week.

The first article had outed the Department of Eugenics as a hate group that had based its scientific findings, its so-called proof of racial inferiority, on long-discredited research practices. It linked Herman Wall to several influential Congressmen, as well as connected the operation with several of the wealthiest families in the United States of America. Marty depicted Wall's involvement with the KKK and exposed Luther Tower as the Imperial Cyclops of the Klan and his involvement in the attempted burning of a young Black woman.

The second article had tied Herman Wall to Heinrich Funk, and by extension, Adolph Hitler in Germany, and suggested that he was but a go-between connecting Kellogg, Carnegie, Harriman, and at least three senators with the Nazi party in Germany. That article had gotten Marty called into the office of top brass of the *Brooklyn Eagle* with a threat that he would be fired. That had been five days ago. Marty had called him the day before and suggested that he should make sure to read today's newspaper.

With a sigh, fairly certain that it was probably not much more than an apology for having accused men of power and riches of wrongdoing, 8's eyes flickered to the front page.

The KKK, the Department of Eugenics, Congress, & Adolph Hitler

The Links that Bind Them Together

Eleanor Roosevelt has demanded a Congressional investigation into the connections made here in the *Brooklyn Daily Eagle* between the deceitful nature of the Department of Eugenics and several Congressmen who have championed their false science. Amongst other things, Roosevelt has demanded a second look at the recent Reed-Johnson Immigration Act.

The assistant director of the Department of Genetics, Herman Wall, is still missing. It is believed that he may have fled to escape the shame of being exposed as a charlatan pulling the wool over the eyes of good Americans such as W.K. Kellogg, Andrew Carnegie (before his death), Mary Harriman Rumsey, and Senators Reed and Johnson.

Another missing man, Luther Tower, has been exposed as the Imperial Cyclops of the Ku Klux Klan, and is wanted for questioning regarding an attempted murder.

Captain Archipoili of the Fort Greene Precinct has been working closely with the Park Slope Station to round up a number of local men of German origin for plotting insurrection against the United States of America. So far, seven men have been deported, and rumor has it there will be more. The ringleader, one Heinrich Funk, a close associate of Adolph Hitler, is still on the lam.

It is thought possible that Wall, Tower, and Funk might be together, but the association they attempted to foster has been smashed. The Klan has been exposed as

the evil organization that it is, espousing hatred, akin to
the German fascist, of all non-Aryans, be they Roman
Catholics, Blacks, Jews, Irish, and Asians.

"Hey, Bo, anything good in the *Eagle* today?"

8 looked up to see Pearle in a wheelchair, but unlike the past eight
days, back in his snazzy street clothes, a lavender suit jacket and
waistcoat that matched the feather in his fedora.

"It looks like things are getting shaken up a bit, but Marty had to
put in a good word for the rich and powerful, suggesting they were
misled by the grifter, Herman Wall." 8 stood up and held out his
hand. "Let's get you out of here."

Pearle clasped his hand and stood with a grimace. "I could use a
Scotch and a steak."

8 chuckled. "Doubt the doctors have okayed that."

"Doctors aren't high on my list right now," Pearle said. "Not after
what they did to Bettie."

"She still at your place?"

"Yeah. I told her that she and the kids can stay until she can get
her own place."

8 nodded. "Nice of you."

"Woman has had a rough life. Least I could do is give her a hand."

"She work things out with Smack?"

A nurse held the door as 8 guided Pearle outside. Pearle gave
the woman a broad grin, the ole' Hill charm he called it, and
she responded with a shy smile. "Damn." He shook his head and
continued to hobble down the steps. "Bettie has her first gig tonight
at the Roseland. Maybe we can swing by later?"

"Let's get you home first."

"Hey, you got my Nash fixed up."

The automobile was back to its pristine condition. "Figured it was
my fault it was all banged up, so yeah, I got some fellows to make it
look new again."

"Heard from that wise cracker friend of yours? Dorothy Parker?"

"Dottie and her husband went off to some cabin in the woods. Upstate I think, to lick her wounds, or something like that."

"Man, I can't believe you gave that priceless gold eagle to that double-crossing manipulating Theda Vogel."

8 settled Pearle into the passenger seat and went around to the driver's side. "I suppose if anybody owned the thing, it was her. I don't think the Italians have any claim to it anymore, and I wasn't giving it back to some fanatic Germans, especially once we connected them with that lunatic Hitler."

"You didn't think about keeping it for yourself?"

"Wasn't mine. I was just hired to find it."

"Any word from Bugsy?"

8 shook his head as he pulled the motorcar into traffic. "I'm sure when he needs a favor, I'll get a visit. Until then? I could use the quiet."

"The police still looking for Wall, Tower, and Funk?"

8 nodded his head. "The police and several government agencies. But I don't think they're going to find them."

Pearle laughed. "In the end, the leaders of the so-called master race became fish food."

"Not kosher, one would think." 8 observed.

"Fish don't care, man. Fish don't care."

Acknowledgments

If you are reading this, I thank you, for without readers, writers would be obsolete.

I am grateful to my mother, Penelope McAlevey, and father, Charles Cost, who have always been my first readers and critics.

Much appreciation to the various friends and relatives who have also read my work and given helpful advice.

I'd like to offer a big hand to my wife, Deborah Harper Cost, and children, Brittany, Pearson, Miranda, and Ryan, who have always had my back.

I'd like to tip my hat to my editor, Michael Sanders, who has worked with me on fourteen novels now, and always makes my writing the best that it can be.

Thank you to Encircle Publishing, and the amazing team of Cynthia Bracket-Vincent, Eddie Vincent, Chris Wait and Deirdre Wait for giving me this opportunity to be published. Also, kudos to Deirdre Wait for the fantastic cover art.

About the Author

MATT COST is the highly acclaimed, award-winning author of the Mainely Mystery series. The first book, *Mainely Power*, was selected as the Maine Humanities Council Read ME Fiction Book of 2020. This was followed by *Mainely Fear, Mainely Money, Mainely Angst*, and the newest, *Mainely Wicked*. He is also the author of the Clay Wolfe / Port Essex Mysteries, *Wolfe Trap, Mind Trap, Mouse Trap, Cosmic Trap*, and the latest, *Pirate Trap*, was published by Encircle in March 2024.

I Am Cuba: Fidel Castro and the Cuban Revolution was his first traditionally published novel. His other historical fiction novels are *Love in a Time of Hate* (August 2021), and *At Every Hazard: Joshua Chamberlain and the Civil War* (August 2022). His love of histories and mysteries is combined in his 1920's Brooklyn 8 Ballo Mystery series, which begins with *Velma Gone Awry* (April 2023) and continues in *City Gone Askew* (July 2024).

Cost was a history major at Trinity College. He owned a mystery bookstore, a video store, and a gym before serving a ten-year sentence as a junior high school teacher. In 2014, he was released and he began writing. And that's what he does: he writes histories and mysteries. Cost now lives in Brunswick, Maine, with his wife, Harper. There are four grown children: Brittany, Pearson, Miranda, and Ryan. A chocolate Lab and a basset hound round out the mix. He now spends his days at the computer, writing.

If you enjoyed this book,
please consider writing your review
and sharing it with other readers.

Many of our Authors are happy to participate in
Book Club and Reader Group discussions.
For more information, contact us at info@encirclepub.com.

Thank you,
Encircle Publications

For news about more exciting new fiction, join us at:

Facebook: www.facebook.com/encirclepub

Instagram: www.instagram.com/encirclepublications

Sign up for the Encircle Publications newsletter:
eepurl.com/cs8taP

Printed in the USA
CPSIA information can be obtained
at www.ICGtesting.com
CBHW020254210724
11863CB00006B/59